DRAGONFLIES

Also by Andy Straka

A Witness Above
A Killing Sky
A Cold Quarry
A Night Falconer
A Fatal Ground
A Trigger Within
Record Of Wrongs
The Blue Hallelujah

DRAGONFLIES

A THRILLER

ANDY STRAKA
(WITH DURRELL NELSON)

LLW MEDIA

Copyright © Andy Straka 2015

Print Edition

ISBN: 978-0-9848438-6-2

Published by LLW Media/Fountain Hill Books

PO Box 6608

Charlottesville, VA 22906

E-book (Part 1) distributed by Trident Media Group – New York

In Memoriam:

Corporal Bradley T. Arms, USMC
KIA November 19, 2004
Fallujah, Iraq

ACKNOWLEDGMENTS

Many thanks to Jeanne Siler, David Moody, Major Robert Schuett, USA (ret.), and loyal family and readers Chris, Julia, Kelci, Lily, Mason, John, Deborah Prum, Jennifer Elvgren, Michele Veillon, Lucy Russell, Judy Bushkin, and Denny King. Many more thanks to my wife, Bonnie, who does it all. I also owe a debt of gratitude to the dozens upon dozens of non-fiction authors, journalists, and others who have written, published, and/or produced books and stories about unmanned aerial vehicles—more popularly known as drones—and robotics over the past couple of years. Their work continues to ignite incendiary currents in this fiction writer's imagination.

Praise for the novels of Andy Straka

"A breath of fresh air."
— Jeffery Deaver

"A talented author."
— *Publishers Weekly*

"Highly recommended."
— Michael Connelly

"Characters you feel in your bones."
— Julia Spencer-Fleming

"A first rate-thriller."
— *Mystery Scene*

"Once he's got you in his grip, he never lets go."
— Rick Riordan

PART 1
"SHADOW OF DRONES"

1

CHIEF WARRANT OFFICER Raina Sanchez dropped the nose of her Kiowa Warrior as the chopper prepared to jump the ridge. Leaning back in her seat the midnight darkness seemed to embrace her. The high peaks of the Hindu Kush were barely silhouettes against the star-filled, moonless sky.

Raina loved this kind of action. The adrenaline rush from flying Air Cav was like nothing else—the fight close to the earth, as close as a pilot could get. For a moment, she felt as though she were one with the helicopter, the controls responding to her gloved hands and booted feet like deftly falling angels, the flight of the machine a synthesis of her years of training with decades worth of technological add-ons to her Vietnam-era Kiowa.

Cresting the rise, she fired a burst from the .50 caliber guns, her eyes coming to focus on the target. Captain Skyles ran the mission in the seat next to her, pinpointing their Hellfire missiles with the laser rangefinder, JTAC squawking him guidance, both of them gritting their teeth to keep from chipping them due to the shudder of the guns.

"I make about a half dozen," he said.

"Copy."

In her thermal viewfinder the insurgents looked like

miniature green phantoms skittering among a clump of buildings atop a small plateau at four hundred yards. She held steady for a three count while Skyles sent their missiles roaring downrange, knowing most of those phantoms were about to meet their virgins in paradise. The Op was already beginning to feel like a success. She swooped the chopper over her own advancing infantry, the cockpit swaying as they moved into fire support.

Thunk

"What the...?" They felt the near-miss blast as much as heard it.

Skyles turned his head. One of the advantages of the Kiowa over the larger Apache was that it allowed the pilots to see out the doors.

"RPG. Tangos to our right."

Rocket propelled grenade. Where'd the shooter come from? She banked hard, swinging the copter back and forth in an evasive maneuver.

Raina knew what she was doing. She hadn't been flying a racetrack or any other identifiable pattern, but the flash of another RPG launch to their left knifed into her being like a sharp blow to the stomach.

Skyles swore out loud. "They've got us bracketed."

Vra-boom

This time they felt the full impact of the shock wave, jolting them violently to the side, the booming detonation so close it nearly ripped the cyclic control from Raina's hands.

Only her helmet and restraints saved her. She recovered to find their cockpit humming with warning lights and alarms.

"Status report."

Skyles twisted around to have a look. "LTE," he said, his voice tense but composed.

Loss of Tail Rudder Effectiveness. Nightmare time for any chopper pilot.

Already the ship was feeling balky. She pushed on the pedal controls. The Kiowa yawed left instead of right, against her will.

"We've got a problem."

She knew Skyles was already beginning emergency procedures, engaging his own controls, helping her as best as he could to bring the chopper back under their command. But they had only one way left to go, and that was down, still traveling at close to a hundred knots, with precious little air between them and the ground.

"Hold on to it."

"I'm trying."

"Mayday, mayday," Skyles spoke into his mike. "Dragonfly 16 is going down. Repeat. Dragonfly 16 going in hard."

She searched in vain for signs of hope in the darkness below, but saw none. Willing herself to stay focused, she could still see the outlines of the plateau ahead. For a moment she thought she might have felt a response on the rudder, but it was all happening too fast. The Kiowa was beginning to spin beyond their reach with the blackness of the mountain looming.

"Fight it, Raina," Skyles egged her on and perhaps himself as well, straining against the centrifugal force as he dumped fuel and discharged the last of their ordinance.

If there was to be any saving grace, she would think later, if there was to be any occasion for her to fly again, she would gladly give it all away for the chance to take this one flight back.

The implosion of glass and steel snatched the useless stick from her hands as their spinning blades bent like flower petals into the rocky earth. The chopper broke into pieces, lethal projectiles of rotors flying off in all directions, the cockpit collapsing, smashing to one side and threatening to crush her before flipping over, driving at an angle into the ridge, blacking her out.

She awoke seconds later to the smell of aviation fuel and

fear, gagging for breath as the howling pain at the bottom of her leg began to drag her into shock.

She saw nothing until the tall American infantryman was there, leaning over her in the blur of his headlamp, ignoring the tracers punching the rock and sand all around them, the whites of his eyes embedded within his camouflaged face, focused on cutting her from her seat and dragging her to safety, and all the while her trying to scream for Skyles, all the while her trying to cry out with words that wouldn't come....

Raina shook her head, jarred back to reality as she stared into her darkened video screen.

She turned to look around. Her butt wasn't parked in her Kiowa anymore, but behind a computer console in the safe confines of the back of a windowless van parked along a Northern Virginia side street.

"You all right, Rain?" she heard a voice in her headphones.

"Yeah." She stretched her shoulders to break the tension.

"Lost you there for a minute."

"I'm fine."

She reached for her joystick and made the needed corrections to put her reccee—as in reconnaissance—unit back on course.

Outside the van, a beautiful autumn afternoon was blooming into full display, the crisp air punctuated by sunlight and the reflection of brightly colored leaves. Not that she noticed.

Half a mile away, her hover angel whispered through the pitch-black interior of the ventilation duct, guided by its mini CCTV night vision camera, moving deeper into the building, undetected. Barely bigger than a mosquito, the tiny drone—more correctly known in military parlance as a MAV or micro air vehicle—had been guided into the structure through an outdoor grate and carefully maneuvered through a maze of conduits and vents to the main elevator shaft, where it had risen under her control to the target floor.

This fancy office tower may have offered class A plus commercial space and the best security measures money could buy, including a pair of armed guards keeping watch on multiple surveillance cameras, but they were no match for Raina's angel. The miniscule flyer was nearly translucent and almost silent, virtually impossible to spot except up close. Its miniaturized systems, from power and propulsion, to imaging and detection—had they been available to the general public—would have put even the finest Silicon Valley chip developers and Swiss watchmakers to shame.

Inside the duct, the natural light began to grow as the angel approached the ceiling vent above its objective. She switched from night imaging to the angel's regular CCD computational camera system. Directly below the imagers, a white-haired man sat behind a large desk talking on a mobile phone.

Gingerly, she landed the angel on the edge of the vent for a moment, before allowing it to drop, unseen, into the room.

2

TYE PALMER TRIED not to betray any emotion as Nathan Kurn's two security men patted him down. They waved an electronic wand over his clothing, looking for weapons or surveillance equipment, and one of them spent a good deal of time looking through Tye's wallet before handing it back to him.

Not that he was too worried about them finding anything. The microscopic listening device in his ear canal would pass any such superficial inspection—or so he'd been told. Same with the tiny microphone tucked inside his gum, although he shouldn't have need of it, as long as things went as planned.

One of the guards nodded an okay to Kurn when they were finished.

"Thank you, gentlemen," the white-haired man said, the legendary figure himself, waving them from the room.

Tye waited. The man also waited until his security people left, closing the door behind them.

"Welcome, Mr. Palmer," he said, turning to shake Tye's hand. "It's nice to meet you in person."

"Nice to meet you, too, sir."

"In your email you sent me background on both you and your partner, but I don't see her with you today."

"Good thing," Raina spoke into Tye's ear where only he could hear. "I'd have to work too hard to keep from puking on the guy's desk."

Tye addressed himself to Kurn.

"I'm sorry. Raina doesn't get out in the field all that much. It's not always that easy…with her prosthetic and all."

"Great." Raina sounded annoyed. "Go ahead and saddle me with the gimp excuse."

"Mmmm." Kurn grunted his assent. "I'm sorry for the frisking. But I'm sure you can appreciate a man in my position can't take too many chances."

"No problem."

"I'd have asked you to sit down, but I'm on a tight schedule. I've already had you vetted by my security people and, given the sensitive nature of our discussion, I thought we'd better get right down to business."

"Fine by me."

A TV remote lay on the desk blotter directly in front of Kurn. It was, in fact, the only thing on the blotter at the moment. Kurn picked it up and pushed a button, turning to point it at a flat panel television display mounted to the wall behind him.

"Let's get started then." He stepped around the desk to stand next to Tye as the screen flickered to life. He pushed another button on the remote and a video began to play. No sound came from the film. The display showed merely images.

It took a few moments for Tye to fully process what he was seeing on the screen. He was shocked by what he saw, but he kept it together. Kurn let the film roll on.

"Do you know who this is in the video?"

"No, but I'm sure you're going to tell me."

"Big problem," Raina whispered in his ear. "Where he's

standing is blocking my view of the screen. And my audio is acting up. Have to reposition. See if you can stall him."

The film on the wall kept going. The footage had apparently come from the inside of a college fraternity house. Not exactly cinematic quality and the lighting wasn't good. But it was good enough to tell what was happening.

"This is my only son we're talking about," Kurn said. "His name is Derek."

Tye nodded. From the tip Major Williamson had given them, he'd already guessed the identity of the male on the screen and Kurn had just confirmed it.

On the tape, a strapping young Derek Kurn could clearly be seen rising from the bed in what appeared to be his room at the fraternity. He wore no clothes. An attractive, naked girl lay on the bed beneath him. She was tied down. But she didn't appear to be struggling at all, and the closer Tye looked it was obvious she had either had far too much to drink or been drugged.

It was a clear case of date rape. The picture looked as ugly as it sounded.

"Pretty disgusting. I can see you've got a big problem." Tye played along. "So what do you want us to do about it?"

"Simple. I want you to go in, gain his confidence, and a have a confidential discussion with the boy, if you get my drift, about his behavior. We need to put a stop to it."

"Confidentially."

"Yes. Indeed."

"What about the girl?" Tye asked.

"What about her?"

"Do you know who she is?"

"Some coed, most likely."

"Have you thought about trying to find out who she is, to try to make amends?"

"Make amends? What good would that do? She clearly

won't remember what happened anyway. Trust me, it will just open up a whole can of worms."

Tye said nothing.

The tanned big game hunter and self-described tennis addict stood gripping the remote while the film kept running. The links on his French cuff shirt probably cost more than what Tye had ever earned in a month.

Tye didn't know what else to say. He glanced around Kurn's elegantly appointed corner office, which occupied a sizable piece of the twelfth floor in the glass office tower in Roslyn, Virginia. The walls were filled with framed photographs of Kurn and various presidents, senators, and other celebrities, a potent reminder of his status as one of the most colorful and influential broadcast figures on the planet, an A-list invitee to all the important beltway-insider gatherings. Just across the Potomac, in all its glory, stood the hive of politicians and political dealmakers in Washington, D.C. that Tye, though he was no longer a soldier, still found worth defending.

"Okay," Raina said. "Back online again. I've got a little bit better angle. Try to keep him from moving around."

What was Tye supposed to do, bear hug the guy? He'd been dubious about using the little snooper drones from the beginning. He could see with his own two eyes what Derek Kurn was guilty of and how his powerful old man was trying to keep it quiet and cover up for the kid. He didn't need a drone to tell him that.

Kurn looked impatient. "You're back working on your degree and even though you're older you can still pass as a student. You think you'll be able to get in and do what I need, or not?"

"I think so. Yes."

"Good. I can't abide this type of behavior. I don't know

where Derek ever learned such things. But something has to be done about it."

The man seemed more than a little on edge. Maybe he was having second thoughts about letting Tye, and by extension Raina, in on his dirty little family secret.

Tye was half-tempted to walk out and just report what he'd seen to the police. But he knew if Raina continued to run into technical difficulties, it would simply be the word of a lowly former Army grunt against a media celebrity's like Kurn. Tye would be discredited, or slandered, if need be, and the case would go nowhere. Kurn didn't get to where he was without knowing how to play hardball. And even if Raina did manage to record some good copy of the tape, they still might be on thin ice.

"I think that's quite enough," Kurn said. "You get the idea." He punched a button on his remote and the screen went blank again.

3

WATCHING AND LISTENING blocks away, Raina flexed her arms and rolled her shoulders to keep her hands from beginning to quiver. From where she'd landed the MAV she had thought she could get the best camera angle on both the screen and Kurn. But whether consciously or unconsciously, the man kept moving back and forth, blocking her view of the video. Turning his back to the MAV also muffled the sound of Kurn's voice, and it forced her to fly silently along the seam of the curtains to find a better location along the hanging curtain rod.

It was like piloting a plane or chopper at treetop levels over hills and valleys—nap-of-the-earth on a micro scale. And without a co-pilot, all the while she needed to continue to position her ship and manage her camera equipment and sensors to maintain visual contact with the target. One slip of the controls and she risked detection, either by creating a sound or an obvious movement in the fabric.

This was really happening. There was no going back. When Major Williamson had approached her about this operation, he'd warned her she should be prepared for something different. He also didn't have to work too hard to convince her of the rightness of the cause.

"Hey, if it isn't the new drone girl," Tye had said when she walked into the abandoned warehouse he and Williamson had specially set up for her to practice flying her new little machines. "That's all you can say to me after saving my life and not seeing me for what, four years?" She had punched him playfully in the arm. It was like hitting a rock.

She'd been amazed at how seamlessly they'd fallen in to work together as partners. Tye despised the drones, and sometimes she couldn't blame him. He didn't think they were needed, but she was beginning to realize how shortsighted he was being.

The past three weeks of daily planning and training, learning how different flying the MAVS could be from the type of flying she'd been used to—at times, it almost seemed like nothing more than some kind of training exercise. As if the MAVs she was piloting were little more than some pimpled-faced nerd's pipe dream. They couldn't be actual crafts with genuine operational status and purpose, could they? They were so small. Sometimes guiding them through the air felt surreal.

She'd seen Nathan Kurn on television and read news articles about him since she was a child. They weren't messing with John Q. Citizen here. The charismatic Kurn knew things around Washington. He must have held dozens of markers with powerful and important people he could call in whenever he wanted. Yet based on Major Williamson's recommendation and a series of pre-interview emails, Tye and Raina, a couple of ex-Army outsiders, had managed to infiltrate Kurn's inner sanctum and gained enough of his confidence to be entrusted with what for him must have been the most sensitive of missions, protecting his reputation and that of his son, the truth be damned.

She had to work hard to keep herself from trying to digest all of these issues at once and stay focused on her flying.

Even with daily, intense hours behind the screens, piloting

what she'd dubbed the angel and its slightly larger relative the dragonfly—she'd named the bigger ones after her AirCav unit—wasn't like controlling any helicopter or plane she'd ever flown. The proximity of her location to the MAV themselves minimized any delays to the signals she relayed to the device, but becoming accustomed to the miniature environment the angel traveled through was proving far more daunting than she'd expected.

Door frames became narrow ridges on cliff faces; table and floor lamps proved to be giant, incandescent torches to be avoided; deep pile carpets looked like elephant grass; while passing along the edge of a picture window was like navigating the shoreline of some kind of clear blue ocean. Before leaving the military, she'd met and talked to an Air Force Predator pilot one afternoon at a conference. She remembered him describing the type of pressure operators experienced flying a full-sized, armed UAV over the battlefield. Major Williamson, who had experience training Predator pilots, had warned her about this. She was beginning to understand what they were talking about. She knew Tye must have been sweating bullets in Kurn's office. She wondered if he understood, let alone appreciated, that she was doing the same.

Facing Kurn in the office, Tye kept his manner relaxed but business-like. They needed more intel. Who knew what surprises this dude might have in his bag of tricks?

"Is this the only copy of the video?"

"Yes," Kurn said. "And I plan to destroy it after you leave. I only wanted you to see it so you would know what we're dealing with."

What they were dealing with was a young woman who'd been violated without her knowledge or consent. There had been enough of her face visible on the screen that Tye was hopeful he and Raina could make a positive ID from her Facebook page or college records. They could approach the girl and see if she wanted to press charges.

If she remembered anything at all. If she even wanted to come forward. Two big ifs.

"How'd you manage to shoot the video?"

Kurn shrugged. "I've been a long time benefactor and booster of the university. A maintenance man was well paid to hide the camera and then retrieve it and ask no questions. You know they make these little nanny cams now. You can really keep an eye on things with them."

"Really," Tye said. *If the weaselly old pirate only knew.* "When was the video taken?"

"Last weekend. But I've suspected something like this for a little while. There was another girl whose family came to me with their suspicions last month. We were able to come to an arrangement in that situation, but this needs to stop."

An arrangement, no doubt, that involved a good deal of money, Tye thought. Their eyes met for a moment as a long silence hung between them.

"He's probably slipping the drug into the girls' drinks," Tye said. "The police—"

"No." Kurn held up his hand. "I don't want the police involved. I want this matter dealt with privately." He laid the remote control on his desk and ejected the disk from his computer, handling it as if it contained pornographic images of children before tucking it into a drawer. "And I want it done quickly, quietly, and efficiently." Kurn's eyes narrowed. "You've been a professional soldier. I expect you and your partner...Ms. Sanchez, is it?...to act professionally."

"Without prejudice," Tye lied.

He glanced out the window for a moment at the Theodore Roosevelt Bridge, the distant Washington Monuments and the top of the Capitol dome. Thousands of his fellow "professional soldiers," as Kurn had referred to them, a couple of whom had been well known to Tye, lay buried among the sea of white headstones in Arlington only a mile down the highway between Roslyn and the Pentagon. That was at least one thing the politicians had gotten right: putting the National Cemetery up close and personal to D.C. where they'd have to be near them every day.

"You're back in school I see," Kurn continued, "Which I very much respect. What are you studying?"

"Military history."

Kurn chuckled. "Good for you. Something you must know a little bit about. Here's what I'm thinking. You can tell my son and his fraternity brothers that you're a transfer student, hoping to check out their house. I was a Zeta Phi over there at the university myself back in the day, and, if the need arises, I can easily drop your name with a recommendation about a promising prospective fraternity brother."

"Probably won't need it. But doesn't posing as a potential pledge violate some kind of fraternal code or something?"

"You let me worry about that."

Much as he hated to admit it, these alpha Greek fraternity-types pushed buttons in Tye's brain he'd just as soon didn't exist. He figured most of them for overeducated hibernators; adolescent, asinine products of special privilege, their souls fat and inebriated. Stick them in full battle-rattle in 110-degree heat and the bark of assault rifles and some hopped-up Hajis in the neighborhood, and you'd find out how they really measured up.

Then again, maybe Tye was missing something. Maybe Nathan Kurn's status was so exalted he didn't need to worry about such things as fraternal loyalty. Maybe the man's son was just a regular old Joe of a rapist. The subtleties of higher education and big media executive power plays probably represented too much of an enigma for a simple door kicker like Tye.

"So you want me to cozy up to your son and try to catch him in the act or something, maybe raid his little stash of pills?"

"I want you to pretend you're a police detective and arrest him."

"You want me to impersonate a cop?"

"If that's what you want to call it. But not just any cop, a cop who has connections. Specifically to me. Derek knows I have friends in law enforcement. All you need to do is tell him you're working undercover or something."

"Last I heard, there are pretty serious laws against that sort of thing."

"Of course, but this is just between us. Once you've sufficiently shaken him down, you can let him know you're working for me."

Tye didn't like the idea of shaking down anyone for the likes of Nathan Kurn, but he kept quiet.

"Okay," he said. "Then what?"

"That's it. We put the fear of God and prison into my son and tell him we'll be watching his every move. And if I so much as hear a breath about him doing this kind of thing again, I'll cut him off. No more financial support, and if he faces prosecution, I won't protect him."

Really? He knew the last threat was a bluff. Any man who went to this much trouble to mess with his son's head wasn't going to sit by and let that same son trot off to rot in prison without the best kind of fact-spinning and motive-bending defense money could buy.

"With all due respect, Mr. Kurn, you said Derek is your only son. Why don't you just go down there and confront him about the situation yourself?" He thought it was a logical question.

But Kurn made a face and rubbed at the back of his neck, apparently uncomfortable with the query. "That, um, that gets rather complicated. My relationship with Derek is private, for one thing. And I have other issues to consider. Like I said, I want no publicity and no one else at the school should ever know about our intentions or actions." Kurn turned to look out the window at a view of the D.C. skyline. "Believe me when I tell you this, Mr. Palmer. I know my son and I know how to best handle this issue."

"But why are you doing all this?"

"I have my reasons. Not the least of which, as you may have heard about in the news, I'm involved in a major merger at the moment, and the last thing I want is for some of my son's youthful indiscretions to botch up the works."

Youthful indiscretions. Tye wondered what other skeletons Kurn might be hiding. Maybe the apple didn't fall very far from the tree.

Maybe fearful he'd said too much, Kurn turned to look him straight in the eyes. "I've spent some time looking into your backgrounds, you know. You and your partner, I mean." The man stepped over to his desk, looked down, and scanned an official looking piece of stationary. "I understand you both served in Afghanistan."

"Yes, sir."

"And Ms. Sanchez was a pilot. All sorts of commendations. Shot down. Lost a foot. Must have been horrible. You were awarded a Bronze Star for pulling her from the wreckage under heavy fire."

"Yes, sir."

"Well that's certainly good enough in my book. A pitiful old TV man's dilemma over his boy's sexual dalliances seems a far cry from the valor of military service."

Pitiful old TV man? Who was this guy trying to con?

"No argument there," Tye said.

Kurn moved another folder off of a pile on his desk and flipped it open to reveal a photo. "Tell me more about your partner. She's quite attractive, or so it appears from her official photo."

"Oh, please," Raina whispered in his ear. "Now I really am going to puke."

"She's very skilled at what she does," Tye said.

"She's not a student like yourself?"

"No."

"Well, I would very much like to meet her, too, before all this is over."

"I'm sure that can be arranged."

"Mmmm." Kurn smoothed out the sheet of paper he held in his hands.

"So I suppose the only question left to ask from my end is how much you two are going to charge me for this little job."

Tye didn't flinch. "Ten thousand."

"Ten thousand dollars?"

"Half up front as a retainer, plus expenses."

Kurn cleared his throat. "That's a lot of money for a couple of days' work for a college student. You know I could get a regular private investigator working on an hourly basis for less."

He and Raina had agreed upon the amount because they didn't think Kurn would respect them if they asked for less. He wasn't backing down. "If you could find one who could pull this off. You're asking both of us to take a big risk."

Kurn seemed to suppress another smile. "All right, Mr. Palmer." He spun his desk chair around and sat down in it. "I'll pay you your retainer." He reached down behind the chair and came back up with what looked like a leather portfolio. Folding it part way open, he pulled out a stack of hundred dollar bills, peeling off the number he wanted. "But I expect results."

"Absolutely."

Kurn handed him the stack of money. Then he opened one of his desk drawers, pulled out a small card, and handed it to him. "I want to be kept informed at all times. I'll be checking in with you soon. That's my personal cell phone number and the contact information for my executive assistant. If for some reason I don't answer my phone, she'll know where to find me."

The network chieftain leaned across the desk and extended his hand again. Tye took it and with it the measure of an opponent whom up until today he'd only known as an abstraction. Kurn's grip was as firm as his gaze, brimming with charismatic arrogance.

Tye had read accounts of Arab Muhajadeen in Afghanistan years before, anxious to get in on the fighting against the Soviets, the vast majority of which was actually being done by the Afghanis. Upon meeting the wealthy and magnetic Saudi, Osama Bin Laden, the wannabe jihadists would pledge themselves to martyrdom on the spot.

He felt no such inspiration shaking hands with Kurn.

Kurn released his hand. "I'm late for a conference call. You won't mind showing yourself out?"

"Not at all."

In the end, Tye supposed, all wars became personal. Otherwise, who would do the actual fighting?

Not the political leaders. Not the strategic thinkers, nor the talkers and writers. Not the film and TV people like Kurn with all of their trappings and camera crews. No, it was left to the head knockers and the grunts like himself to undertake the discipline and to suffer the physical and emotional scars of being the tip of the spear.

He and Raina had no intention of contacting Nathan Kurn again. Leaving the room, he glanced back over his shoulder to see the man picking up his phone.

4

RAINA WAS WAITING for him in the van.

"Did you get the recording?"

"Some of it," she said.

He climbed into the front passenger seat, closed the door, and buckled his seat belt. "You don't sound confident."

"Look," she said. "These little MAVs aren't perfect."

"Do you have him on disk or not?"

"Yes. I have most of what he said to you."

"What about the movie he showed me of his son?"

"Some of it, like I said. But I had to reposition the angel several times because he kept moving, and the picture is a little dark." Raina shifted into drive, engaged the turn signal, and, glancing over her shoulder, eased out into the line of cars flowing along Wilson Boulevard. Only her left foot had been lost and replaced by a prosthetic, so driving was no problem.

"You think it's enough?"

"I don't know. I haven't exactly had time to review the recording."

They drove in silence for a few moments. Tye didn't like it one bit. He'd put his butt on the line with Kurn and now they weren't even sure if they had solid evidence against the son. He knew Raina was good, the kind of pilot you wanted behind the controls if you had to go into any kind of hostile situation.

But he was still uneasy about using the MAVs. Never trust a machine—plus, how did he and Raina know they wouldn't become a target themselves? There could be a ShadowHawk a few thousand feet overhead right now keeping tabs on them and they wouldn't know it. All anyone would see, of course, was a lean young man in a blue sport coat and khakis climbing into a silver camper van. As for the dark-haired woman behind the wheel, he and Raina might have been two lovers or even husband and wife, just another young couple perhaps meeting for lunch. The odds that they were under surveillance were slim, but you could never be too cautious.

He didn't allow himself to breath easier until they were well away from the building.

"At least you had him convinced. Congratulations," she said.

"Thank you."

"You were a pretty smooth operator in there."

"I was lucky."

"I don't think he suspected a thing." She smiled, her dark curls flowing over her cheeks to frame her full lips and bright teeth.

"Let's hope not."

"I know a good place we can talk," she said.

They turned on to Ft. Meyer Drive and drove further into Arlington. It was a sunny day, warm for late October, the temperature reaching the high seventies. With the heat from all of her equipment in back, Raina had the van's air conditioner running at full tilt.

The juice bar and sandwich shop she had in mind stood in a nondescript strip mall, wedged between a used bookstore and a tax preparation service. The proprietors, a Sikh husband

and wife, had just opened for the day. It was still too early for lunch, even for a Friday, so Tye and Raina had the place to themselves. They bought a couple of smoothies and found a back corner booth where they could keep their voices low and speak in private.

"This is it then," she said.

Tye nodded. "We're committed either way. Looks like we're on."

"I'm going to need a couple of additional pieces of equipment. I've already started working on a list. I'll email it to you and Williamson once it's ready."

"More toys?"

"They're not toys." She was supposed to do all the flying while he handled the ground work, which included requisition.

"I know, I know. Just teasing. But no email," he said. "Let's just print it out or write it down, and we can discuss it with Major Williamson and burn the list afterward." He lowered his voice. "We don't want to leave any kind of electronic trail in case we get caught."

"We won't get caught," she said under her breath.

He nodded before taking a quick sip from his drink. "I'm sorry for doubting you. We won't get caught as long as you keep flying the way you just did in there. Look, the equipment is what it is. I get it that you know what you're doing with all this techno wizardry, sometimes I guess I just—"

"Don't worry," she said. "I can handle it."

"No worries about using this stuff against civilians?"

"Sometimes," she admitted, trying not to dwell on issues that would just confuse the situation even more. "But I figure the way things are going in the world these days, the genie's already out of the bottle on this stuff."

"We're going to have to take this whole thing with Williamson one job at a time. The mission with Kurn is good. It's a righteous thing."

"No doubt about that," she said.

She crossed her legs beneath the table and her foot bumped his knee.

"Sorry." She looked down for a moment, embarrassed.

"No worries."

"Don't mean to sound like I'm lecturing you, either."

"You're not."

"What about the cash?"

Tye took out the roll of hundred-dollar bills and set it on the table. "I guess we put it in the slush fund in case we need it."

She nodded, and he stuffed the thick wad of money back into his pocket.

Her fingers lay on the table. For a moment, she wondered if he might reach across and put his hand on them to reassure her, but he didn't.

They were still trying to understand one another. When she'd shown up in the warehouse with Williamson a couple of days after the major had recruited her for the job and seen Tye, she could hardly believe her eyes. It was like fate, or God maybe, had put him in that burning Kiowa to pull her out years before.

Maybe there really had been a reason she'd survived, and that reason was here and now. She'd wanted so badly to get back into the air again. Flying the MAVs was fascinating, vexing, and thrilling, all at once. Seeing Tye again, and getting to work with him, had been like the icing on the cake.

Tye stared at Raina across the table. *What did she think of him?* he wondered. There was only one thing he knew for certain: he wanted to know more and more about her. What really made her tick?

He'd heard she'd been one of the best of the best before getting shot down. Didn't even want to try to imagine how hard it must have been for her since. All he knew was Williamson had plucked her out of working behind a desk for some defense contractor to recruit her for this job in the same way he'd recruited him. The first day, she'd joked she'd been feeling like a drone working in a cubicle for the past couple of years so she might as well learn to fly some more interesting ones.

He'd watched her struggle at first with the new technology. Flying by remote control was obviously different than flying live in the cockpit. But Williamson apparently had spent some time training Air Force Reaper pilots and seemed to know what he was doing when it came to the MAVs. He could be hard, but he was patient, and Raina was obviously a quick study. Whether the equipment Williamson was providing them would be up to the job remained an open question, but there wasn't a whole lot either Tye or Raina could do about that. Just like being back on deployment.

"No second thoughts yourself about what we're doing?" she asked, gazing out through the empty shop front for a moment before looking back at him as if she were reading his thoughts.

"None at all," he said.

"Good." She raised her foam smoothie cup in toast to his. Maybe he was imagining things, but he thought he saw a hint of a sparkle in her dark eyes.

5

LATER, THEY DEBRIEFED with Williamson over a secure video link.

They were in Raina's Fairfax apartment. It was on the second floor of a nondescript garden complex, almost identical to Tye's on the other side of the building, both sublet for a month under a pseudonym. A small, one-bedroom affair, there was a computer desk and chair, a couch, and a single, back window in the living room. The branches of a big maple tree obscured most of the view outside. Sunlight filtered through the canopy, flashes of orange and red blooming from the peaking autumn leaves.

Seeing the major always brought Tye back to leading his squad at their forward operating base in Nangarhar and the operation against the Taliban that had led to his pulling Raina from her burning chopper, the death of her commander co-pilot, and the loss of two good infantrymen from his squad.

Soon afterward, Major Cameron Williamson, tall, bald as a bowling ball, dressed in clean desert camouflage uniform, had choppered in for a day and introduced himself. The FOB was still reeling at the time from the aftereffects of the battle. It was unusual but not unheard of for an Air Force officer to show up at such a frontline position. As far as Tye was concerned, he and his squad bled in the dust and muck while the flyboys and all their A- 10s, F-16s, B-1s and drones normally kept their panties dry overhead.

But Williamson made an impression on Tye. The man carried an uncommon air of authority and he seemed to instantly get Tye and his soldiers the way a lot of superior officers didn't. Williamson told them he was on a "fact-finding assignment." Most of Tye's platoon had figured him for CIA, except he didn't wear a beard and dress like a Pashtun.

Raina told Tye she had met Williamson, too, soon after the battle that ended her flight career. He had made a pass through the hospital where she was being treated, specifically asking about pilots.

Now, years later, Williamson had reached out to Tye and Raina like some kind of ghost from their mutual past.

"How'd things go on your first go-round with the MAVs?" the major asked, his image filling Raina's laptop screen.

"Not bad," Raina said. "We had some technical difficulties, but I was able to work around them."

"Good. That's why I picked you for the job. Did you get what you went in for?"

Raina hesitated, so Tye jumped in.

"Yes, sir. Not quite as much as we'd hoped, but we're in position to proceed."

He and Raina had gone over their recording of the video Kurn had shown him on his office wall a dozen times. It was far from perfect. Coupled with Kurn's statements and photos they'd obtained of his son, Derek Kurn could be identified in the grainy, partially blocked video. But if the video were required to stand on its own, there was plenty of room for doubt.

The view of his victim, on the other hand, was clearer, and he and Raina were already trying to identify her.

"Remember rule number one," Williamson said. "What

you're doing with our MAVs must remain secret. You've been specifically chosen due to your backgrounds. I hope you understand from a civil liberties perspective we're playing with dynamite."

"So we're just throwing civil rights out the window now, Major?" Tye looked across at Raina. Drones like the Predator may have more than earned their place on the battlefield, but he still mistrusted the capabilities of the MAVs; the challenges Raina had faced in Kurn's office earlier in the day only reinforced his doubts. Plus, he was no longer in the Army and he felt like pushing Williamson a bit. The major had let slip in one of their earlier conversations that Tye hadn't been his first choice for this op. He wished he could have known who'd been the top pick. No one liked to be relegated to second team.

"You know better than that, Palmer. You know what we're dealing with in Nathan Kurn."

"But what are we doing here? Are we working for law enforcement, is that it?"

There was a pause. "I can't answer that. Officially, you're private investigators."

Great.

"Look," Tye said. "If you really want to nail Kurn, why not just use the FBI or something? Why even bring us into it?"

"This is a fluid situation," Williamson said, suddenly sounding like a bureaucrat. "As I told you, we chose you people because of who you are. For your own protection that's all I can say for the moment."

"You picked us because you knew we'd be on board with this mission. Isn't that about all there is to it?"

"That was a factor in my decision-making, yes." He looked across at Raina. Her face was a blank. "This is a distraction, Mr. Palmer. You need to stay focused on the mission at hand."

"Okay," he said finally. "Just wanted to get that out there on the table." He glanced at Raina. "I guess we stay on a need-to-know…for now."

"All right then…As far as Kurn and his son, I trust you two already have a further game plan in mind?"

"We do."

"Good. I don't want to know any of the details. You both know how to contact me should you need any more technical resources or support."

Raina shifted a little in her seat. "What about funding?"

"Our arrangement still stands. All expenses paid as they occur. Payment in full on completion of the mission."

"What about the money Kurn paid us?" Tye asked.

"If you succeed, I doubt he'll be coming after you for it."

"Yeah," Raina said. "Especially since we're the ones who could end up in jail."

There was a long pause. "…Let me know when you've completed your objective," was all Williamson said.

"If things work out the way I've drawn them up…" Tye said, "that's one thing you won't have to worry about finding out."

"Very good then."

The picture went dark. Raina and Tye were left staring into the laptop screen together.

"Not exactly the warm-and-fuzzy type, is he?"

"Hardly." Raina grunted in agreement. "But I probably wouldn't listen to him if he was."

"The day after tomorrow is Halloween. They'll be having a big party at the frat. We can make our move then."

Raina pressed her lips together. "All right."

She'd placed a little plastic jack-o-lantern on one of her computer monitors, but that was it as far as the decorations. Neither of them would be doing any partying.

"You don't need more time to practice with your little drones, do you?"

"No. No, I'm good to go."

"What's wrong then?"

"I'm putting an awful lot on the line with Williamson," she said. "And so are you."

"Yup. So?"

"You say it so cavalierly. Like you're willing to just throw your whole career away."

He shrugged. "I guess I left all that kind of stuff back in Jalalabad."

"What kind of stuff?"

"Concern for career."

"But you're back in school."

"That's different." He shrugged some more. There was no sense in arguing about it. Nothing could be like the ragged edge of bravery and terror that came with being downrange. The dust and sun and cold. The hot smoke. The smell of goats, the sights of brightly mosaic prayer mats, and the fear in people's expressions.

"What about you?" he asked.

"I'm here, aren't I? Instead of filling a space in some corporate cubicle."

He nodded. In her Kiowa, Raina had been about as close to the ground fighting as it was possible to get from the sky. She was Air Cav. No matter what happened, he would never question her courage.

She looked him in the eyes. "We both know why we're in this. We fell into the same crapstorm over there. I can never repay you for what you did. But right now I need to know you can complete your part of this job. I'm relying on you."

He nodded.

"You think we can really pull this off?" she said.

"Piece of cake." He offered her a dubious smile.

"No. Tell me."

He wouldn't lie to her.

Nathan Kurn had been featured on the cover of *Time*. The man had a lot of powerful friends. His son Derek was playing major college football—maybe not a star or even a starter, but a scholarship player and the kid was president of his fraternity. The younger Kurn inhabited a rarified atmosphere: he was both a jock and the son of a celebrity. They were trying to expose the Kurns through the potentially illegal use of what was no doubt classified and possibly untested military technology. They had their work cut out for them, and though their cause may well have been righteous, they were in uncharted territory.

A thousand things might go wrong.

6

THAT NIGHT, RAINA dreamed of flying again. Back in the left seat of her helicopter over the kill zone, watching the thermal imaging focus on some steep, nondescript moonscape. Into the picture strode the dark silhouettes of a pair of Afghan mountain horses, navigating the harsh terrain.

They were small but powerful Lokai, beautiful creatures staged for battle and put to good use by Afghan Northern Alliance fighters and the first covert U.S. troops dropped into the mountains in response to 9/11. They reminded her of the horse her father had bought for her on their small ranch in New Mexico, a beautiful Appaloosa, the year before he came down with cancer and they ended up having to sell the pony to help pay for his treatments.

Raina watched the horses for what seemed like a long time through her scope, until it happened as it always did in the dream. The sudden loss of control. Like falling off a cliff. The fall into darkness and the horror of impact. The feeling that she couldn't get out of her seat, that she could never get out.

She awoke in a cold sweat. She was alone in her bed in the temporary apartment. Tye had similar digs in another building in the same complex. He'd fallen asleep on her couch while she continued to work away at her keyboard, so she'd thrown a blanket over him and retreated to the bedroom sometime after one a.m.

The bedside clock read a little after four. She knew she had to be sharp for the new day about to break. She had to be sharp for Tye and for Williamson, whoever they all were working for now, because their mission was good and was on target. But she also knew sleep wouldn't be coming again, at least not for tonight, not for her.

She crawled out from beneath the covers, fumbling in the dark for the crutch she needed to make it to the bathroom without her prosthetic foot. Sometimes the frustration of it all brought tears to her eyes, but she felt as if she were all cried out.

She finished in the bathroom, pulling her bathrobe around her, and stumbled to her desk to check on her computers. Everything seemed normal and quiet—all systems go.

One of the tiny hover angel MAVs lay on the table next to the computer. She picked up the drone and gently turned it over in her hands.

What a marvel of engineering, she thought. Its translucent wings acted as miniscule rotors, not unlike those on her helicopter; except these were made of some ultra-thin but strong membrane-like material she'd never seen before. The tiny control hinges were even more elegant; she'd marveled at them when she first examined them under the microscope.

The brains of the unit were housed behind its miniature camera. She fought against the temptation to try to disassemble the board to examine the circuitry for fear she might damage it. The thing must have cost a fortune to develop. Had to be government. The CIA, NSA, or some other spook agency must be behind it. Or could it have come from overseas? Nothing on the units themselves or their components gave them away, unlike any other drone she'd ever seen. Hell, any Tom, Dick, or Harry could buy a little drone these days and fly them around their backyard using their smartphone as a controller. The off-the-shelf components were manufactured all over the world—China, Russia, Israel. But these little babies were way beyond that.

Her experience as a pilot had given her a healthy respect for flying in combat, so she felt like she understood both the positives and pitfalls of weaponizing unmanned aircraft. She knew many foreign governments, not all of them friendly to U.S. interests, were continuing to develop and deploy their own military drones. In the armaments world it was nothing short of a drone frenzy.

Even so, the camera system on this little baby was more advanced and of far smaller form than any she'd ever seen. When functioning properly, it could almost reconnoiter an entire space, looking at it from multiple different angles.

She'd read articles about autonomous drone systems, employing advanced pattern recognition computer algorithms to fly independently, and she shuddered to think of the possibilities. Eye-in-the-sky surveillance systems like the Army's Constant Hawk or the Air Force's Gorgon Stare were already changing the way military strategists looked at warfare.

But the miniaturized MAV she held in her hands took things to an entirely different level. She could provide intimate surveillance of anyone, almost anywhere. She could infiltrate a corporate boardroom or someone's bedroom. The possibilities were almost as endless as they were sobering.

On the other hand, maneuvering undetected through suburban neighborhoods and even inside buildings was far from easy, as she was learning. It required a special set of talents she was being forced to develop as she went, beyond anything she'd ever had to worry about flying for the military.

Feel the plane.

She could still hear Major Williamson's voice from only a

few weeks before admonishing her through her headset to get control of her tiny drone, as if she were actually aboard the flight. She was finding she liked the challenge of piloting the tiny devices. The larger dragonflies were sometimes more fun to fly, zooming nap-of-the-earth or darting in and out among buildings. They were designed for use outdoors and could track far greater distances. But they also made more noise, a faint but persistent flutter. The hover angels, like the one she held in her hand, were especially effective indoors, but were more easily thrown off track by extremes in temperatures, a stiff wind, or even hot or cold air blowing from an air conditioner or room vent.

"Best little private eye in the world."

"Oh," she said, almost dropping the drone on the desk. She set it back down carefully.

"That thing in your hands, I mean…it's a pretty good investigator."

Tye, all six-feet-four of him, leaned against the doorframe of her bedroom. His shirttail hung out. His jeans looked like he'd slept in them, which of course he had, and his short hair was pasted to one side of his head.

"You startled me."

"Sorry. I heard you rummaging around in here and wanted to make sure you were okay."

"You look like hell."

"Good morning to you, too. Don't you ever sleep?"

"I slept…some," she said, sounding a little more defensive than she'd intended.

"You're really obsessed with those things, aren't you?" He looked at the little drone.

"I am," she admitted. "You have to admit they're pretty amazing."

She picked up the MAV again. She was coming to consider the little drones as extensions of herself. MAVs were something she could control, unlike people. If the public knew the kind of things they could do with these little gems, would they be fascinated? Or horrified?

"Well, you know what they always say," he said.

"What's that?"

"A pilot's first love always has to be their ship."

"What do *you* know about being a pilot?"

"My dad was a pilot. For a little while at least. Before he left me and my mom. But that was a long time ago and it's a long story."

She set the drone down again and turned away, embarrassed. She felt disarmed sometimes by his candor.

"Me," he went on. "I'd rather be standing face-to-face with someone, looking them in the eyes."

He smiled at her from across the room.

This was the man she owed her life to, but there was a part of her, she had to admit, that sometimes wished he hadn't been so heroic, that wished she'd died in the crash along with Skyles.

Her long recuperation and the counseling that went along with it had been painful and slow. She'd been left to pick up the pieces of what was left of her life and the inevitable self-questioning about what she might have done differently. Now here Tye was, suddenly, improbably, back in her life.

Staff Sergeant Tye Palmer had seen two tours in Iraq and another two in Afghanistan. His special technical expertise, he jokingly claimed, was functioning as a homing device for trouble.

Had he come to rescue her again? Rescue her from what?

"I guess robots will never truly think and act like humans," she mumbled, half to herself.

For now, Williamson had assured them, their MAVs were strictly surveillance platforms. But it didn't take much of an imagination to realize that these little flyers were bound to be weaponized and more, sooner or later. And when that happened, there would be few places an assassin, or counter-terrorism team for that matter, couldn't penetrate. Counter-measures, along with the drones themselves, would become huge business. For all she knew, maybe they already were.

"Let's hope not. Otherwise, we're all doomed. You had breakfast?" he asked, stretching and yawning.

"No, I—"

"You got any eggs and bacon around this place? I fry a mean over-easy."

"Sorry, I haven't had time to shop."

"Okay. We both need some fuel in the tank. Why don't I slip back over to my apartment and jump in the shower. I'll be back in a jiff and we can head out and find something to eat."

"Sounds like a plan." He lingered in the doorway for a moment.

"Oh, and thanks," she said.

"For what?"

"For checking on me."

"Somebody's got to do it, Chief."

For an instant, she was sure she was looking at the ghost of Captain Skyles.

She glanced down at the drone on the desk in front of her again, wondering if, with all of the technological wonders happening these days, someone somewhere in the world was actually developing a workable time machine.

But when she looked up at the doorway again, Tye was gone.

7

A COUPLE OF HOURS later, Raina stepped back into the apartment. Closing the door behind her, she tossed the van keys onto the desk next to her computer, laying her cell phone next to them, and sighed.

She and Tye had gone out to breakfast at a local diner where they'd eaten bacon and eggs and good hot coffee and alternately shared pages of a daily newspaper. This was their day to get all of their planning and preparations together before Derek Kurn's frat party tomorrow night, but Tye had said little while they ate. Maybe he was just hungry; at times he didn't seem to be much of a conversationalist.

She'd dropped him off at a Wal-Mart a half-mile down the highway from the apartment complex where he said he needed to pick up a few things. He said he would walk back to the apartment and they would meet up again in an hour to finalize their plans.

Moving awkwardly across the room, she turned and flopped down on the couch to think. Lucky for her it was her left foot she'd lost, her Army rehabilitation therapist had cheerily assured her. At least she could drive a car without special equipment. Maybe not a helicopter again, but....

Oh, who was she kidding? She'd become a freak of nature;

that was all there was to it. The pretty—at least she still hoped—young woman seated in the corner at the bar all the guy's would try to come on to…that is, until they got a look at the foot. Then their eyes would skip away. Even if they stayed to listen to her story, they'd treat her more as an object worthy of a respectful distance, like some kind of monument—unless they were soldiers themselves—to the men they maybe thought they should be. The juxtaposition didn't exactly spark an avalanche of potential romance.

But enough of the pity party.

She started to push up from the couch when she heard, almost sensed, the slightest creak of the floor from within the darkened kitchen, and felt an iciness slice through her like a knife.

She wasn't alone. She didn't know exactly how she knew, but she knew.

She tried to fling herself across the room to where her old Army sidearm hung in its holster on the coat rack, but she was too slow.

"I wouldn't do that if I were you," a voice said.

She froze, down on one knee. A pair of men, dressed in blue jeans and collared shirts with their heads covered by ski masks, appeared, rising up from their crouch around the corner into a shooter's stance. In their hands were Colt semiautomatics, pointed at her head.

Her heart leapt into her throat.

"Who are you?" She instantly figured by their bearing and demeanor they were either military or ex-military.

"You don't need to know that, ma'am. Please return to the couch."

"And what if I don't?"

"It's not a request." She looked into the eyes of the one doing the talking, the taller of the two, and could see he meant business. She worked her jaw in a circular motion. How could she have been so stupid as to let these two get the jump on her?

"Okay, a polite command then," she said. "I guess I'll take the couch option."

She stood upright and returned to the couch.

The man spoke to his accomplice. "Cuff her and hood her."

"What?" She didn't like the sound of this.

But before she could react the other man moved behind her and pulled her hands together behind her back, securing them with a pair of plastic handcuffs. Then a black hood came down over her head, throwing her into the dark.

"What's going on?" she asked. "Why are you doing this?"

"The less you talk and the more you listen the easier this is going to go. Turn around and sit down on the couch," the first man said.

She could hear him moving toward her. She felt the briefest touch of something hard against her head and realized to her horror it was the barrel of his Colt. At least she could still breath.

"Okay. Okay. Let's not get trigger happy." She did as he instructed. It was a little difficult without the use of her arms or her sight, but she managed to drop down heavily onto the couch again. The two men were silent for a moment, but she could hear them moving around her. She wondered what they were doing.

The answer came a moment later when she felt the sting of a needle in her hip.

"Hey!" She instinctively tried to shake away, which made it hurt worse.

"Don't move."

"What are you doing? What did you just give to me?"

Visions of the video she'd just recorded from Nathan Kurn's office flashed through her mind.

"You won't be harmed as long as you cooperate."

"Why should I believe you?"

"This is for your own protection." The drug was already taking effect. Like a gray curtain, sleep pressed down on her like a curtain, spreading through her shoulders, arms, and legs. Noting the effects as if examining them from a great distance, she could no longer feel her appendages, nor the rest of her body—not ever her mouth, her lips, or her tongue.

"You're treating me like a terrorist," she managed to mumble, the voice not like hers at all.

The last words she heard sounded something like a dream, as if the man, too, were speaking from far away.

"Maybe you are."

8

TYE KNOCKED ON the door to Raina's second floor apartment again and waited.

Still no answer—where could she be? The rental van was still in the parking lot. He seriously doubted she'd gone anywhere on foot. It had barely been an hour since she'd dropped him off at the Wal-Mart.

He shifted the bag of groceries from one hand to another and took out the spare key she'd given him. They'd agreed to exchange keys on the off chance, as part of the job, one might need to get into the other's temporary apartment. They'd also agreed he would come by her apartment to go over things after picking up the food at store. He knocked one last time just to be sure.

Turning the key in the lock, he had the funny feeling he was opening more than just a door. Just a little while before they'd been celebrating their success at penetrating Nathan Kurn's office, at opening a potential new chapter in their lives, fraught with risk and reward.

Over the past few days, he was beginning to notice a new side to Raina, a truer confidence, and a freer spirit. Was it because of the MAVs? *Because she was flying again?* Raina was also incredibly efficient and thorough at her job. Reliable as the day was long—she could multi-task with the best of them. Why hadn't she called him if she was planning to go out somewhere? It wasn't like her. He smelled trouble.

He pushed on the heavy door and let it swing open.

"Raina?"

Nothing.

"Raina, you here?"

The soldier in him peered warily through the doorway. From inside the small apartment, the refrigerator motor purred. He caught a faint whiff of something antiseptic and vaguely familiar. For some reason, it made him think of her artificial foot.

In the time they'd been working together Tye had been careful to be as casual as possible about it. He instinctively knew she was self-conscious about her disability, and he didn't want to force her into a conversation to address it; he wanted to give her whatever time and space she felt like she needed. But maybe that was a mistake. Had she fallen or been hurt?

"Anybody home?" He stepped into the living room.

To one side was a desk with a computer on it; the computer and screen were turned off. Opposite the window stood a small couch with its cushions in disarray. That didn't seem like the Raina he knew.

He checked the kitchen and bedroom for any sign of her, but found nothing. Back in the living room, his eyes came to rest on the desk again. A pile of aviation books and software manuals lay beside the computer monitor. Between the books and the monitor he found the keys to the rental car, but that wasn't all. With the keys was the cell phone she'd been using. Raina knew they needed to be in constant contact. Next to her jacket Raina's handgun also still hung securely in its holster from a peg on the wall.

What could have caused her to leave the apartment without

at least her phone? Maybe she just needed a break after the stress of flying the MAV into the building and had gone outside to sit on the lawn or something.

He stepped back across the threshold and looked down at the sidewalk, but he saw no sign of Raina. Their van was the only car in the narrow parking lot at the moment, and a tall hedge blocked any view beyond. He walked down to the end of the balcony where he could get a better look at a patch of grass and a small pond that abutted the apartment complex. The grass was empty and the pond was still. On the other side of the pond, through a stand of pine trees, traffic flowed along a lightly traveled Boulevard.

"Huh," he muttered to himself. Back in the apartment, he stood in the living room looking around. Maybe he was worried over nothing. Maybe Raina was a closet cigarette smoker and had snuck off, forgetting her keys, into some outdoor cubby hole down the way to enjoy a puff; she would be back, embarrassed, in a couple of minutes. But in the few weeks they'd been working together, he'd spotted no sign of such a habit.

His gaze came to rest on a thin strip of sticky paper that looked like it had torn off and fallen between the couch cushions. He reached down to pick it up.

Sticky to the touch, it looked like a piece of a label that been torn on one edge. But the typed wording was still readable: *Diisopropylpheno.*

Tye had no idea what the word meant. But it sounded like a scientific name. Was it some kind of medication? Maybe Raina was dosing herself for pain—she wouldn't be the first vet addict to come down the pike.

There was that faint antiseptic smell again. Could something have gone wrong? Could she have accidentally OD'd and wandered off down the complex or into the woods? He shuddered to think of the possibilities.

But something didn't add up. Why had her door been closed and locked tight when he arrived? Her keys still lay on the desk. That meant someone else besides Tye had a key.

He sat down at the desk, pulled out his smartphone, and opened up a search engine, carefully typing in the letters from the label. It didn't take long to find what he was looking for. Only one letter was missing. *Diisopropylphenol* —more often known as Propofol, a common general anesthetic agent.

He turned and looked over the couch cushions again, seeing in his mind what must have happened. The faint leftover smell wasn't from the drug. He'd smelled it often enough—it was from the alcohol rub swiped over the skin in preparation for an injection. Maybe someone careful and well trained had drugged Raina. Maybe they'd opened the box containing the medication, begun the injection, and she had struggled for a moment, which was when the piece of label was knocked free.

Was Raina all right? Had their mission been blown?

9

RAINA AWOKE TO near darkness. She was lying on a narrow cot in a small, dimly lit room. Above her was a concrete, bunker-like ceiling, and on every side painted concrete walls with no windows. Her body still felt stiff and heavy, her throat as dry as parchment. She felt her wrists. Her hands no longer seemed to be cuffed.

"Glad to see you're awake, CWO Sanchez."

She turned her head slightly to see a handsome, dark-haired man in expensive looking clothes—tailored khakis, oxford shirt, and stylish sweater—standing over her.

"How do you feel?"

"Like someone hit me over the head with a fence post. What is this? Who are you?"

"My name is Lance Murnell, special advisor to Homeland Security."

"Homeland?" She massaged her forehead, still feeling a little woozy.

"That's correct."

"Since when is DHS into abduction?"

"Uh…yeah. Sorry about that. It wasn't my call."

"Got anything to drink in this place?" She felt like she was about to die of thirst.

"Sure." He reached toward a table behind him and came back with a Styrofoam cup filled with ice chips, which he held out to her.

She took the cup from him, put it to her lips, and began to suck on a mouthful of ice.

"Take it easy. You don't want to induce vomiting."

"What are you, a doctor?"

"Not a medical one, no." She looked him up and down. He could have easily posed for the cover of *GQ*. Not that she ever paid too close attention to such things. He seemed like a nice guy, too—nicer than the kidnapper cyborg-types who'd stuck a needle in her vein anyway, although that wasn't saying much.

"Why am I here?"

Murnell smiled. "You get right to the bottom line, don't you? That's one of the reasons we picked you."

"Picked me? Picked me for what?" She already had a new job and a stark righteous mission with Tye Palmer, thank you very much, she wanted to add, but figured she'd better not. If they were in her apartment, they must have already known about that.

"It's for a new type of technology I'm about to show you, if you're up to it. A program I think will be of great interest to you."

"Oh, yeah? Why all the secrecy? What's it for, repelling alien invaders or something?"

He smiled again. "Not exactly."

This really was one seriously good-looking dude.

Raina didn't normally swoon over men—she was attractive enough in her own right. But Murnell was off the charts. She wondered if they'd purposely sent him in to be here when she woke up, a walking talking genius hunk of male pheromones.

"Okay. What is it then?" She tried to sit up, but immediately felt dizzy, and laid her head back down.

"In a minute. Give yourself a little more time for the medication to wear off."

"I don't have more time."

"Why, you have some pressing appointment?"

Actually, yes, she thought. *With a pretty boy college rapist and his scumbag cover-up of a father.* She glared at Murnell, wondering if he might just fit into the pretty boy category himself.

"All right," he said getting the message. "If that's what you want…But if you fall and crack your skull, don't say I didn't warn you."

"Can I have some actual water?"

"Okay." He reached around and picked up another cup, turning to hand it to her. This one contained only liquid.

She took a couple of sips. It tasted heavenly.

"Stomach okay?"

She nodded.

"Good. You think you can stand?"

"Time to find out," she said.

She raised her head again, and though she felt the same dizziness, this time it was a little better. She pushed through it and sat all the way up. He steadied her momentarily—she caught a faint whiff of his aftershave—before stepping away.

"Everything all right?" he asked.

"Whoa. What'd you people give me?"

"It's an anesthetic. Just like you were having a surgical procedure. There should be no long-term ill effects."

"Priceless." She shook her head. "Who were the guys who snatched me?"

"One is a medical corpsman. The other is a squad leader. Both special forces."

"Great. Now they can add seizing woman against her will to their resumes."

"Again, I apologize. But I hope you'll come to see it was worth it."

"Right," she snickered.

"Still feeling okay?"

"I'm fine. Let's see what you've got." She swung her legs off the cot and placed her feet on the floor.

"You can walk okay? ...I mean with the prosthetic."

"That's the general idea. Titanium, carbon fiber, and biomechanical electronic feedback—state of the art. Though it's not exactly the same as Mother Nature."

She pushed off the cot and rose into a standing position. The room seemed to swirl for a moment.

He was there by her side, taking hold of her arm again.

"Don't get any bright ideas," she said.

Again he offered her the smile, this time with a slight guffaw. "Don't worry. Can you make it okay?"

She nodded, waving him off, and he let her go. "Which way to the Emerald City?" she said.

He looked at her quizzically for a moment. "Funny you should say that," he said.

10

THERE WAS A loud click as the door in the corner of
the room angled open. She followed him through it into
a brilliantly lit hallway. After the dimness of the room, the light
was almost blinding.

"Give your eyes a moment to adjust." He paused, waiting
for her to catch up.

"Where are we going?"

"You'll see. Stomach still okay?"

"Okay enough." She felt like crap but wasn't about to give
her jailer the satisfaction of knowing it. He laughed. "Spoken
like an Air Cavalryman."

"Woman, you mean."

"Of course."

Raina noticed right away that, unlike the room with her
cot, the walls here were made of a more high tech substance,
a kind of steel she'd never seen before, polished like glass, with
a faint greenish tinge. The walls and the ceiling contributed to
the corridor's brightness. At the far end of the hallway, maybe
fifty yards away, stood a soldier with an M16 in full combat
gear. What *was* all this?

Upon reaching the soldier, they were confronted by
another, far more substantial entrance. The soldier continued to

stare straight ahead, paying them little to no attention, except to nod slightly at Murnell as they approached the large door. On the wall was a small display panel with the screen at eye level. Murnell turned to look directly into it.

"Dr. Lance H. Murnell, P-Q-1-2-7-5-B-4-4."

Facial and voice recognition no doubt—Murnell continued to stare into the screen. But Raina also got the distinct impression it might be more than just a computer looking back at him, perhaps even, at the two of them.

"What have you got going here, Murnell?" she asked.

The large door slid silently upward.

The Homeland Security scientist turned back to her with a sardonic grin. "Welcome, Ms. Sanchez," he said with a sweep of his hand and a slight bow. "To the Yellow Brick Road."

The door opened wider to reveal a gymnasium-sized space with huge, reinforced rafters overhead and darkened walls of the same type of material as the hallway they'd just traversed. But it was what stood at the center of the space that immediately drew attention. It was a sphere, maybe ten feet in diameter, anchored to the floor with large struts and what she guessed might be hardened power and communications conduits. The surface of the sphere glowed green but also looked to be at least partially transparent.

"What is it?"

"Come and see," he said.

They stepped through into the cavernous room, the large door silently closing behind them.

Raina pulled her gaze from the sphere to look around. There seemed to be no one else but them in the entire space. Murnell was like a kid in candy store, egging her on, apparently eager to share with her what no doubt was probably in part his creation.

Drawing closer, she made out what appeared to be a small door in the side of the sphere and a pilot's seat inside.

"Is it some kind of a ship?"

"More like a cockpit."

"Where's the rest of the craft?" They circled around to the door in the side. "Hold on. You'll see."

There was a metal ramp leading up to the door. Murnell climbed it and pulled the hatch open. Raina held back for a moment.

"You coming?"

"Yeah." She clambered up beside him.

"Go ahead." He was holding the door open for her.

"You first," she said.

He shrugged and climbed through the hatch into the sphere.

She grabbed the door from him as he went through, feeling its polished, hyaline surface. It was room temperature, neither cool nor warm.

"What material is this thing made of?"

"Sorry," he said from inside the bubble. "That's beyond classified. I'm not even sure I understand all of its structure myself. But what it can do... come on inside and I'll show you."

She'd come this far. Why not?

She stepped through the opening into the sphere with him.

"Reminds me a little of the old bubble canopy helicopters," she said.

"It does, doesn't it?"

The curvature of the floor made her feel slightly unsteady. There seemed to be no access ramp or step to the single seat.

"This is still a prototype, not yet fully operational. We've yet to add a few of the finer comforts, I'm afraid. But why don't you go ahead and sit down in the chair? I'll show you what she can do."

She looked at him for a second or two. Was this guy crazy? Putting her in the command seat of who knows what?

"Are you a pilot, Dr. Murnell?"

"Me? No. And it's Lance, by the way. Just call me Lance."

"You're not going to brief me on your ship before putting me behind the controls?" Not that she could see any instrumentation. None appeared to be present—only the empty seat, apparently of major league aerospace manufacture, looking like it had been transplanted from the space shuttle.

"Trust me. It's better just to show you." He pulled what appeared to be a small remote control device from the pocket of his sport coat. He pushed a button and the chair came to life, turning part way toward them.

"Don't worry," he said. "It won't bite. Go ahead and have a seat."

She did as he instructed and edged to the chair, turning awkwardly to sit down.

Murnell stepped up to stand beside her. "Now hold on for a second. This can be disorienting at first."

He ran his fingers across a small touchpad built into the arm of the chair.

The world went black for a moment. Where the transparent sphere had been and the cavernous room beyond, she could see nothing but darkness. In the next instant, however, they seemed to be transported through time and space to another world. An arid landscape, punctuated by sage bush and cactus with brown mountains in the distance, spread out before her.

She could still see her own body and the shadow of Murnell's standing next to her but the image seemed to swallow everything else.

"What is this?"

"The Mojave Desert."

"In California?"

"Nevada actually. Just across the border."

"This is from a UAV or a MAV?"

"Good deduction. Yes, the picture you're experience is

generated from a small cluster of them, to be more precise. More advanced, but not all that different from the ones you've been playing with for the past few weeks."

"Oh. You know about that, do you?"

"We might know a lot more than you think we know."

Wonderful. It was the first acknowledgement that, whoever Murnell was, he and whomever he worked for knew about her activities with Tye and Major Williamson. Were these people really from Homeland Security? The thought unnerved her. How much did Murnell actually know? Unless he pressed her about her activities, which he obviously hadn't done, she decided she better remain mum for now.

Thankfully, her host didn't press her on the point. He went on: "You know we've had something of a debate going within the research community about the future of UAVs and MAVs, or drones, as the public likes to refer to them. Besides the obvious ethical issues regarding weaponization, territorial sovereignty, privacy rights, etc., the more fascinating technical debate revolves around artificial intelligence and the merits and drawbacks of the deployment of so-called autonomous drones versus maximizing the information available to the remote operator. I and my colleagues fall into the latter camp."

"You mean you always want a pilot."

"Exactly. Our position is that artificial intelligence—at least for the time being—is best suited to gather information to be provided to human decision makers."

She couldn't help focusing on the 'for the time being' part, but decided she just needed to listen.

"How much information are we talking about?" she asked.

"That's rather obvious, isn't it? Look around you."

She swiveled her head to look in all directions. The images all melted into one to form a completely immersive experience. It was as if she were actually standing in the middle of the desert at that very moment. Flying her single hover angels or dragonflies was like controlling a joystick while looking through a straw by comparison. What Murnell was showing her was a leap into science fiction.

"It's an advanced outgrowth of full dome immersive technology," he said. "If we're going to take you into somebody's neighborhood or down the stovepipe into the kitchen where they're assembling the latest generation of improvised explosive devices, you better be able to have a good look around. Wouldn't you agree?"

She nodded. How could she not?

"But that's only the beginning," he said.

He made another gesture on the touchpad, which, she noted, seemed to wrap around the entire arm of the chair. Instantly, the desert scene was replaced by a large collection of separated images showing different settings, from street scenes to countryside, even, from high overhead, an entire city.

The screens seemed to hang suspended around here in a floating constellation of pictures. In one moving image over what appeared to be Afghanistan a battle was even taking place. As if by magic, the shadow of Murnell's hand reached up and pulled one image away, replacing it with another and then another.

"How are you doing all this?"

Murnell said nothing.

"All of this technology has to be classified."

He chuckled but still said nothing. Instinctively, she felt her hand start to move toward the control pad on the arm of her chair, but she held it back.

"Think of all the possibilities," he said.

"I can see that."

"What if we could drop you anywhere in the world you wanted to be? In real time, so you could have a good, close-up look at the place and what was happening there. All while seated right here in this chair."

"I'd say it would be very cool."

It also sounded a lot like Big Brother, but she figured she better play along.

"The experience is almost as good as sex," he said.

She could feel his eyes on her in the darkness. Okay, now she was getting creeped out.

Thankfully, he moved on: "We believe this technology has unimaginable possibilities—and, in the right hands, tremendous potential to protect people and do good."

"Okay. So why kidnap me to show it to me? Are you trying to recruit me to do something?"

"Maybe." He hesitated for a moment. "But I prefer to think of it more as an evaluation."

"Your evaluation of me? Or my evaluation of you?"

"Ha!" He laughed out loud. "I like that about you, CWO Sanchez. You don't pull any punches."

In a whisper, the darkness swept away and the images all disappeared. She was back in the transparent bubble again with Murnell standing next to her. The empty, cavernous space stood still all around.

"Wow," she said softly.

"So here's my deal." He turned back to look at her, put his hand on the back of the chair, and leaned so close she caught an even more unmistakable hint of the aftershave. His voice took on a conspiratorial tone. "In exchange for your silence about what you've just seen, I'm willing to give you unfettered access to this technology for the next couple of days, and as much training on the spot as you think you can absorb."

"What? You're kidding…right?"

"Not at all."

"But…why?"

"That should be obvious, shouldn't it? Because I'm hoping to entice you into joining us. The missing link for much of our efforts is qualified pilots. And with your background flying not just helicopters but now MAVs…need I say more?"

She looked into Murnell's clear blue eyes. Was he for real? What about the mission with Williamson and Tye? She couldn't abandon them in midstream.

"So if I accept this deal of yours, I take it I'm stuck here for a while."

"Nope." Murnell reached in the pocket of his coat and pulled out a mobile phone. "You're free to come and go as you please. With only one condition: You can't know the where-abouts of this location. I'm calling a car to take you home right now, in fact.

"We'll have to take some precautions, naturally. You won't be drugged again, but you'll need to be hooded and seated behind blacked out windows for any trips going and coming to this facility. It's less than a half hour ride back to your apartment, so it shouldn't be too unpleasant."

"Are you for real?" She almost started to laugh.

"I think you'll come to see that we're not about some deep, dark conspiracy. We're only trying to do what's right for our country, not to mention the rest of the people on this little globe of ours."

It sounded a lot like what she and Tye were shooting for, only their mission with Kurn was a lot more specific. She was almost at a loss for words.

"So what, I'd be working for Homeland?"

"Yes, you would. At least, in a manner of speaking."

"What do you mean in a manner of speaking?"

"That just means I'm not free at the moment to give you any more details than what I've already offered. I think you'll agree, under the circumstances, it's a pretty generous offer."

Again she wondered just how much he and the other people working in this facility knew about her activities with Kurn and the MAVs. Part of her wanted to lay her cards on the table, but another bigger part told her to hold back.

"Okay," she said. "Can I have some time to think it over?"

"Sure." He reached in another pocket, pulled out a different mobile device, and handed it to her; it was a small flip phone. "This phone only dials certain numbers and one of them is mine. Go home and get something to eat and drink, take a nap, do whatever. Call me later this afternoon with your decision. But I need to know something today. We're on a very tight schedule and are trying to get all of the pieces in place."

On a tight schedule for what? she wondered.

"And if I decide to say no?"

"Then we have to kill you, of course."

He stared at her with a straight face for a moment. Then he broke into a grin.

"No, I'm just kidding you, of course…don't take yourself so seriously…If you decide what you've seen isn't for you…well, let's just say we'll cross that bridge when we come to it, okay?"

"Sound pretty vague to me."

"I really don't think you're going to say no anyway, so it's not worth worrying about. Oh, and one other thing. What you've just been exposed to is absolutely top secret. You're a dedicated soldier so I don't have to remind you what that means. You can't speak to anyone about what you've just seen here today. It could endanger both you and whomever else might come into possession of such information."

So there it was—a shot across the bow. She got his message, loud and clear.

"Understood," she said.

"Again, I'm very sorry for the unpleasantness earlier with

our Special Forces friends. It was necessary for the sake of expediency."

"Expediency, huh?" She looked at him.

He nodded.

"All right. I'll think it over."

The truth was she would have said almost anything at that point to get out of the place. As interesting and attractive as this technology all seemed—not to mention Murnell himself—she sensed he was lying.

Nothing added up. Why kidnap her if they only planned to let her go? Had Murnell been simply counting on the gee-whiz factor of his out-of-this-world sphere to recruit her, or was there something more?

She felt an urgent desire to leave.

"I'd like to go now," she said.

"Very good. Whatever you wish." He raised his phone to his ear. "I'm calling your car."

11

"YOU CAN'T JUST bail out on me like that!" Tye glared at her with a blatant mixture of anger and concern.

They were seated across the small kitchen table from one another in her apartment.

Raina said nothing.

She hated lying to him, but what choice did she have? She took Murnell at his word about his threat to their safety.

She didn't fully trust Murnell—a lot about him made her uneasy—but, after thinking things over, at least part of what he said made sense. Were she and Tye playing for the wrong team?

Maybe they were in over their heads with Williamson. She'd never seen or heard of anything like what Murnell had shown her, but that didn't mean whatever top secret projects Homeland Security might have going didn't bear at least some stamp of legitimacy.

Maybe it was time she thought about stepping up to the big leagues once again.

"Where were you?"

"I told you. I just needed to get out for a little while. I needed to clear my head."

"Clear your head? You were gone for over three hours. You left your cell phone and your keys. I had no way to get in touch with you. I've been sitting here waiting around on you all morning. I was just about to call up Williamson to talk about aborting the mission."

"What are you now, my babysitter?"

He pursed his lips and shook his head. They stared at one another for a few moments.

"I'm sorry," she said. "I shouldn't have said that."

"Let me see your arms," he said.

"What?"

"Roll up your sleeves. I want to see your arms."

"Why?"

"Just do it."

She shrugged and did as he asked. Lucky thing for her the Spec Ops guys had stuck her in the hip. Her arms were free of any marks.

But why was Tye asking to see her arms? Did he know more than he was telling her? Maybe she wasn't the only one keeping secrets.

He examined her skin.

"Okay," he said, sighing with what almost seemed to be relief.

"What are you talking about? What were you looking for?"

"Just wanted to make sure you weren't addicted to something. You know, wigging out on me and shooting up."

"Are you kidding me? We've been working together every day for weeks and you knew me way before that. Have you ever seen anything to suggest I'd even think about becoming a junkie?"

"No," he admitted, looking sheepish. "But who does? A lot of guys, coming back with blast injuries, have run into problems with pain killers and the like."

"Well, I'm not one of them. Look. I appreciate your concern for me, and all. But I'm a big girl and I can take care of myself. And sometimes I just need some space to get away and think."

"Right. I get it. But you and I gotta be more communicative when we're on point with this mission. We're into some high stakes mojo here, and we could both end up with a one-way ticket to Leavenworth, or worse. You understand what I'm saying?"

Tell me about it, she thought, as their gazes locked a moment longer.

"I know," she said. "You're right."

"You're still committed?"

"Of course. I'm all-in just like you when it comes to this job."

Was she? She couldn't afford to let him see she might be thinking differently all of a sudden, at least until she had more information.

"All right," he said, draining the last of his mug of coffee. He pushed his chair away from the table. "Let's get going and figure out what we're doing this afternoon."

12

THE YOUNG WOMAN'S name was Stacie Hutchinson. A junior majoring in business, she lived in an off-campus apartment complex called University Crossings. Standing next to Tye on the stoop of Hutchinson's apartment, Raina felt a lump rise in her throat about how to break the news to the pretty coed that she'd been raped.

She and Tye had used facial recognition software to make a positive ID from the Kurn video. Stacie Hutchinson certainly had a distinctive appearance. The girl could have been a fashion model with her long brunette hair, slender figure, and slim face. Not to mention a thin nose with dark, narrow eyebrows, and her smooth, apparently suntanned skin. Completing the beauty package, Hutchinson's bee-stung lips seemed to wink at the camera inquisitively in the photo from her Facebook page. Raina was curious to see if the girl looked the same in real life.

She couldn't help absent-mindedly running her fingers along the scars on her neck, her gaze instinctively dropping to the oddly shaped end of her pant leg that draped over the top of the sneaker covering her artificial foot.

The garden apartments were tucked into a quiet neighborhood between a public park and a row of upscale stores. The tenants were mostly upperclassmen or graduate students. Tye and

Raina were dressed like students as well—wearing blue jeans and casual shirts.

"It'll be okay," Tye reassured her.

How did he do that? They'd only really known each other for a couple of weeks, yet he already seemed to have the ability to sense what was going on in her head.

She smiled and nodded as he rang the bell.

They had argued over who would talk to Hutchinson. Tye thought she, as a woman, should go by herself, owing to the nature of the crime. She could see his point of view, but she preferred to stay with her computers and take care of intelligence and flying the drones, letting him do all the fieldwork.

In the end, they'd struck a compromise. They would both go. But since Raina spent most of her waking hours these days holed up behind a computer screen, she couldn't help feeling like she was missing out on something not being plugged in to the Internet or flying her MAVs.

No one seemed to be coming to the door after the first ring, so Tye pushed the bell again.

"Just a minute!" A young woman's voice sounded faintly through the heavy door.

"Your lead, rookie." Tye whispered. He'd taken to teasing her about the fact she'd "only" been a pilot, not down with the ground grunts like him.

"Rookie, my—"

"Uh-uh." He held up his hand. "Let's watch the profanities. Remember we're live and in living color."

Even without the drones, they were still recording, forced to rely on a hidden camera for Tye and a simple sound wire for her. The audio and video twins, Tye had joked. Yin and Yang.

Was wearing such surveillance equipment without a court order legal in Virginia? Raina didn't even know. She wasn't sure she wanted to know.

They were definitely tracking under the radar.

She wondered idly if she and Tye were the only "operators," as Williamson had started referring to them. She needed to start thinking about counter-measures in case they found themselves under remote surveillance. The bad guys in Iraq and Afghanistan were always trying to hack into drone control systems and the Iranians had even succeeded.

Murnell and Homeland must have realized that Williamson had managed to reactivate her Top Secret clearance. She had access to what she considered was a treasure trove of encrypted files and potential MAV strategies. Whoever Williamson was plugged into, they had connections, but what he'd shown her so far couldn't come close to what she'd seen in Murnell's sphere.

Still, she liked knowing she and Tye were considered independent—even if it was an obvious move by Williamson to generate plausible deniability to protect himself and whoever else they might be working for. She and Tye could refuse any mission for any reason they liked. That was sure different than any job she'd ever had working for Uncle Sam.

The door finally opened. It was Hutchinson.

"Yes?" The girl wore a pair of baggy sweatpants bearing the college logo and a sleeveless tee. Even without makeup she looked stunning.

"Stacie Hutchinson?"

"Yes?"

"My name is Raina Sanchez, and this is Tye Palmer. We're investigators and we wondered if you could spare a few minutes to answer some questions."

Raina flashed her Virginia private investigator's picture ID and Tye did the same. Williamson had provided them with official-looking, laminated cards made up for each of them, exact duplicates of the real thing. He'd even gone so far as to somehow get their names listed in the Commonwealth's PI database.

"What's this all about?"

"Derek Kurn," Raina said.

"Derek?" Hutchinson stared at them for a moment.

"You know him?"

"Yeah. Sure. Everybody on campus knows who he is."

"You were with him at a party last weekend."

More staring. "Umm…yeah." She ran her hand across her slender neck. "But what—?"

"Do you mind if we come in, Ms. Hutchinson? We just have a couple of questions to ask you about Derek and we really don't bite."

The girl looked them up and down for moment, her gaze lingering for a moment on the slight ankle bulge in Raina's jeans, before making eye contact with them again.

"Yeah, sure. Okay."

She opened the door wider and moved to one side as Raina stepped across the threshold with Tye in tow.

Raina's first impression of the apartment was one of clean but chaotic housekeeping. Hutchinson and her roommates had added some nice decorating touches to the place—a blue glass vase on a table and a couple of modern paintings. But there were also baskets of dirty clothes lining the hallway wall.

"It's my roommate's turn to do the laundry this week," Hutchinson apologized. "The machine's just next door in another building, but she hasn't gotten around to doing it yet."

"Not a problem," Raina said. She needed to do some laundry herself. "Is your roommate in?"

"No. She had a class."

Hutchinson closed the door and led them through the foyer into a small living room containing a threadbare but still serviceable couch, a couple of rocking chairs, and a credenza with a small flat-screen TV. Lacy, makeshift curtains framed the windows. *Not bad for college students on a budget.* Hutchinson put a hand on one of the rocking chairs and motioned for Tye and Raina to take the couch.

When they were all seated, Tye and Raina sitting forward on the edge of the sofa, Hutchinson said, "So you have questions about Derek?"

"Yes."

"What, did he do some kind of a prank? He's actually a pretty sweet guy underneath it all."

Raina glanced at Tye. "Underneath all what?" she asked.

"Well, you know. Him being on the football team and his dad being such a celebrity and all…Sometimes he and some of the other guys feel like they have to put on this kind of front."

"Sure. Have you been dating him long?"

"Oh, we're not dating. I've seen him at a couple of parties and hung out with him."

"Okay. What else do you know about him?"

"Not much."

"He ever mention his dad?"

"Oh, yeah. He hates his dad. I mean, I think his dad treated him really badly growing up. Derek hardly ever saw Mr. Kurn while he was in prep school, his dad never even showed up to any of Derek's games. But now that Derek's on the team here at college and his dad's this bigwig alumni, his dad's started trying to talk to him and coming around more."

Raina looked at Tye for a moment, who was nodding, before looking back at Hutchinson. "You say you've hung out with him…Does that include having sex with him?" she asked.

"What?" The girl sat up a little higher in her chair. "No! I mean, I like the guy and he's sort of cute and all. But we've never hooked up. Is that what this is about?"

Raina took a deep breath. "You can confirm you were with him at a party last weekend?"

"Yes."

"I need to ask you something…How'd you get home from the party?"

Hutchinson stared at them for a long moment. You could almost see her mind trying to process what happened that night and the consequences of the leading question.

The girl's demeanor turned serious. "I…I don't remember, really. It was super late. I kind of had a bit too much to drink and I think I fell asleep. My roommate Karen was there, too, and when I woke up she was helping me out to another friend's car."

"Did you feel ill that night?"

"A little, I guess. But I never threw up or anything."

"Where did your roommate find you?"

"In the den at the fraternity. I guess I passed out on a couch. It's pretty embarrassing, actually. But what's any of this have to do with Derek Kurn?"

Raina felt a deep-seated anger rising up from within her. She glanced over at Tye before turning her attention back to the coed. "Ms. Hutchinson…can I call you Stacie?"

"Sure, yeah. Of course."

"Stacie, I'm afraid we have something potentially disturbing to show you…."

The girl's eyes grew wide. "Okay…I guess." She sat forward in her chair, biting her lip.

Raina turned to Tye, who pulled out his smart phone. They'd already cued up the video and she took the phone from him. She stood and walked the phone over to Hutchinson so the young woman could hold it and watch for herself as it began to play.

Hutchinson palmed the phone, already beginning to look toward the screen. "What is this from?"

"Just watch, please."

Hutchinson stared into the screen for several seconds. At

first, she seemed to have trouble comprehending what she was seeing. But then her face turned white.

"Oh, my God." The hand holding the phone began to tremble as her other hand covered her mouth. "Oh...my God."

"Can you confirm it's you in the video?"

The younger woman nodded, tears filling her eyes and running down her pretty cheeks. She started to sob. Her hand was shaking so much Raina had to move in to sit beside her and take the phone from her, gently putting her fingers on the girl's arm.

"I'm so sorry."

"That bastard...I mean..he..."

They sat like that for nearly a minute. Stacie Hutchinson's quiet crying seemed to fill the room. No one spoke. Tye kept a respectful silence and distance. Raina was glad now that she'd come.

The student's sobs brought Raina back to one of the many scenes that continued to haunt her from the war. In this instance, she was in her Kiowa again, flying convoy recon with another chopper. Below where she hovered momentarily, the convoy was passing a stone wall, behind which a man and girl, who looked to be his daughter, were leading a donkey toward a field.

The girl must have said or done something her father didn't like. In a flash like a snake the man came out with a cane and began to brutally beat his daughter about the head and shoulders. She slumped to her knees, but the father continued the beating.

The chopper was moving forward, so Raina couldn't see what else happened, but she spoke to Skyles, who ordered her to circle back around over top of the stone wall, if nothing else to intimidate the beater into retreating. The father did just that, lowering his cane, turning away from the girl as she scrambled away, and raising his head upward to look at the chopper directly above.

Raina would never forget the look on the man's face. He smiled and waved his hand at them in greeting, business-as-usual, everything a-okay. She couldn't help wondering if Stacie Hutchinson was feeling a little bit like that girl had felt.

After the initial shock of the situation appeared to have washed over her, Hutchinson started to pull herself together. When she felt the girl's sobs diminish, Raina took her hand off her arm and stood back up.

"I'm so sorry," she repeated.

Hutchinson wiped tears from her cheeks. "I knew something was wrong, after the party, I mean. I just felt funny somehow. But I felt so sick and embarrassed I just wanted to push it away. I guess I just didn't want to think about it."

Again no one spoke. They waited until Hutchinson further regained her composure.

"But how do you know for sure this is Derek? I mean, I was with him that night and it looks like his room and all, but you can't really see his face all that well in the video."

"We know it's him, Stacie," Raina said.

The young woman nodded. "How'd you get this video?"

Raina glanced at Tye, who must have felt it was the right moment to enter into the conversation.

"That gets a little complicated," he said.

"What do you mean? Who sent you? Do you work for the police?"

"No."

"Who then?"

"We can't say. But now that you've confirmed you're the woman in this video, we can certainly talk to the police. But that's going to be up to you."

Hutchinson nodded. "Has Derek seen this video? Does he know you have it?"

"Not yet. But he will as of tomorrow."

"Okay…" She hesitated, rubbing her hands together before wiping them down her legs from her waist to the tops of her knees.

"What's wrong, Stacie?" Raina asked.

"I don't know. I just feel so…so dirty."

"I understand."

"I'm scared."

"Of what?"

"Of this getting out. Of what might happen. My name and his name in the papers and everything."

"Of course. But you know, you may not be the first young woman he's done this to…or the last."

"I know, I know…But, I mean, I'm still not sure if I can go through with it all…."

"You mean press charges."

"Yeah…You know who Derek Kurn is, don't you? His father—"

"We know who he is."

"Then you know if I come forward I could just as easily end up being the one accused…It's so embarrassing. I mean, I don't know…the pictures and the stories will be everywhere."

There was no denying that. Raina wondered if she herself could stand up under such scrutiny.

"You saw the tape," she said. "It's pretty hard for anyone to argue with what's shown there."

Hutchinson nodded. "I know. But I need to talk with my parents."

"Sure. Absolutely."

Raina felt sick to her stomach. It wasn't just the girl's humiliation and the violation of her body the rape represented. Now Hutchinson and her family had to the weigh the prospect of accusing the son of a prominent public figure and the inevitable media circus that would follow. Whatever Stacie Hutchinson did, she and Tye would have to figure out a way to complete their overall mission.

Raina pulled out a blank business card with only her name and temporary cell phone number written on it in black ink. There was also a web address for a secure message board.

"Here," she said, handing it to Hutchinson. "This is my contact information. The cell phone number won't be any good after the next two days. Please call us and let us know what you decide by tomorrow. And if you ever need to reach me in the future, you can always leave a message for me on this web message board. Anytime, day or night."

Hutchinson took the card from her. "So you're planning to show what you showed me to Derek tomorrow, right?"

"Yes. And hopefully elicit a confession from him. But we won't go public without your say-so. You and your parents need to decide whether you want us to take this to the police."

"Thank you." The girl rubbed her eyes. "It's just all so confusing, you know?"

"I understand. And again, we're terribly sorry."

"You know what?" Hutchinson's face grew cold and her tone bitter.

"What?"

"Tomorrow's Halloween."

"Yes, it is," Raina said.

"Some holiday, huh? Trick or treat."

13

IT HAD ALREADY been dark for a few hours. Raina had to wait until Tye returned to his own apartment to go to bed before calling Lance Murnell at the number he'd given her. She wasn't exactly sure what she was doing, but she'd made up her mind.

She needed to find out more about what Murnell and Homeland Security were up to.

"I thought you were going to leave me at the altar," the scientist joked when he came on the line.

"Is it too late to start on some training?"

"Not at all. We're open twenty-four/seven over here."

Wherever "here" was. Murnell obviously knew more about Williamson and the MAVs she'd been flying than he'd let on. For all she knew, maybe Homeland was aware, if not intimately familiar, with their mission, although she doubted the department would ever officially be in favor of, let alone somehow involved, with what she and Tye were doing.

Worse case scenario, she and Tye might even be on the wrong side of some sort of internal civil war. Either way, covering up a rape could never be justified—in anybody's book.

Twenty minutes later, she sat in the darkened back of a government sedan with a hood pulled over her head again, hearing the sounds and feeling the vibrations of the car moving along a major highway, then smaller roads with turns, a few potholes, crossing what even seemed like several sets of railroad tracks.

She wasn't fond of the hood, but her hands were free and at least she could breathe.

She felt little fatigue. She'd eaten dinner after Tye left, and was still raring to get some work done learning more about the technology Murnell had shown her that morning. A part of her couldn't help but feel like she was sneaking out on Tye after their confrontation earlier about her initial disappearance, but she pushed the thoughts away. She'd sensed a tension between them all afternoon that hadn't been part of their relationship before. Was it because of her own doubts or because of his toward her?

Regardless, for both of their sakes she needed to know more, and she owed it to herself to at least follow things through with Murnell. Maybe she wouldn't even have to choose one way or another. Maybe she could continue to help Tye and Williamson complete their mission and move on to something bigger at the same time.

She hoped she wasn't deluding herself about such a possibility. The psychologist she'd seen for a while after the crash would call that magical thinking.

The vehicle paused. She heard the driver say something. It sounded like they were passing through some kind of checkpoint. Then they appeared to enter some kind of garage, the roll of their tires echoing off pavement and concrete. The car finally came to a stop and one of her escorts shut down the engine and climbed out while the other opened the back door for her and gave her a hand to help her stand.

The hood was removed. She blinked in reaction to the bright light and saw that she was back in the same indoor parking area from which they'd transported her, after hooding her, from the facility earlier in the day.

"Welcome back, Ms. Sanchez. You made the right decision."

She looked up to Murnell, looking as handsome as ever, this time dressed more like the casual scientist in blue jeans and a sweater, approaching her from the landing above while her two guards—a pair of men dressed casually undercover in blue jeans and jackets—melted into the background and disappeared through a side entrance.

She hadn't really thought through, until now, how skillfully and effectively Murnell had baited the trap, whetting her appetite to work with all of his gee-whiz techno-toys. But seeing the facility and him in person all over again put her on her guard. She wondered if, in addition to whatever technical work he was doing for Homeland, he'd had psychological operations training. He certainly had a knack for timing and for doling out the selective information.

"I'm ready to get to work." She told him the truth.

"Good. So glad to hear it. Can we get you anything to eat or drink before we start rolling?"

"Nope. I'm good to go. Let's saddle up the ship."

"Like a true pilot," he said.

He led the way back down a series of corridors, passing two different pairs of armed guards along the way, to the same cavernous, empty room she'd seen several hours before. It looked no different now than it did then. The outside world could have been eating lunch at noon or sleeping at midnight—to the room and the sphere it was all the same. Once inside, the only reality existed on the screens, in the virtual environment, a full immersive world.

Raina suddenly realized why such a thing appealed to her, drew her even. It was a chance to really feel like she was climbing back into the cockpit again, even more than she did with the dragonflies. She knew she missed flying her helicopter in person. She just hadn't processed how much.

"She's all yours," Murnell told her as he helped guide her into the chair inside the sphere. She also couldn't help noticing how his hand seemed to linger under her arm a fraction of a second longer than necessary.

For the next couple of hours, under his guidance and patient instruction, she learned how to control and manipulate a series of apparently different MAVs via multiple MAV-generated images. She loved the freedom Murnell's drones seemed to give her, the sensation of the craft in her hands, responding instantly to her control as if she were actually on board.

But the amazing thing was the vision. The information these drones provided was astounding, as close to being there as she could imagine. She wasn't even sure what the drones she was flying looked like, except for his occasional reminder that there was more than one, all working in concert, from the desert in Nevada to the desert over Baghdad, from a city in Northern Africa to the mountains of Pakistan, eventually even, a live feed of a downtown section of Beijing, in all its splendor and smog, not too far from the Forbidden City.

She felt exhilarated, empowered, and even a little frightened. While she sat in the near midnight darkness of Northern Virginia, on the opposite side of the globe hazy lunchtime sunshine filtered through a busy urban neighborhood.

"Don't the Chinese know we have this technology?" Raina asked.

"Oh, they know," Murnell said, "At least in principle. But for now we've managed to keep the details away from their prying eyes—no easy task, I can tell you, given the persistence of their cyber-snooping. To the rest of the world, most of these toys are years from being operational."

Yet here he was handing the keys to the kingdom to a disabled, retired Chief Warrant Officer.

Raina wasn't stupid. She had the same gut feeling as before. Something didn't add up.

"Why me?" she asked him again. "Why recruit me to fly these things?"

"Because you fit the profile." He shrugged, offering an impish grin. "Sometimes we don't like to work with former pilots. We've found they too often come with detrimental ingrained habits from logging too many hours in the air. But you're a quick study, and—if you don't mind my saying so, CWO Sanchez—you come with the whole package."

She felt his eyes on her again, as if they were undressing her. It made her feel vulnerable. Not that having some guy hit on her was any kind of new experience—she just hadn't allowed it to go on like this since Afghanistan.

Was it only the flying and the rush of incredible technology she was after?

"In fact." His voice jolted her back to reality. "I think you're about ready to solo."

His shadow moved away from the chair.

"What?" She'd only trained on a desktop computer simulator under Major Williamson's guidance before starting to work with the MAVs. Sitting along in the sphere was an entirely new experience.

"It's all right." He was already moving toward the door. "I'm going to step out of here for a few minutes. But don't worry, I'll still have an eye on you and you'll still be able to hear me talking. Go ahead and try some different venues on for size."

"Different venues?" She wore no headset or other communications gear. "But how—?"

She turned to look at the door, but Murnell had already exited through it.

"Hello?"

"I'm here," he said matter-of-factly. "Can you hear me okay?"

"Roger."

"Good." The voice seemed to come from above and behind her. "Now just relax."

The images surrounding her still put her on the street in Beijing. But now, at the edges of the street scene on all sides were a collection of other, smaller screens, showing other video screens from different parts of the globe.

She feathered her fingers across the control pad and took control of whatever it was she was flying. It shocked her to realize that whatever form these MAVs took, their existence seemed to disappear from her consciousness. The drones were nothing more than a means to an end: secretly placing her in the heart of a foreign nation.

"Fly straight along the street for a bit. Let's see how you do."

So Murnell, wherever he'd moved off to, was seeing everything that she saw.

Maybe there was another sphere or some kind of a master display where he could track her movements in real time? There seemed to be so much information pouring into her own environment, she couldn't imagine what it would be like to manage an even larger array.

She did as he instructed and the images began to change, slowly or rapidly, depending upon how fast she slid her fingers. She could walk, she could run, she could zoom upward to fly. She wondered, if she decided to dive headlong into the pavement, if she could even crawl—maybe the drones under her control were so advanced they possessed such capabilities. But she was too new at this type of flying to make such a potentially risky move.

"Excellent," Murnell encouraged her. "Two streets ahead, you'll be turning to the right."

"Copy."

After two more blocks the street opened into a wide intersection where it crossed a busy boulevard jam-packed with buses, bicyclists, and cars. She was high enough in the air to avoid hitting anything, but did no one take note of her presence? Were the MAVs she was flying virtually invisible like the tiny hover angels she'd been deploying with Tye?

"Okay," Murnell said. "We're going to try something different. Remember, this is just an exercise…I want you to cross this intersection and once you reach the other side move to the sidewalk on the right hand side of the street. You'll need to watch out for the buildings to your right. They're taller here."

"I can see that," she said.

"Stay focused."

She flew as he directed over the intersection, entering a residential street lined with multi-story apartment buildings on either side. Swerving a little to the right, she began moving over top of the sidewalk.

"Nice," he said. "If you look ahead of you, you'll see a man walking with his wife and two small children, a boy and a girl. Look even more carefully and you'll notice they're being flanked discreetly on all sides by secret police. Those are the guys doing their best to try to look like businessmen or tourists in dark suits."

"Who is the man with the family?"

"For now let's just say he's a very high-ranking Communist party official. If you zoom in for a close-up, you'll notice a seventy-thousand dollar Jaeger LeCoultre watch strapped to his wrist."

"I'll take your word for it."

She could make out the middle-age man approaching her on the sidewalk ahead, tall for an Asian, in a dark, expensive looking suit. The woman next to him was beautiful. The children were dressed like American prep school kids. They were laughing, as kids often do, especially the boy, but they remained a respectful distance in back of their parents.

"All right." Murnell's voice seemed to drop an octave. "Weapons going live."

"What?" For a moment, Raina thought she must have been hearing things. "Are you insane?"

"Relax, Chief. Remember, this is only an exercise. Focus on your flying."

No time to play twenty questions. Unless she was being bamboozled by some elaborate video game, this was as real as it gets. Like what she'd heard Predator pilots and sensor operators experienced, weapons hot, tracking a moving target—times ten. She nudged her drones a little to the left to avoid a building overhang.

"Stay on target." "You are certifiable, Murnell. Putting a newbie into a situation like this."

"It's not a situation, Sanchez. As long as we don't get caught. And you're no newbie. Show me what you can do."

"What kind of weapon am I supposed to be carrying?"

"That's classified. But I will tell you it's miniscule in comparison to the hellfire missiles our military drones are using—though every bit as deadly and a lot more surgical."

"Surgical. You mean as in assassination."

"Focus, Sanchez. The target is the tall man in the suit."

"What about his wife next to him and the two children?"

"Do your job and they'll all be mourning at his funeral." An orange dot appeared in her field of vision. "You see the target finder?"

"Got it."

"Move it left or right a little, but not too much. The computer is doing the heavy lifting. You're there for the fine tuning."

Fine tuning, all right. Fine tuned to a kill.

"Who's making the call on the shot?"

"That's above our pay grade. Fifteen seconds out."

"But am I in the kill chain?"

"Not yet. Keep the orange dot on the man in the suit."

The family filled the screen directly in front of her now, the dot jumping and darting with the micro-motions of the MAVs. Even the slightest movement of her fingers caused her to move slightly off target, but she focused all of energies on the man's face, and it seemed to be working. Was she starting to get the hang of it?

"Five seconds."

The woman was saying something in what Raina assumed must be Mandarin Chinese to her husband, the words faint but audible. She wore a tasteful pearl necklace and dark suit jacket over a stylish pencil dress, stockings, and high heels. Raina felt like an invisible murderer, walking right up to her husband with an invisible gun. She was so close she could see lines in the man's face and the subtle pink shade of the woman's fingernails.

But just before she passed over top of the target, everything disappeared.

Raina blinked and found she was staring through the glassine surface of the sphere into the dark emptiness of the surrounding space. She looked around the chair and ran her fingers back and forth across the touchpad, trying to bring the images back, all to no avail.

"What just happened?"

There was no response.

"Murnell?"

"I'm here," he finally said.

She breathed a sigh of relief. "What's going on?"

"Nothing good," he said.

14

TYE AWOKE WITH a start at dawn. He'd fallen asleep on the couch again, but the one in his own apartment this time. Stretching his legs and rubbing the sleep from his eyes, he sat up and looked around at the Spartan furnishings.

He had no plans for staying here, so why add anything? Out of habit, he dropped to the floor for his morning AFPT calisthenics. As his thoughts came together about the day and the mission at hand, something wasn't sitting right with him.

He was nervous about continuing to work with Raina—no use denying it. The idea made him uncomfortable and he tried to push it away—maybe because he felt such an attraction to her—but she was definitely keeping something from him. Something had gone on yesterday morning when she disappeared, and she had lied to him about it.

Taking down Kurn may not have been quite the same as going to war, but in many ways it wasn't all that different, and one thing Tye knew for certain: you don't go into battle with soldiers you don't have faith in to watch your back. Raina had breached his trust and they needed to have a frank discussion about it.

He finished his exercises and turned toward the bathroom, but stopped. His watch read six a.m. and Raina's apartment was just across the complex. Was it too early to call? He unplugged his mobile phone from the wall where at least he'd remember to charge it the night before, scrolled to her number and punched the button.

She answered before the second ring.

"Hey," he said.

"Good morning, Sergeant," she said with a hint of mocking familiarity. "How'd you sleep?"

"We need to talk."

"I know," she said. "Big day ahead."

"No. I mean we need to talk about what we're doing before this whole thing goes any further."

"Oh." She seemed surprised. "All right. Is something wrong?"

"Yes. And I need to talk to you about it in person."

"Okay." She hesitated. "You eaten yet?"

"Nope."

"Why don't you come on over? The coffee's on and I'll throw together some scrambled eggs and toast."

"Thanks. I'll jump in the shower and throw on some clothes."

As the hot water revived him he thought about everything that could go wrong tonight at the fraternity. Derek Kurn might already be wise to their plan. Maybe the kid was smarter than his old man gave him credit for. Tye figured he could pass himself off well enough as just another student—after all, that's what he still was—but when the time came to confront the younger Kurn with his crime he'd be relying on Raina's mobile spy video to give him an edge. Take it away and the risk of something going south would be greatly amplified.

He knew he could handle himself in a fight, but Tye had no training as a detective or law enforcement officer. The bottom line was if he and Raina were going to pull this off they needed one another.

Meeting him at the door minutes later, Raina looked concerned. "Are you okay?"

"Not really"

"Come on. Your eggs are ready."

He followed her inside and they sat once again at her kitchen table, this time eating and drinking coffee in silence.

"All right," she said after a couple of minutes. "I think I know what's eating at you. This is about yesterday morning, isn't it?"

He considered his words carefully before speaking. He took a deep breath and looked her in the eyes. "You're lying to me."

She looked back at him for several moments before nodding. "You're right, and I'm sorry."

"What's going on, Raina?" He cupped his hands against his chin and leaned his elbows against the table.

Raina looked around. "Listen."

"What?"

"Hold up for a second. Come into the bathroom."

"What are you talking about?"

She made a circular motion with her fingers, indicating he should say no more. He got the message. This was growing stranger by the moment.

Once they were both inside the small bathroom, Raina stuffed a towel into the crack in the door. He also noticed there was water in both the sink and the bathtub with the drain plugs closed.

She sat down on the edge of the tub.

"I swept this room just before you got here. We should be able to talk without being heard."

"Are you saying we've been bugged?"

"I'm not taking any chances. Some important people are on to what we're doing with Williamson."

This was not good news, not good at all.

"What kind of important people?" he asked.

"Homeland Security."

"Are you kidding me? Are you sure?"

She nodded. "I've been talking with them."

"Homeland? You've been talking to Homeland?"

"That's right."

"And you didn't think you needed to share any of this with me?"

"I'm sorry. But trust me, it didn't start out by choice."

Tye thought back to the torn label he'd found yesterday between her couch cushions.

"They drugged you," he said.

She looked at the floor and nodded again.

"You sure these people are who they say they are?"

Her eyes turned to meet his gaze. "That's what they said, and from what I've seen so far, they've got all the resources and tools to back it up."

He took a deep breath. If their activities were running afoul of Homeland then they really were pushing out on a limb. Did Williamson know? Was Williamson a part of it?

"How much do they know about Kurn?" he asked.

"I can't say for certain. But they must have a fair amount of information. Why else would they come after me and know exactly where to find me? They've also been making vague references to what we've been doing. Nothing too specific, but enough to make me worry."

"Yet they let you go."

"Yes."

"And they came after you and not after me," he said.

She pursed her lips and let out a deep breath, locking eyes with him. "It looks like they're trying to recruit me."

"Recruit you? For what?"

"Another job."

"What kind of job?"

Raina tented her fingers on top of her lap. "It kind of defies description. I really can't tell you any more than that. There's no need for you to get dragged into this any more than you have to."

"Don't give me that. I'm already dragged into it whatever you're talking about. We both are."

"Yeah. Okay," she said.

"I don't believe this. We're trying to take down one of the biggest media honchos in the country and you're sitting here in a tiny bathroom with towels stuffed under the door. How do you know Kurn didn't get wind of our plan and sic these people on us?"

"I don't. But if he did, then he's got a lot more pull than we even imagined."

Tye leaned back against the edge of the sink, shaking his head.

He wasn't surprised Homeland, if they knew anything at all about what he and Raina had been up to, might have a keen interest in what they were doing. It explained a lot. Raina was probably telling him the truth—most of it, at least.

"We need to talk to Williamson," he said.

"All right. But wait…"

"What?"

"How are you so sure we can trust him either?"

He looked at her for a moment. "I'm not so sure we can trust anybody. What about you?"

"You can trust me, Tye," she said. "I didn't have to tell you everything I just told you, did I, about what's going on between Homeland and me? I'm playing it straight with you."

"You withheld information form me."

"I didn't have to tell you that either. But I just did."

He nodded. At least he knew he could still count on her. They were still in the fight together.

"We still have to talk to Williamson," he said. "He's the one who set us up with all of this equipment and your little miniaturized Air Force."

"You think the phones he gave us are still secure?"

"I noticed they didn't take yours yesterday when you disappeared. But

still...Here, we'll use mine." He pulled the device from his pocket and dialed the number.

Williamson answered right away. Tye put him on the phone's speaker, explained where they were and that he and Raina had been having a discussion.

"What do you need?" the major asked.

"We've got a problem," Tye told him, looking at Raina.

"Okay. What's going on?"

"Question, Major. Have you been playing us?"

"Say again?"

"I asked if you were playing us."

"Playing you? No. Why would I want to do that?"

Tye listened over the speakerphone while Raina gave Williamson the same rundown of her encounter with Homeland Security she'd given him. Williamson grew increasingly quiet the more she told him. The major waited until she was finished speaking before saying anything else.

It was difficult to read his reaction over the phone.

"Is that it?" the man said finally.

"Yes," Raina said. "That's what happened."

"You said the individual with whom you spoke seemed to be aware of your activities with Mr. Palmer and the MAVs."

"Yes."

"Did he offer any details?"

"No."

"Did *you* offer him any details?"

"No. I wouldn't."

"Good. And you don't know where you stand with him now?"

"No. Like I said, something bad happened."

"But you said they were trying to recruit you."

"Yes. I don't know. Maybe I didn't make the cut or whatever. What is he after?"

"He was fishing. I think I'm acquainted with the individual you're referring to."

"Murnell?"

"Yes."

"What do you mean?" Raina asked. "You know him?"

"We've never met, but I know who he is."

Tye had to interrupt. "What's this all about, Major? Are you and whoever else we're supposed to be working with on the up-and-up or not?"

Williamson was silent for a moment. "I suppose that depends on what you mean by on the up-and-up," he said finally.

"Great. Now you sound like a politician."

"I'm sorry I can't give you more information at the moment, but look, when I first came to you with the tip about Kurn I was up front with you...You know about our mission and you know about the risks."

"Yeah. But if Homeland is snooping around then we might all be compromised."

"Don't be so sure," Williamson said.

"What's that supposed to mean?" Raina asked.

"Just that the government and our national security apparatus are complex. I don't need to tell either of you that. And groups with competing interests can sometimes collide with one another. Sometimes worse."

"Worse? How worse?"

"All I can tell you for certain is that a lot's going right now, and there are forces at play with differing agendas."

"Will the mission with Kurn have an impact on that?"

Williamson seemed to hesitate. "Quite possibly," he said.

"I'm pretty sure this guy Murnell works for Homeland," she said.

"I've no doubt he does. At least nominally. But you and I both know how things look on a piece of paper or in official department records usually varies quite a bit from the reality on the ground."

"Are you saying we may be caught up in some kind of turf war and that's why they're trying to recruit me?"

"This is about something much bigger than that," the major said.

"Like what?" Tye asked.

"I can't say any more right now. I need to get off this line. But I'm going to find out."

15

F RUM UNIVERSITY WAS a top-ranked, private liberal arts school with Division I athletics and hundreds of millions of dollars in federal research grants, among many other things. It didn't hurt that the campus was situated within a stone's throw of the nation's capital beltway.

The sun angled lower in the sky as Tye walked across the University Commons in the waning afternoon light. He stopped for a moment to watch a gaggle of Smurfs, Angry Birds, and princesses—kids in their costumes—working some of the dorms for early trick or treating.

Tye wasn't that familiar with the school. He probably never could have gained admission, let alone have afforded the tuition. He wondered if undergraduates giving out candy had become a Halloween tradition. Regardless, the college's administration must have supported it. Such gestures must have made for good "town-and-gown" relations—the students, from mostly wealthy backgrounds and from out-of-state, connecting with the locals in a way that made up for noisy wee hours partying that no doubt created problems with their neighbors.

The weather was especially nice for trick-or-treaters this year, too, with the temperature hovering near the sixty-five degree mark, warm for the end of October. Judging by the number of kids in evidence, parents must have liked bringing their kids on campus for the annual candy orgy too, maybe because they could get the bulk of their night's work done all in one place and before dark.

"Did you bring your bag for treats?" Raina teased him through his hidden earphone.

"Wish I did," he said.

He wondered what the parents with their trick-or-treaters would think if they knew a nearly invisible watch bird was keeping an eye on their every move from overhead. Raina was camped out a block from campus with her computers and joysticks in a different van they'd rented thanks to Williamson's seemingly unlimited budget.

They were still waiting to hear back from him about Raina's encounters with Homeland. According to Raina, there'd been no more contacts from her strangely benevolent Homeland captors either, so they were still all systems go with their plan.

It had taken the better part of the day to set things up.

Raina never complained, even when helping as best she could with the grunt work of moving the computers. What made her so beautiful, Tye realized, wasn't just her figure or face, attractive as they were despite the scars. It was something else—deep, dark, and dangerous, burning within her soul. Tye wished he could identify its source. He was afraid he might never get near it, let alone understand it. She'd pitched right in and pulled her weight when it came to setting up the van and all of her equipment.

Tye was on his way to try to meet Derek Kurn face-to-face before the party. Since the younger Kurn was the current president of his fraternity chapter, Tye wanted Derek to feel comfortable with him so no suspicions would be raised later. The idea of setting someone up for a takedown made Tye uncomfortable, but he realized he better get used to it if he were going to be effective at this line of work.

"Should I wear a costume for the party later?" he asked through his hidden mike.

"Probably," Raina told him. "Something minimal. Although you look scary enough as it is."

He smiled before pushing off again. He had seen a poster on the student union bulletin board about the Halloween party at Zeta Phi. It was bound to be a big blowout since the date this year fell on a Thursday, which most of the students treated as the start of a long weekend. One of the things that amazed him in going back to college was how few students actually attended class on a regular basis anymore, especially in the big lecture courses.

Unless you were an engineering geek or pre-med, a lot of students considered their Friday classes mostly optional. They'd pick up whatever information they needed or catch the lecture online.

He moved beyond the Commons dormitories and along a sidewalk between a pair of newer academic buildings. The sun was less intense here and a chill swept through him. He was glad he'd worn a hooded sweatshirt and jeans, which didn't include the hockey jersey and goalie's glove he was hoping to pass off as a costume later for the party. It would turn quickly colder as darkness approached.

At the end of the long, tree-lined walkway, he started down a stairwell that led to a broad avenue that cut through the center of the small college town. He passed a harried mother leading two young children up the stairs in the direction of the candy gorging fray on the Commons, one dressed as a bumblebee, the other, slightly older, as a ninja.

The ninja reminded him of a woman wearing a *burka* he'd encountered on a street during his first Iraqi deployment.

Most Iraqi women wore *abayas* instead of *burkas*. *Abayas* at least allowed for the entirety of the face to be seen.

But the woman Tye had encountered that afternoon was dressed in full *burka*, and he couldn't help but feel alarmed at the sight of her. Suicide bombers wearing *burkas* to disguise their deadly cargo had only recently attacked a mosque in the region, and Tye was momentarily separated from his patrol and feeling vulnerable. He'd reflexively disengaged the safety on his M4 Carbine and tried to read the woman's eyes as they neared one another, but she quickly averted her gaze. Out of fear? Out of anger or hatred?

He could never say for sure.

In any event, he'd moved safely past the woman that day without incident. He never would've thought something as innocuous as a child's play mask could dredge up such a memory years later and thousands of miles away. But there it was.

At the bottom of the stairs, he almost bumped into a couple of coeds starting to head up the steps with their backpacks. One blonde, one brunette. They had to be at least six or seven years his junior, with lithe bodies, made-up eyes, and dressed to attract. They smiled at him in turn, before moving on up the stairs.

"Let's stay focused here, Palmer," Raina chided him.

"I'm focused. I'm focused," he whispered.

The Zeta Phi house was perched on a corner lot at the end of an otherwise quiet street dotted with only a couple of other fraternities and sororities. The site was a couple of blocks from the center of campus, close enough to be part of the school but also standing independent, an entity unto itself.

Preparations for the party seemed to be in full swing. Three or four guys kicked and tossed a football to one another on the lawn, testing out a makeshift set of goalposts consisting of a line draped between a couple of trees, while a couple of others were attempting to "slack-line" or walk across the same flimsy rope in the latest college fad.

Another group was busy setting up a ping-pong table, sawhorses with long tables holding steel kegs of beer, and huge stereo speakers draped with ghoulish decorations on the patio. From his online photo and what he'd seen in the video, Tye recognized Derek Kurn among the students next to the house. He approached the group.

"Excuse me. Is this Zeta Phi?"

"Yeah." One of Kurn's companions answered.

"Heard you're having a big Halloween party tonight."

"Yup. Starts at ten."

"I'm a transfer student. Was hoping I could crash the party and maybe check out the fraternity."

"You a Zeta Phi?"

"Not yet."

They stared at him for a moment.

Derek Kurn, *el Presidente* himself, stepped forward.

He was shorter than Tye but in better physical shape. Biceps bulged from the sleeves of his Polo shirt.

"You look too old for college, dude," Derek said. In person, he not only bore a great resemblance but also sounded like a younger version of his father.

Tye paused for a moment. "I was in the Army, Iraq and Afghanistan," he said.

Derek nodded. His jaw jutted out to show he was impressed, as did those of several of the others who had stopped whatever they were doing to look. "Cool, man. C'mon ahead then later. We'll show you around."

"Sounds good. Thank you."

"See you later." The group went back to their preparations as Tye moved back down the walkway.

Mission accomplished; he was no longer a stranger to them.

"That was easy," Raina said.

Maybe too easy.

Derek Kurn might check into his story about being a transfer student, but he was banking on the hope it wouldn't happen right away. All the really desirable pledges, the new varsity jocks and guys who handled themselves with the right amount of moxie and lack of posing, were no doubt already on Derek's and his fraternity brothers' radar screens. What was one more potential pledge coming to a party? Plus, Derek seemed like he had a lot of other things on his mind at the moment.

Whether that included another foray into date rape at tonight's party remained to be seen.

16

INSIDE THE VAN a mile away, Raina stood to adjust her headset and stretch her arms. One of her little watch birds was giving her trouble, the controls balky and sometimes seeming to skip a beat. She'd be lucky if she could keep the thing flying long enough to get it back to the small base camp they'd established on the roof of a utility shed in a wooded area near their apartments.

One of the often unspoken realities of bigger UAVs was that they crashed a lot, compared to other aircraft—even the multi-million-dollar Predators and Reapers the Air Force was flying—and Raina had found her little hover angels and dragonflies to be no exception.

She wondered if Murnell and all his high-tech wonders had made any progress in overcoming this issue, but the Homeland scientist had remained tight-lipped regarding any details about the type of crafts she'd been piloting. A part of her already missed what she'd experienced in the sphere. Manipulating her sometimes flighty, and by comparison archaic, joystick and controls in the back of the van soon became a frustrating experience; she had to work hard to focus on the skills she'd acquired and to maintain her discipline.

She sat back down before her console and watched as Tye

walked down the street. He really wasn't a bad-looking guy. Maybe not as movie-star handsome as Dr. Murnell, but he had a different quality about him—rugged, dependable. She could see that their relationship was going to be complicated no matter where this all went. Sitting back down at her console, she spoke into her mike.

"Hey, soldier. You need to hoof it back here. I'm having a few technical challenges."

"Something critical?"

"Nothing I can't handle."

Anyone watching Tye would think he was having a hands-free conversation with someone on his mobile phone.

"All right. No more word from your Homeland buddy?"

"He's not my buddy, and no, nothing."

"Maybe that's good. Maybe they just wanted to check you out and now they'll leave us alone."

"Don't sound stupid."

"Wishful thinking, that's all."

"Does it ever freak you out knowing I'm watching you?"

"A little. But not that much as long as I know it's only you."

"You need to sit in this chair a while. I wish you could see what it's like from the other end."

"Maybe I will."

But Raina was thinking not just about what she was seeing on her computer screens in the van but the inside of Murnell's sphere and the type of virtual reality it created. Was it even real? Had she actually been flying some kind of a miniaturized drone down a street in China the night before? The screen in front of her told her that it was all too real, and she wondered what Homeland was planning to do with their apparently secret technology. But if it was so secret, why had Murnell allowed her, even welcomed her to work with it, only to let her go when she was done?

She wasn't working for Homeland. She was no longer even an employee of the federal government, her veteran's health benefits notwithstanding. Other than Tye, whom could she trust? And a part of her was beginning to wonder if even the soldier who had once saved her life could be compromised. Why hadn't they heard back yet from Major Williamson?

17

TYE DIDN'T CLUE into the guy following him until he was almost back to the van.

He'd seen the stocky African American man out of the corner of his eye, walking along behind him on the opposite side of the street when he left the frat house, but he'd paid him no attention. Raina either hadn't seen him or must have discounted his presence, too. As he rounded the third and final corner, however, he realized the man was still with him; hanging back a little, it seemed, but definitely still there.

Tye had a bad feeling. No matter how many high tech gizmos you brought to the party, they couldn't replace the gut sensation you got from being from being right there on the ground.

He decided to continue walking past the van without looking or stopping.

"What are you doing?" Raina asked.

"I think we may have company."

"What?"

"Just sit tight."

He turned the next corner and proceeded along the block. At the next turn he glanced casually behind him. Sure enough, the man was keeping pace, about seventy yards behind him. He scanned the street for any signs of police or campus security and saw none. A large university building loomed ahead on his right, with an adjacent alleyway formed by a retaining wall against a steep hillside. The sun was about to set and long shadows were overtaking the street.

"I see what you're talking about. I've got eyes on him if you need them," Raina said.

He thought for a moment.

"What's the layout with the alleyway up ahead?" he asked.

"It parallels the building all the way around back. Must be for fire department access."

"Windows?"

"Hang on a second."

"Haven't got all day here, Rain."

He was drawing nearer to the alley and he didn't want to slow down or appear to alter his gait in any way.

"Right," she said. "Sorry. I see no windows or doors in the back of the building. None down the alley either."

"Security cameras?"

"Don't see any."

Sounded like a good a place to draw the guy in and find out what he was up to. It might be the only chance he'd get.

"Okay. I'm going to try to reel him in," he said.

"You sure?"

No more time for chitchat. Moving briskly as he approached the building, he abruptly turned and ducked down the alley. The entire alleyway was framed by the tall concrete-enforced retaining wall that had to be at least twenty feet in height. The narrow opening to the blue sky overhead let in minimal light.

"Okay. I see what you have in mind," she said.

It was good to have her eyes in the sky.

"How am I doing?" he asked.

"He's closing on you."

Breathing harder from the adrenaline, Tye hurried to the end of the building, and slipped around the corner.

"Am I good?" he whispered.

"Okay, you're fine," Raina said. "He's just coming into the alley now."

Tye willed himself not to move. Whatever was happening here would become apparent soon enough.

"He's stopping for a moment to check things out. Must be wondering if you went into the building."

Tye waited.

"All right, he's moving again. Slowly. He's still looking around. I'll tell you when he's just about made it to your corner."

He liked the tactical advantage Raina's gave him. It allowed him to magnify his capabilities in ways he'd never considered. He counted to fifteen, trying to project back to how long it had just taken him to move along the wall.

"He's just about on top of you," Raina said.

Here we go.

Tye stuck his leg out and stepped directly into the man's path.

"Hold up, friend."

"Wha—?"

The man took a quick step back. About five-ten, two hundred and fifty pounds, he wore a dark gray sweatsuit with big pockets. Up close, Tye realized, he was neither African American nor Latino, as he'd suspected—maybe Middle Eastern or Filipino, maybe something else. He had a small scar on his lower lip, a tattoo on the side of his neck, and dark, set-back eyes. Mr. Sweatsuit neither looked nor carried himself like a student.

The heavyset man came out of his pocket with a handgun cradled in his right fist. Tye immediately made it as a large caliber, not the type of weapon typically brandished by your everyday gang banger.

"Whoa," he said. "No need for that." Alone and unarmed in what he now realized was a stupid place to confront the guy, he instinctively edged forward a little, closing the gap between them.

"I'll decide if there's a need," the man said.

His accent was distinctly American. Not Southern or New York. Midwest? Chicago? Maybe the west coast? Maybe L.A.?

"You were following me, Amigo," Tye said. He was still kicking himself for not anticipating the gun. He could imagine Raina's panic at the moment, watching on her video feeds. Should she call the police? They both knew she couldn't do that.

"Who you callin' Amigo?" The man trained the barrel of the gun directly at Tye's chest.

He raised his hands in the air, feigning panic, moving closer. "Don't shoot. Please don't shoot me."

The big man looked disgusted. "What are you? Some sort of psycho fag?"

A few inches more. "I was just…I was just…"

A sound like the flutter of wings burst from somewhere above. The big man's eyes flicked up toward the noise, all the opening that was needed.

Tye spun his hands in a clockwise whip, grasping the top of the barrel with his left hand to push it away while breaking the man's grip with a powerful chop from his other, executing a clean *Kiaido Ryu* gun disarm. He pulled back with the gun in his own control before the guy even knew what hit him.

The man lost his balance for a moment, but Tye wasn't fooled. The guy came right back at him with a switchblade from somewhere, aiming for Tye's midsection. Making a snap decision not to use the gun, he blocked the thrust with a kick to the man's groin and a static hold, which the guy must have counted on.

Whoever he was, he must have been a wrestler or something. A strong one at that, and he wanted his gun back. He wasn't about to give up this fight, and Tye realized the guy was ready and willing to kill.

The next knife charge, fueled by anger and fear and who knew what else, started from above where Tye held his arm in a partial clasp. Tye had no choice but to redirect the force of it. The big man tripped over his own feet, his huge body whipsawing toward the ground, but as he did, his lower body slammed into Tye, knocking the gun away, as they both rolled to the ground.

The gun clattered to the pavement. The guy was a step closer and pounced on it.

Tye rose up to move toward him, but it was too late, he saw the black barrel angling toward him again, knowing this time the guy was going to pull the trigger.

But before the big man could squeeze off a shot, something whistle-zipped through the air and the guy's head exploded. Some kind of high velocity round went right through him, splaying blood and bone against the building.

"Holy..."

Tye leapt back, moving to take whatever cover he could against the bare brick wall. He dropped to one knee. Seconds went by. Mercifully, there appeared to be no more bullets on the way, at least for the time being.

The man had been killed instantly and the result wasn't pretty. Tye's heart felt like it was about to pound out of his chest.

"Did you see that?"

"I saw it," Raina said.

He looked up. "Where the hell did that come from?"

"I have no idea. It sure as heck wasn't from me."

The attacker who a moment before had been about to kill him was now well beyond dead. Half his brain had been plastered against the wall and ground.

"Sniper?" Raina asked.

He searched the fading blue above and the surrounding rooftops to see if he could tell where the shot had come from but saw nothing except the gathering darkness and a distant cloud, crawling mist-like across the small patch of sky.

"I don't see how," he said. "No angle for anyone to shoot from. You see anything on your screen or thermal imaging?"

A pause. "Negative."

Again, he forced himself to slow down and calm his breathing. "Okay. Let me think."

"You need to get out of there."

"First, let me see if this guy has any kind of ID on him."

He bent over the body, now slumped like some grotesque marionette against the brick side of the building. There was blood everywhere, more continuing to ooze out, but the guy's heart must have stopped pumping soon after his brain exploded. He'd seen as bad in combat, but this was different.

He checked the pockets of the bloody sweatsuit and found nothing. No wallet. No money. No keys or anything else. Whoever this guy was, he sure traveled light. He looked over the rest of the body to see if there might be any unique identifying characteristics. Not a thing. Other than the fact the dude had been in need of some dental work.

"Your prints will be on the gun," Raina said.

"Thanks, Sherlock." He should have thought of that. He was going to have to start thinking more like a cop. He tore off his varsity style jacket and used it to wipe down the handgun—a big Beretta he realized now—that had dropped back to the pavement.

"Wait a minute," he said. "Why don't I just take the thing? It hasn't been fired. There's no forensic trace."

"Sure. Whatever. It's starting to grow dark. Just get the heck out of there."

Maybe the gun would help lead him back to its source. He engaged the safety on the Beretta and jammed the weapon into the back waistband of his jeans, covering it with his sweatshirt.

Who was this dude? And, more importantly now, who or what had taken him out? All he knew was he had to get moving again. He realized he was sweating, even though it was growing cooler.

Tye started to make his way out of the alley, glancing overhead as he went.

18

"WHAT WERE YOU thinking?"

Raina glared at him over the top of her computer screen from the back of the van. Tye was driving slowly so as to not call attention to their vehicle. No doubt someone would be finding the body in the alley soon enough.

They came to a stoplight and Tye looked at Raina in the mirror. She was still upset. She had a right to be. It would have been much smarter of him to confront the guy out on the street where he would have been less likely to pull a gun.

"I wasn't thinking," he said. "I was reacting. Never should have let him pin me in that place, and once the fight started, I shouldn't have let him get the gun back. He was about to send me packing to Never-land."

"I saw that."

"You think he was he was from Homeland Security?"

"How should I know? I'm not exactly on DHS's team. Now we have people trying to kill us, and bullets flying out of the sky and we have no idea why."

"Which only confirms the fact that we're messing with some important people. You think the shot came from another drone?"

"Had to be. The alleyway was too narrow for anyone or

anything else to have a view from above. But not a normal military drone like a Predator. If a Pred had taken him out, you would have been smoked along with him, and so would most of the side of that building."

"So a smaller one maybe. Something new. Like the ones we're flying."

"It's possible. But the MAVs aren't supposed to be weaponized, and they're too small to pack a punch like that," she said.

"Maybe it was from some sort of an automated gun."

"That's was my first thought…But how would they have taken the shot unless it had a platform and was positioned directly over the alley? Only way to do that is with a drone… But there's a big problem."

"What's that?"

"There was nothing else up there. Believe me. I checked from every angle I could find."

Tye thought things over for a moment.

"You want to pull the plug?" he offered. "We can abort right now. Return the equipment, tell Williamson to take a flying leap, and disappear. I know a place out in Idaho where we can lay low for a while."

"I don't think it's that simple," she said.

"What do you mean?"

"I've been thinking about this. We know too much. And what about Stacie Hutchinson and Derek Kurn? Are we supposed to just forget about the recording?"

"We could just send it in to the police and FBI as an anonymous tip."

"Which Nathan Kurn would promptly find a way to explain away or pay someone to have buried."

"Maybe the guy worked for Kurn."

"You think Kurn's on to us?"

"Could be."

"I've pulled in my MAVs," she said. "Got them parked in a safe spot for now."

"I want to know where that round came from."

"What kind of bullet was it?"

"I didn't exactly have time to stick around for a ballistics analysis but it had to be a larger caliber."

Tye's cell phone went off in his pocket. He pulled it out and looked at the screen.

"Figures. Anonymous," he said.

He put the phone to his ear and answered.

"Drive to the following location," a voice said. It was Williamson. He pushed the button to speaker, so Raina could hear it, too. The major's instructions ended with a set of GPS coordinates, which she wrote down.

"Was that you who fired the shot?" Tye asked.

"Drive to the location," Williamson repeated before abruptly clicking off.

"There's your answer then. He had to have been the one to make the kill," he said.

"We still don't know that for sure."

"He obviously knows about it. Why else would he be calling us? Where's he talking about meeting?"

"Hang on a minute." She typed the coordinates into her keyboard. "Looks like it's a few miles from here…." She typed some more, staring into her screen. It's a group of warehouses over near NIH."

"It's getting dark. Rush hour should be over. Should we take the beltway?"

"No. Too visible," she said. "Stick to surface streets where we at least have some tree canopy cover. I'm already plotting a route."

19

THE INDUSTRIAL PARK stood empty, its ghost-like buildings illuminated only by a few glowing street lamps and limited security lighting. The van's headlights swept across a real estate agent's sign at the entrance. A hundred and twenty-five thousand square feet of warehouse and light industrial space was available for lease; yet one more casualty of a stagnant economy.

A chain link fence topped with razor wire barred entrance to the property, but the apparently remotely controlled gate slid silently open to welcome them. Someone was obviously expecting their arrival.

"This place looks like fun," he said.

"Better keep our eyes open." Raina, who'd moved next to him in the front passenger seat, swiveled her head back and forth, scanning the shadowed hulks and darkened windows of the empty structures.

"A little nervous, are we, without your drone babies watching over us?"

"After seeing what happened to that guy in the alley...you bet I am."

They rolled into the main intersection of the complex. From down one of the side streets, a dark, low-slung vehicle approached. Tye turned the van to face it. He gave the accelerator a little more gas.

"Who do we have here? James Bond?"

You could tell the approaching automobile was some sort of low-slung sports car, but not much else was apparent behind its gleaming Xenon headlamps. The car rolled to a stop about fifty yards ahead of them. Tye braked the van to a halt as well.

The door of the sports car opened and a man climbed out, stepping forward into the glow of their lights. Clad in dark blue jeans and a black leather jacket, he was of medium height but quite thin and completely bald.

Tye raised an eyebrow. "Forget Bond. Looks more like an anorexic Vin Diesel. It's Williamson."

Raina nodded.

"Here we go."

He felt for the Beretta he'd placed on the seat next to him. Leaning forward, he shoved it back in his waistband.

"I'm coming, too." Raina pushed open her door as he opened his.

"Of course you are," he said.

They climbed out and approached Williamson on foot.

"Little upgrade in the lifestyle, huh, Major?" Tye said.

Williamson nodded. "You might say that. Good to see both of you in person again."

Tye glanced at Raina, around the perimeter, and overhead for any sign of something awry.

"You summoned us here."

"That I did."

"You just murdered that man in the alley," Raina said.

"Regrettably, I took the shot. But since you were watching with your MAVs, I'm sure you agree he was about to pull his trigger. It was a clear case of defending Mr. Palmer's life. I wouldn't call that murder."

"You used another type of drone?"

"Yes."

"What did you find out about the guy who's been romancing me from Homeland Security?"

"I've confirmed most of what you told me was accurate."

"Did the dead man in the alley work for him?"

"Quite possibly. We're still trying to find out more, just like you."

Tye screwed up his mouth. "Who are you, and we, really working for, Major?"

"As I've told you before, this is mostly a private effort."

"Mostly…why would DHS have such an interest?"

"Quite possibly because we may be employing some of their technology."

"Whose side are we on, the government's?"

"I'm afraid it's not that simple anymore. There are elements all throughout the government, all over the world for that matter, involved in the kind of thing we're doing. A lot of us have had to become freelancers. Just like you, we try to judge each individual situation as best we can when it comes."

"So how have you gotten me such high security clearance?" Raina asked.

"I'm afraid I can't tell you that."

"We know you were Air Force and you've told us you used to be with the Company, but you can't be doing all this alone."

"I have help."

"Who provides the money?"

"We're self-funded. We prefer to work off the grid."

"Who heads up the organization?"

"I can't tell you that either. Not yet anyway. But I do want you both to understand the gravity of the situation we all now find ourselves in."

"Yeah, well I kind of got that message loud and clear when that guy's head blew up in my face," Tye said.

"What *do* you know about the dead man in the alley?" Raina asked.

"He was a former soldier like yourselves. On the wrong side, I'm afraid. We didn't think they'd act so quickly, but you must have tripped a wire that alerted them."

"What do you mean *they*? Who are they?"

"I'm sorry to have to be the one to tell you this, but you two have been dropped into the middle of another war. It's being waged with both public and independent resources, and it can be dangerous at times. No one will hold you responsible if you elect to walk away right now."

"What kind of a war are we talking about?" Raina asked.

"Think about the mission you're on right now."

"You mean against people like Nathan Kurn and his son?"

"That's part of it, yes. Look. We all know there are people among us, some of them very prominent people, who have gotten away with things... who continue to get away with things."

"That's what this is all about? Taking down people like that?"

"To some extent. Either way it's a big collateral benefit."

"What about the law?"

"Laws can be bent, circumvented, or ignored. Happens every day. Sometimes we tiptoe on the fringe of that as well. Takes some getting used to, but I grew accustomed to it working for the Company. It's not that I don't believe in the rule of law. It's that when the law fails....that's why a few of us have spent so much time and money on developing some of the technology you're employing."

"You said we tripped a wire," Raina said. "Maybe it was because we identified the rape victim and went to talk to her."

"Let me guess. And she wanted to talk with her parents," Williamson said.

"Yes."

"Who no doubt would've contacted their lawyer…that's probably what called the dogs on you," he said.

"Not Lance Murnell from Homeland Security?" Raina asked.

"The two may not be mutually exclusive."

Williamson paused, maybe to let the weight of what he'd just told them sink in.

"So wait," Tye said. "You're trying to tell us the guy in the alley worked for Nathan Kurn and maybe DHS, too?"

"Maybe. But not directly."

Tye rubbed the back of his neck. "So you've gotten us all deep into this thing, whatever it all is."

"No," Raina said. "We've gotten ourselves into it. No one's been twisting our arms."

"Let me just tell you this," Williamson said. "We may not be perfect, but if you're working with us, as far as I'm concerned you're on the side of the angels. Anytime you disagree with that assessment, you're free to quit."

"Really?" Tye said. "No questions asked? Sounds too simple."

Williamson shrugged.

"If what you say is true, it wouldn't matter if we quit right now. Some of these people might still be coming after us."

"Very likely."

"I smell a rat with Nathan Kurn. He's mixed up in all of this."

"Well we've known that all along, haven't we? It's part of the reason we started down this road."

"Which means we have to keep moving against his son before it's too late to do anything about it."

"I agree," Raina said. "But if we're in some kind of a war, as you say, Major, what if we get caught? We could all go to prison. If nothing else, the FAA has yet to legalize the use of drones for the kind of thing we're doing here."

"Unless they're private…and operated below 400 feet in altitude. There's a lot of gray area in the rules right now. As far as the FAA or anyone else is concerned, we're all still hobbyists…"

"Some hobby," Tye said.

"Look," Williamson told them. "There's a lot going on in the world these days. Riots overseas. Unrest here at home. No one really knows yet how to handle all of the implications of this next generation of security and war fighting technology. Not the President or the Joint Chiefs. Not the Director of Homeland Security. No one with the NSA or the Company. Certainly no one in Congress. And what they all fail to appreciate is that it's already here. Military UAVs have been making flights over American soil for years. Law enforcement is already deploying them, crude as they are compared to what you two are flying. We're just a few clicks out in front of the curve."

"More than a few clicks, I'd say," Raina said. "Who else knows about the MAVs and the kind of thing Murnell was showing me?"

"Enough people to make the technology very volatile at the moment. These things aren't like nuclear weapons. Not so easily containable."

"We could expose your whole operation," Raina said.

Williams shrugged. "I would think you've both known me long enough, Raina, to know I've made contingency plans. The question is, do you still believe in what we're doing? After all, you've come this far…"

There was a long pause as they stood inside the glow of the headlights looking at one another.

"We're on the side of the angels, huh?" Tye said.

"I like to think of it that way, yes."

"What if the President of the United States ordered you to shut down right now, would you do it?"

Williamson smiled. "I'm not going to speculate about hypotheticals. The fact is he hasn't ordered us to shut down and he's not about to."

"Does the President even know about what you—about what we're doing?"

"You're kidding, right? I hate to burst your bubble, but that's not the way this game is played. Too much is happening too fast for it to be otherwise. I never said it was going to be easy. But I will tell you this: while we may not technically be public servants, we will never do anything, ultimately, to subvert our country. I would also hope you'd know me well enough by now to understand I mean what I'm saying."

"Even when people are dying?" Raina asked.

"Especially when people are dying."

Tye looked at Raina. She looked back at him and nodded.

Tye said: "The police are going to have an interesting time trying to figure out how the guy died in the middle of town from a shot like that."

"We've already made sure there were no security cameras linking you to that alley. As for any witnesses, well, we'll just have to hope for the best on that one. At least it was beginning to get dark."

Tye thought about the irony of someone watching them when he and Raina were the ones who were supposed to be doing the watching.

"How long have you been running surveillance on us?" he asked.

"Just since I picked up on the fact you were being tailed. It actually started a couple of hours before you ended up in the alley. You're lucky I intervened when we did. Otherwise, you wouldn't be standing here right now."

"Are the other people you're working with ex-military or ex-Company, too?"

"Sorry. I can't tell you that either, but as you might imagine, we've all got our share of friends and supporters we can call upon when needed."

Another long silence hung between them.

"So what happens next?" Raina asked.

The major folded his arms. "I believe in delegating authority. I'm here to give you some reassurance, but I'm trusting in you to make the right decisions. You people are running this op on the ground, not me."

Tye thought for a moment. "We might need a favor when it comes to the cops. Not about what just happened in the alley. Something else...."

Williamson stared at him for a moment. "All right. We'll see what we can do."

"What about any other people who might be after us?"

"I'll do my best to try to keep them off your backs ... Speaking of which..." Williamson looked at his watch. "It's time we hightailed it out of here. The police patrol this place regularly and they're due to make another check in a few minutes."

"WHAT'S ALL THIS?" Raina asked.

After leaving Williamson they had returned to the apartment complex to get ready for the late night ahead on campus. Tye had insisted she accompany him her over to his apartment where he led her to a utility closet behind the kitchen. Its heavy door was secured with a pair of beefy padlocks Tye was in the processing of unlocking.

"I've had a feeling we might be headed toward trouble, so I went out earlier this morning after we talked and picked up a few things. Figured I'd put some of Nathan Kurn's money to good use."

She squinted into the darkness of the small space as he opened the door to see a cache of firearms, body armor and ammunition—two AR-15s, a pair of Mossberg tactical shotguns, and four or five semi-automatic handguns, from 9 mm up to .40 caliber.

"What, are you planning an invasion?"

Tye shrugged. "Williamson did say we were back at war."

"How did you buy all of this stuff at once?"

"Williamson may have friends. Well, I've got some, too. Plus I had the cash from Kurn."

"Are you checked out on all of these weapons?"

"Yes, ma'am. Plus, I've got that sweet Beretta I took from the dead guy. How about you?"

She looked over the selection, picking up a mid-sized Glock and turning it over in her hands. "Most of them," she said. "Enough to get by."

"That'll do."

"Hopefully, we won't have any need of them."

"Always pays to be prepared."

By eight o'clock they were back in Raina's apartment, having talked things through and formulated what they hoped would be the right approach. When Raina's cell phone rang on the table beside her computer desk, Tye almost reached for it. He waited for her to pick it up.

She looked at the display. "Stacie Hutchinson," she said.

She pushed a button on the keypad and put the phone to her ear. If Hutchinson got cold feet about exposing Kurn's son, or if her parents had talked her out of it, they'd have to figure that into their plans.

Raina sat listening to whatever Hutchinson was telling her. "Thank you," she said finally into the phone. "You're sure?" There was a long pause. "Okay. Thank you for letting us know. You'll be hearing from us shortly."

She broke the connection and looked up at Tye.

"Well?"

"She's in. She talked it over with her parents, and she's willing to press charges…but only if we get a taped confession or come up with better proof than what we've got on the recording."

"Oh, is that all?" He pulled in a deep breath. "Dang, woman."

"Well, you can't blame her, can you? She and her family are looking at having to go to war, too. And with Kurn, we all know it's bound to get very, very ugly."

"All right then," Tye said. "I guess we know what we have to do."

"I'll try to give you enough advance warning if anything bad looks like it's coming your way."

He chuckled. "Hey. It's just a frat party, right? It ain't Fallujah. I get in there and nail this turkey and we're done. At least for now."

"It's like being downrange again a little, isn't it? Even when the threat appears, it isn't always so obvious."

"I guess that's one way to look at it."

Raina looked at the floor. "You ever read *Ender's Game?*"

"The book? Sure. Back when I was in high school. Seems like a long time ago."

"You know I feel a little bit like Ender sometimes when I'm flying the MAVs. Like it isn't even real."

"The dude thought it was all a training exercise or something, didn't he? Didn't know he was really killing people."

"Yeah, and even though I know this is all real, sometimes I can't help but feel disconnected. I still have all the emotions. Like I'm here with you in this room right now, but I'm not really here."

"Sounds kind of weird when you put it like that," he said.

"I wish I could be in there with you when this goes down."

He didn't quite know how to take what she was saying. He thought he knew her well enough to realize she was focused on the job at hand and didn't mean what she said in any romantic way, but that's how it sounded.

She stood up from her chair and walked awkwardly to the refrigerator. Maybe she sensed what he was thinking, and it made her uncomfortable. She was obviously stiff from hunching over her keyboard, and her prosthetic didn't make things any easier.

"It will be just the same as if you were in there," he said.

"Not really. You're the one who would've been dead in that alley if it weren't for Williamson." She grimaced as she twisted the top off of a beer. "You want one?" She tilted it in his direction.

"Why not?"

He stepped over to her, his palm brushing against the back of her hand as she handed him the cold bottle. She turned away and took out another for herself.

Tye took a long sip. He hadn't drunk beer in a few days. It tasted good. He rummaged in one of the cupboards and found a jar of peanuts.

They sat down across from one another at the small kitchen table. He opened the jar and placed it between them.

"You ever wonder if it was all worth it?" she asked.

"What do you mean?"

"Over there, in Jalalabad. Wherever."

"Sure. Who doesn't? But we went over there and did our jobs. We did what we were supposed to."

"They gave you a medal," she said. "You deserved it."

He shrugged. "We all did."

"Maybe. I don't know about that."

"You got a medal, too."

She made a face. "I never wear mine. Probably breaking some protocol or something."

They each took another drink and stared into their bottles.

"You know I had another bad dream about it last night," she said. "Like a lot of the others I've had before."

"Yeah?"

"It's dark and I'm looking with my chopper's night vision and I'm seeing those mountain horses they have over there. It reminds me of growing up on the ranch in New Mexico and my father."

"That's cool."

"I should take you out there riding with me sometime. You'd like it."

"Never been on a horse. But I'm game."

"It's a little harder for me get up into the stirrup these days, but I've gone riding a couple of times since I've been out. Virginia's got some beautiful country, but it's not New Mexico."

He nodded. "Sounds nice."

She took another sip of beer and set her bottle down on the table. "You know, when I signed on for this mission with you a few weeks ago, I never figured on people dying."

"Me either. I guess we should have known better."

"Live and learn," she said. "Either way, there's nothing cool about what happened to Stacie Hutchinson, not to mention that guy in the alley."

"Very true," he said.

Their eyes met for a long moment.

"I should start getting prepared," she said, looking away.

"Okay. I'm going to try to get a little shuteye before the main event. Mind if I sack out on your couch again?"

"Be my guest."

She paused for a moment, as if she wanted to say something more but couldn't. She pushed back from the table and turned back to her computer workstation, her movements almost cat-like despite the silent spring of her prosthetic foot.

Raina barely ever seemed to rest. In addition to her many other talents, maybe she took some kind of superwoman pills.

Tye, on the other hand, had been legendary in his platoon for his ability to grab a quick catnap when needed. In less than a minute he began to drift to sleep, smiling at her back as she typed something on her keyboard and stared into her screens.

21

THE SIDEWALK LOOKED like it was made of chalk in the near darkness of the suburban street. Along the curb stood an unmarked sedan with two city detectives seated inside.

Tye approached the car with caution. The night had taken on a chill beneath a thin moon while a hint of wood smoke from someone's fireplace flitted through the air. Even from a block and a half away, the music from the fraternity party thumped through the quiet neighborhood. Laughter from another, smaller student gathering could also be heard from somewhere down the street.

The car window slid down as Tye drew up on it.

"You Palmer?"

"Yeah."

"You're late."

The driver was a big man with a bulldog face. Tye couldn't really tell with him in the car, but the detective looked like he was at least as tall as he, only a lot older and a lot bulkier.

"Sorry."

It was well after ten p.m. and there were no trick-or-treaters left on the streets. The Halloween action, whatever might be left of it, had moved inside.

"Sounds like there's a big party going on down the way," the detective said.

"That's why I'm here."

"What's with the hockey get-up?" He pointed to the colorful jersey Tye wore over his jeans and boots and the big leather mitt in his hand.

"Halloween costume."

"No mask?"

"I figured it might creep people out too much."

"Uh-huh…Chief says some old Army buddy told him you'd meet us here and that you might have some information about a rape."

"Better than that. I plan to give you the rapist and the evidence to prove it."

"You do, huh?"

Tye nodded.

"Just like that."

"Just like that."

He probably sounded too cocky, but he needed to get the guys' attention.

"What, you know the guy in question? He confess to you or something?"

"No. It's a little more complicated than that."

"Mmm. I'll bet it is…You look too old to be a college student."

"Yeah, I've heard that."

"What'd you do, flunk out the first time or something?"

"No. I took a little detour."

"A detour?"

"Yeah. Through Iraq and Afghanistan."

The detective eyed him and up and down and formed a serious pout with his mouth to show he was impressed. He glanced across at his partner and nodded. Maybe they were starting to believe, just a little, that Tye was for real.

"Okay," the man said. "What's the play?"

"Simple. The party down the street's at a frat house."

"So we gathered. You a member?"

"Nope. But they're hoping I might join. I can get into the party."

"All right. Then what?"

"Once I'm in, I'm going to confront the guy with the evidence."

"Before you show it to us? Sorry, it don't work like that, partner."

"It's going to have to in this case and you'll see why."

"What do you mean?"

"The guy's family has some major league pull. There are people who will try to bury this before it ever sees the light of day. I want to prevent that from happening."

"So what does you walking in there and confronting this guy accomplish?"

"If everything goes as planned, a lot. You'll have an open and shut case. No one even needs to know I was here."

"And I should just take your word for it."

"Talk to your chief."

Williamson had helped set this up. Tye hoped the major had fully done his part.

"You got a court order for any of this?"

"Call your chief." Tye looked over his shoulder. The last thing he needed right now was somebody from the party wandering down this back street and spying him with the cops.

The detective glared at him for a moment. The guy pulled out his phone, punched in a single number and stuck it to his ear. "You stand right there for minute," he said. "Don't move."

Tye waited. The detective powered his window up for a moment so Tyce couldn't hear what was being said. Soon the man's mouth was moving in animated conversation.

It wasn't too long before the window came back down.

"Okay, hotshot. Not sure who you are or how you're doing all this, but the chief's given the go-ahead. This has sure been one freakstorm of a night around here."

"What do you mean?"

"Don't you watch the news? Some guy got his head blown to bits a few blocks from here. The coroner's still trying to pick up the pieces. You better watch yourself, Mister."

"Sure thing. Will do."

"Just so you know...the chief told me to tell you anything goes wrong in there, you're on your own. We can just take you all into custody if we have to and sort this all out down at the division...."

Tye nodded and turned to go.

"Hey," the detective said. "I can tell you're not a cop. Why you doing all this?"

Tye looked back at him for a moment. "Loose ends, detective."

"What?" The cop squinted at him with a mixture of doubt and curiosity.

"Just cleaning up some loose ends."

"Must be one big old frayed one..."

"Yeah."

The big cop rubbed his hand across the back of his neck. "Well, hell, son, coming from where you're coming from, I'd imagine you've got a good number of those."

22

THE LAWN IN front of the house lay strewn with plastic beer cups and other trash. A large crowd of students—mostly frat guys but several girls, too—was gathered around a ping-pong table someone had dragged out onto the grass, and a fierce game of beer pong was in full swing. The music was loud enough to mask Tye's approach. He saw no sign of Derek Kurn. Dressed in blue jeans, sandals, and a college t-shirt, no one paid him any attention anyway as he melted through the crowd toward the house.

Raina had briefed him in detail on the layout of the house and the location of Derek's room.

"You in?"

Raina's voice purred into his hidden earpiece as he moved away from the crowd and stepped up onto the porch and behind a pair of columns where he couldn't be heard.

"Not quite."

"Had a little technical glitch with the watchbird I was using on the rooftop across the street, so I lost sight of you."

"Just what we need, a temperamental robofly."

"No need to be mean. My babies get the hiccups sometimes, especially when you insult them."

"I'll try to remember that."

"I've still got eyes in the main hallway and inside the target's dorm room."

"How'd you manage to do that?"

"Don't ask."

"Anything interesting happening?"

"The Kurn kid's in his room, and there's a girl in there with him. It's been like watching the beginning of a slutty movie."

"How would you know?"

"Shut up. This is where what we're doing creeps me out."

"Roger that."

"At least this girl seems to be in possession of her faculties."

"Maybe Derek's making some progress then."

"I doubt it."

"You call the press?"

"Yup. Told them it was a hot tip and to have a TV van in front of the frat house."

"Good. Cops won't be happy about it, but that's their problem."

"I hope you know what you're doing, Tye."

"Me, too."

He stepped out from behind the columns and headed down the porch toward the front door. A group of laughing coeds burst through the entrance and onto the porch, beer cups in hand. They looked at Tye for a moment. He nodded to them, and they smiled.

"Hey, cutie," one of them said.

"Hey yourself."

"Nice hockey shirt. It looks good on you."

He waved his goalie's glove at them and they moved off, giggling, toward the raucous crowd on the lawn.

"My. Aren't we the party-boy now?" Raina said through his earpiece.

"I thought you said you couldn't see me."

"But I can still hear you."

Tye moved on into the house.

From the outside, the building had looked almost regal—Classic Colonial architecture with stately columns circling the porch in front, dark brick with white trim. But the inside offered a different picture. Beer stains marred the wooden floor. The furniture, much of it torn and disheveled, had been pushed back to the walls. Party lanterns and Halloween decorations—witches, skulls, and gory jack-o-lanterns—were scattered throughout the house. Fake cobwebs hung from the ceilings, from the doorways, even the walls. Lights strobed back and forth over the revelers, many sporting masks. The music was deafening.

A muscled mountain of a student—had to be a linebacker—manned a desk blocking entrance to the party.

"Can I help you?" the student asked. The words sounded cheerful enough, but with this dude they sounded more like a challenge than a desire to actually help. Football was animalistic, like combat. For a moment, he was afraid there might be trouble.

He glanced to the side and saw one of the guys who'd been setting up on the patio with Derek Kurn a few hours before. The linebacker followed his gaze. The other guy said to the linebacker, "No problem, Michael. He's cool. Derek met him this afternoon."

The mountain nodded.

"Okey-dokey. Make yourself at home, my friend," the big guy said, stepping to one side. "Don't let any hockey pucks catch you in the teeth."

"Wouldn't mind having you blocking for me," Tye said out of respect.

The guy smiled. In hostile country, you could use all the friends you could get.

Tye moved past him through the foyer and took a look around. The dancing was taking place in the main living room, a large open space directly in front of him. To one side a grand central staircase spiraled upward to the second floor. On the other side, a hallway led to the kitchen and several other rooms. He didn't see any of Raina's little bugs swarming around, but then, he hadn't expected to.

Fortunately, Derek's room was about half way down the hall to his right, a private suite reserved for the fraternity president. He turned and ran smack dab into a rising wall of boxes. Boxed wine. Two guys were just finished building the stack.

"Sorry, buddy. Had to find someplace to stash the empties. We'll carry them out to the dumpster later."

Nice. He couldn't very well go crashing through them without causing a scene, and they blocked off the hall.

He walked through into the living room and made for the wall.

"Talk to me, Rain," he whispered, hoping no one was watching him too closely.

"I see it," she said. "They just showed up with those boxes. Give me a second and I'll try to find a workaround."

"Sure. I'll just stand here putting my rave on."

There was no response.

"Okay," she said after thirty or forty seconds of silence. "Head to your right. About thirty feet along the wall is another open doorway. It leads through the dining room and into the kitchen and back up into the hallway from the other direction."

He began moving, but before he could get very far, he felt a hand on his shoulder. He turned to see the student who'd okayed his entry into the party holding out a red plastic cup.

"Hey, soldier man. Have a beer."

The guy had black curly hair, big ears, and bright teeth when he smiled. He might have been a senior or maybe even a grad student like Tye. He looked a little older and more clean-cut than the other members of the fraternity, which was belied by the fact he wore a Baltimore Ravens jersey over a pair of bright yellow Bermuda shorts, dark sunglasses, and sandals with no socks.

"Thanks," Tye said, taking the cup from him.

The guy held up his beer to Tye's.

"To America," Raven man toasted with a mixture of amusement and sarcasm.

"To America."

Tye took a sip. It was ice cold and tasted almost as good as the one he'd drunk earlier. Another time and place he might actually have enjoyed it.

Thankfully, Raven Man's sunglasses seemed to have a wandering eye and a short attention span.

"Hey. Catch you later, bro. I see somebody I really need to get up close and personal with, if you catch my drift."

"Later," Tye said, watching for a moment as the guy weaved through the dancing throng, holding his full beer cup like an Olympic torch out in front of him above his head.

"Tsk-tsk. No more drinking on the job," Raina teased.

"When in Rome...." Tye said under his breath.

He stood and watched the dancing for a moment. Tye had been a decent student in high school, but never made straight A's. Most of the students at the party were smarter than he was, at least on paper. They didn't have to work nearly as hard. Some had probably graduated from prestigious prep schools where the classes were more rigorous and pressure-packed than the ones they were taking in college. For them, the university was mostly one big party scene, a place to hang their clothes for four years before getting on with the serious business of life.

He found an empty bookcase shelf to place his beer cup on and continued on down the wall. The open doorway Raina had described appeared on his right. He moved through it, past the split off that led to the kitchen and into the semi- darkness of the hall.

The corridor was empty, save for the stack of boxes now blocking the far end. The music made the walls vibrate, almost as if the house itself were in on the party. No doubt the place had seen its share of such noise. Tye had almost forgotten how loud a party could be.

The entrance to Derek Kurn's room was the only closed door along the hall. The others led to a study room lined with desks and carrels, empty, naturally, at the moment, and what looked like some sort of utility room, complete with electrical panels, computer wiring, and blinking switchers and routers.

Tye wondered idly if the house was wired into the campus wide network, but decided probably not. From what he understood, fraternities were private property, and the college's IT department wouldn't want to be responsible for whatever stunts a bunch of half-drunken pledges might be coaxed to try to pull off during rush.

"Okay," Raina said. "I've also got an egress for you if you need it. Derek's room has a bank of casement windows. Looks like all you have to do is roll one of them open and pop out the screen. There's no drop and it leads right into a stand of bushes."

"Easy for you to say."

"Unless you're into scaring topless coeds, you should hurry up and knock on the door now," Raina told him.

"Going in."

He pulled the hockey jersey over his head, tossing it to the floor along with the goalie's mitt to reveal the dark leather jacket he wore underneath. Striding down the hall to the heavy wooden door, he stopped in front of it, and gave it three sharp raps with his knuckles.

There was nothing but silence from inside.

"The girl's scrambling into the bathroom. Knock again."

Despite his misgivings about the MAVs, having Raina's eyes inside the room was like knowing the dealer's hole card in a game of blackjack. He knocked one more time.

"Who is it?" Derek's voice sounded dully through the door.

"Tye Palmer."

"Who?"

"We met this afternoon on the patio. The army guy."

"Oh, Palmer. Yeah, right. What's up, dude? I'm a little busy at the moment. There some problem at the party?"

"No. I need to talk to you."

The door was pulled half way open. Derek stood there barefoot in blue jeans and a dark t-shirt. "Right now? Can't it wait? I'm a lit—"

"It can't wait."

Tye pushed on the door with his foot.

Derek stepped in to stop it. "Whoa, hold up, my man. You don't just barge in here."

"Send the girl out. You and I need to talk."

"Wha? How'd you...?"

They stared at one another for a moment.

"Send the girl out."

"It's okay, Derek. I gotta get back to my friends and the party, anyway," the girl said from behind the door.

"What do you mean?" Derek made a face like his whole stature was being threatened. "No."

"Yes." She appeared behind him in the doorway, wearing shorts, a tank top, and sandals with high heels. "Excuse me, gentlemen." She elbowed her way around Derek forcing the fraternity president to step aside. "I'll just leave you two boys to talk," she said.

They both watched as she traipsed off, a little tipsy, to rejoin the party.

"Not cool." Derek turned on him, gritting his teeth. "Look.

I don't know who the frick you think you are, but we don't do business like this around here."

"No? How do you do business?"

"What's that supposed to mean?" Derek puffed his chest, leaning into Tye and gripping his arm.

He'd hoped he wouldn't have to resort to what came next, but the young football player was not deciding to play nicely.

Derek may have been in top athletic condition, but Tye, no slouch himself when it came to sports, was taller and outweighed him. Not to mention, he'd no doubt had more training and been in far more real fights.

In one smooth motion he chopped Derek's hands from the door and cut off the guy's leverage, strong-arming through the door.

"What the—?"

Derek toppled backward to the carpet.

"Now. That wasn't so nice, was it?" Tye said.

"No violence," Raina cautioned in his earpiece. "Williamson said no violence."

He ignored her.

Derek scrambled back to his feet and held up his hands. "Who are you? What do you want? Get out of my room."

His voice was weaker than a moment before.

"Afraid I can't do that, Derek." Tye moved through the door and pushed it closed behind him. "You and I need to have a little chat."

He reached around his back beneath his jacket and came out with the Beretta. Derek's eyes grew big as saucers and he held up his hands.

"Whoa. Hang on a minute, my man. About what?"

"Sit down."

"What for? What are you going to do?"

"I'm going to show you something."

Derek was on edge. He stood frozen to his spot and Tye was afraid he might pee in his pants.

"I said sit down."

He held the gun loosely pointing at the floor. Reaching out with the fingers of his opposite hand, he gave the athletic frat president a gentle shove toward the bed.

This time Derek took the hint and sat down on the edge of the mattress.

"Do you know who I am?" the kid asked.

"Yes."

"Is this some kind of kidnapping?"

"No. But it might be better for you if it was."

"What's that supposed to mean? Hey, man. This isn't some kind of PTSD psycho thing, is it? You know, you were in all that fighting over there and stuff. I've read about this. Even wrote a term paper about it. You can get help for that."

A term paper, Tye thought. *Seriously?*

"This isn't about post-traumatic stress, Derek. And trust me, there's no cure for what's eating at me." He reached in his pocket to pull out his smart phone, the same way he'd done with Stacie Hutchinson. "I need you to watch something," he said.

"Okay." Derek's voice shook a little. The guy was clearly unnerved. Maybe he should write a paper about *that*.

Tye pressed the phone's touch screen. The display blinked to life. He touched it again and the video began playing.

Derek squinted, his forehead wrinkling with a mixture of curiosity and suspicion. "What's this?" he asked.

"Just watch." He handed the phone to the young man on the bed.

The movie was a montage of news show video clips, war footage, and a congressional hearing, the last part featuring Derek's father testifying before congress. Williamson had sent it to Tye and Raina when he recruited them.

"Do you remember any of this?" Tye asked.

"Yeah. Some of it…I was still in prep school. I wasn't really paying too much attention to the news."

"Do you remember why your father was called to testify before Congress?"

Derek shrugged. "Something about a couple of news stories for broadcast. They somehow got unauthorized video from our own guys and the bad guys got a hold of it or something like that."

"So you *were* paying attention."

"Some."

"Do you remember what happened to your father?"

Again the kid shrugged. "Nothing much, really. Everyone said it was all inconclusive."

"That's right. Because your father lied about what happened."

"How do you know that?"

"Because I was there—on the ground in that action in Afghanistan when it all went down. Your father's network's correspondent and his cameraman were embedded with my unit. The correspondent was a good man. He and his producer didn't realize what that footage revealed about our movements and attack plan until it was too late. They would have never aired that video, but your father overruled them, and two fine soldiers and a helicopter pilot died.

The correspondent and the producer were fired. They took the fall while your father got away with little more than some stern words and a slap on the wrist."

"You're saying my father was responsible for those soldiers' deaths?"

"You got it, partner. And people are still dying."

"What? What are you even talking about?'

He meant the guy earlier in the alley, but decided he better not say anything more.

Derek stared into the video playing on the phone screen for a little longer.

"What's any of this got to do with me?"

"You'll see. It gets worse for you, Derek."

"What?"

"I'm going to need you to look at another video before we continue."

"What, more Senate hearings?"

"Hardly."

He motioned for Derek to give him back the phone and the young man complied. He took the device and flipped to a different app he and Raina had set up, and then watched as the second video began to play.

He handed the phone back to Derek. "Take a look."

The younger man's face as he looked at the screen told the story. At first, he seemed to do a double take, his eyes growing wide as he must have recognized the confines of his own room and even the bed he was sitting on.

"Where'd you get this?"

"Just keep watching."

As the video rolled on, Derek's entire demeanor began to dissolve. He looked like a little boy who'd been caught with a dirty magazine.

"That's you in the video, isn't it?"

"No. I mean, I don't know. You can't really tell from the picture, can you?"

"We know that's you, Derek. The movie was taken right here in this room."

"I don't know, I—"

"That's you, pal."

Derek stood up rubbing a trembling hand across the side of his face. "So what if it is? She was asking for it. That video doesn't show everything. Everything that went on before."

"Why you cowardly little creep." Tye grabbed him by his belt, stood him up, and bull rushed him up against the wall, pushing the barrel of the gun against his face.

"No! Please stop it! Let me go!"

"No violence," Raina scolded again. "It won't look like a genuine confession."

He calmed himself down, let the kid go, and stepped back from the wall.

"Okay," he said. "I'm going to ask you nicely. Is that you in the video I just showed you, or not?"

Derek said nothing.

"It's called date rape, buddy. Is that you in the video or not?"

The kid looked up at him, and for a moment Tye could have sworn he was looking into the eyes of his father.

"I don't have to tell you anything. You just broke into my room."

They stared at one another for a long moment.

"The kid's a hard case," Raina said. "Looks like he takes after his old man."

"Copy that. You see the kind of things I've got to deal with here first hand?"

"What?" Derek said. "Who are you talking to? Did my Dad or somebody send you?"

If nothing else, the kid was no dummy. He was already trying to connect the dots.

"Yes and no," Tye said.

"What do you mean?"

"Your dad hired me. He wants to try to make this all go away."

"What?"

"But I'm here to tell you it isn't going away, Derek. We've

talked with Stacie Hutchinson. You did this. That's your room in the video."

"You think I'm stupid? That video proves nothing."

"So maybe we should just call in the police and let them sort this all out."

"Maybe we should."

"Something's very wrong, Tye," Raina said in his ear. "You need to get out of there."

The roar of an engine could be heard from outside.

What was going on? Tye looked around and tried to think. They also had video of Nathan Kurn paying him off to help cover up the rape. He was no lawyer, but that was obstruction of justice, wasn't it?

A mobile phone rang from the bedside table, a bass melody that sounded almost like a dirge.

"It's my father," Derek said. He started to move but stopped himself.

"How do you know it's him?"

"It's programmed. He's got his own ring."

"Don't answer it."

"What?"

"I said don't answer it."

The phone kept sounding its tone. They waited until the ringing stopped.

But a few seconds later, the phone went off again. Different tone.

"You expecting a text?" Tye asked.

The kid shrugged.

"Go ahead and get it."

Derek went to the table and retrieved his phone. He pushed a button and sat reading the screen.

"It's from my dad. He's here. Right out front on the street… and he doesn't sound too happy."

"We've got major problems," Raina said. "The cops don't seem to be moving at all on this, and the kid's telling the truth. His dad's walking up the front lawn with what looks like some security guards in tow. You need to get out of there right now, Tye," Raina hissed.

The music from the party across the hall abruptly stopped and the walls ceased to vibrate. The sound of boxes being moved and voices came from down the corridor.

Derek looked up with concern.

"The party's over, pal. Open the window," Tye told him.

"What? I thought you were a cop or something."

"Hurry up. Give me the phone and go open the window and pop out the screen."

"Whatever you say."

The young man went and did as he instructed. Then he turned back to Tye.

"What now, man?"

A minor commotion could be heard from down the hall. The security guards were probably rounding up a few overly zealous revelers on their way to arrest not Derek Kurn for rape but Tye for trespassing.

"Hover angel has left the building," Tye heard in his ear.

Things were getting hot.

"Looks like we've got security people starting to circle around from the front of the house." Raina's tone grew tenser. "There's a brick wall that will slow them down, but not for long. You need to hurry."

No time to argue. He pointed the Beretta at Kurn again.

"It may be adios for now, Derek, but you haven't heard the last from me."

He made for the open window and managed to scramble through it for the short drop into the bushes.

23

BEHIND HER CONSOLE in the out-of-the-way construction site alley where she and Tye had set up the van, Raina was wishing she'd gone mobile with her laptop to be of more help. But she still needed to track multiple monitors and the more fine-tuned control over the MAVs her workstation array afforded. She was so focused on watching Tye escape that she almost didn't notice the danger to herself, headlights from a pale sedan pulling into the alley displayed on her exterior security video screen.

She was in for trouble. Before she even recognized the occupants of the sedan, she knew it had to be Homeland. What she didn't expect to see, zooming in the image for a closer look, was Lance Murnell seated in the front passenger seat and a car full of agents with him.

She hoped her com link with Tye was still secure, but she couldn't be sure. She would just have to risk it.

"I've got a problem," she said.

She heard nothing for a moment. Then: "Tell me about it. Little busy at the moment trying to keep from being arrested."

She could see him running now, crossing a vacant lot between rows of houses. On her other screen, the pale sedan was entering the alleyway and heading straight toward her.

"I've been compromised," she said. "I think Homeland's here. Have to dump data before they get to me. Signing off."

"What—?"

She pulled the plug off her headset and cut the main power, her screens going dark. Spinning her server box around, she flipped a set of levers and jacked out the two big hard drives. Next to the console was a set of tools in a canvas bag Tye had been using earlier; along with it a heavy hammer.

She pushed back from her chair and flung the hard drives on the desk. Turning, she picked up the hammer and brought its weight down with all her strength on the drives, crushing their metal housings.

She struck them again and again, the memory components breaking apart and pieces flying through the air and scattering across the desktop. With her arm, she swept the remaining fragments to the floor. She kicked at them with her good foot, sending them sliding and sailing off into various nooks and crannies of the van.

She heard the Homeland vehicle pull up beside her rear door. Not much time. Rifling through the bag of tools, she found a pair of heavy scissors and began cutting and sawing at the server's main power cord; she managed to cut cleanly through it just as a loud bang hit the door.

Smoke filled the air, burning her lungs and stinging her eyes. The door slid open.

Coughing and gagging from the smoke, Raina looked out to see Lance Murnell standing in the darkened alley illuminated only by the glow from his car lights. He wore a light ski jacket and blue jeans and was accompanied by three men, two of whom she thought she recognized, despite the fact they'd been wearing masks the first time she been taken.

"What the hell are you doing blowing up my van?"

Murnell smiled. "Well, well, well, if isn't our good friend CWO Sanchez. Still playing for the wrong team, are we?"

She looked at him. "I have no idea what you're talking about. I'm doing some field studies here for my friend's university project."

"A friend, huh? And field studies? And I suppose there's a reason you need to gather data hidden among construction equipment in the back of an alley in the middle of an unfinished shopping center development."

She shrugged. "It's a good place to study rats."

Murnell said nothing. He motioned to the men beside him who stepped into the van to forcibly if gingerly remove Raina from her chair.

"I thought I screwed up with your special little drones. What do you want with me now?"

She was afraid they might think she already knew too much, and if that was the case she really was in trouble.

"I've got something specific in mind for you," Murnell said.

"Am I under arrest?" She was pulled to her feet and guided from the van.

"That's such an ugly word—don't you think? I try never to use it. But I do have a special test for you."

"A test? What kind of test?"

"You'll see. Your country is really hoping you pass it."

"I think I already passed enough tests for my country, don't you, Murnell?"

"Touché. You most certainly did…"

The men on either side of her pulled her toward the sedan. She decided not to struggle any more or make a fuss. They would just drug her again, and then what good would she be? She hated leaving Tye with no back up or eyes in the sky, but there was nothing she could do about it at the moment.

"What's your game?" she asked. "If you're planning to

24

TYE WAS SEVERAL blocks from the fraternity—away from the campus and walking along the edge of an empty field fronting the capital beltway—before he finally felt safe. He tried talking to Raina again. She failed to respond.

He tried calling her cell phone again, too, and got the same result. Something was definitely wrong. The construction site where she'd set up shop in the van was only about a quarter of a mile ahead. He broke into a hard run.

A couple of minutes later, from a vantage point on the wooded hillside across from the construction project, he crouched beneath a darkened rocky overhang to catch his breath. He could see the front of the alleyway. The complex was lit by rows of new streetlights that, outside of the alley at least, illuminated the areas around the nearly finished buildings as well as daylight. He didn't know exactly what was happening, but Raina's warning had been clear enough: Homeland was onto her and had apparently found the hidden location where she was piloting the MAVs.

The van was also supposed to have offered Tye a means of escape if things went bad. Well, they'd gone bad all right. The van was no longer an option. He could only hope Raina had been able to destroy as much of her equipment and data as possible to escape Homeland's prying eyes.

He watched as a white car slowly emerged from the alleyway with several people inside. Tye wished he had a set of binoculars. He raised his smart phone camera to point at the scene, turning the display brightness as dim as possible so as not to generate much light, and used its zoom function to try to get a better view of what was happening across the way.

The image was grainy and the car kept jumping out of frame, but he thought he could make out Raina in the back seat surrounded by a group of men. The car stopped just outside the alley and was soon joined by a second car and a dark colored Ford Expedition EL with blacked-out windows. One of the men wore a blue ski jacket. He got out of the first car and was soon joined by three or four others from the different vehicles. Blue jacket appeared to be the leader.

So this was Raina's new friend. How cute. The guy didn't even look like he could bench press his grandmother. He took out his phone and punched in Williamson's number, put it to his ear and waited. If ever he needed some kind of aerial support of the type Williamson seemed to be able to provide it was now. Would the man make a move against Homeland, if that really was where these people were from? No better time to find out.

The phone rang again and again and again with no response. Something wasn't right. He tried it again, but Williamson was still not picking up. Just great. Maybe he and Raina were being hung out to dry.

Tye swore under his breath and shut down the call.

Across the way, the man in the blue jacket was talking to the others and gesturing down the alleyway. The car with Raina in it looked like it was preparing to leave and the man was giving instructions to some kind of forensics or follow up crew who would for sure be all over Tye and Raina's van. He scanned the sky overhead. He figured he was mostly safe from aerial surveillance, at least for the time being. Any drones overhead would carry thermal imaging cameras, but in the cool night air the rock around and above him would retain some of its heat from the day; Tye's heat signature would meld with that from the stone, making him virtually indistinguishable from the boulders.

But without help from Williamson, he couldn't stay here long. He was on the run, and he had no idea how many people might be looking for him. He needed transportation, a way to go after the white car below. At least he still had the loaded Beretta and a spare mag he'd slipped in a pocket just in case.

His eyes swept over the terrain around them and the complex below. The sizable construction project took up several square blocks and was flanked on either side by other, established shopping centers, mostly quiet at this time of night, but with the distant neon and halogen of their retail stores still glowing. His hillside formed a graceful curve at the back of the new commercial development; staying in the trees and following its spine would bring him much closer to the alleyway, and there were several construction vehicles parked along side the building that could also provide cover.

The night was growing colder, the air crisp and sharp. His nose ran and his breath turned to steam. The lights of the surrounding suburban campus, crisscrossing streets, and highways lit up the night sky while a siren blared in the distance, reminding him he was being hunted.

Tye measured the risks. It was ground combat tactics 101. Pinned down and potentially flanked on all sides, there was only one course of action left to him.

Attack.

25

B ONE WEARY, SQUEEZED between two men in the
back seat with her hands cuffed and the dark hood still
over her head, Raina was starting to feel claustrophobic. She
closed her eyes. Maybe if she could drift off the nightmare
would soon be over. Sleep couldn't come soon enough.

"We're here." Murnell's voice boomed from the front seat.

"What?"

Already? It had barely been fifteen minutes since they'd left
the alley. Before, when she'd been driven from her apartment, it
seemed to take much longer.

The car came to an abrupt stop. She heard Murnell open
his door and climb out, one of the men next to her as well.
This had to be a different place than before. The van had been
parked only a few miles from her apartment, but the ride to
what she assumed would be the same facility she'd been taken
to before appeared to be over.

The remaining guard next to her unlocked her handcuffs
and pulled off her hood. She waited until her eyes adjusted to
the near darkness of the car— they must have disengaged the
dome light so opening the doors provided no light. The remaining guard exited the vehicle and in his place stood the shadow
of Murnell, who gestured for her to follow. She slid across the

seat and stepped out onto pavement. Stood and took a long look around.

"What is this place?"

They definitely weren't in the same facility Murnell had brought her to before. In fact, it was nothing more than an abandoned parking lot next to what appeared to be a shadowy row of dilapidated warehouses. Just beyond the buildings a stretch of wide, smooth water was faintly visible, disappearing off into inky blackness—the Potomac she guessed. Upriver or downriver, she wasn't sure.

"Do you know where you are?" Murnell asked.

"No. Not exactly."

"Good. You might just have a better chance of living a little longer."

It was the first time Murnell had made any suggestion of a threat against her, and whether or not he or any of his colleagues was the source of the danger to her wasn't clear. But she took him at his word.

Who were they? Genuine Homeland—mainstream, and, she would hope, legal government types? Or some kind of splinter group plucked from within Homeland's byzantine spider web of interests and gone rogue? Whoever they were, she was beginning to have serious doubts if in any way it had been her good fortune to have somehow dialed up their attention and fallen into their net, their seductive technology and handsome scientist spokesman aside.

But then she understood. The answer was so simple it was right there in front of her.

"You people must really be in desperate need of pilots."

Murnell looked at her for a long moment.

"Let's go," he said.

It made perfect sense, didn't it? The world was trending

149

toward trouble all over and drones were taking to the skies everywhere.

Any hobbyist with a smart phone could still pilot a simple one through an empty sky or around a neighborhood. With better technology, more time, training, and sophistication, as with her MAVs, they could hover virtually unseen hundreds of feet in the sky employing the most powerful cameras and imaging capabilities industry could supply.

Wasn't the holy grail of covert surveillance being able to swoop in up-close-and-personal completely undetected?

The possibilities were endless—even pinpoint lethal attacks with complete stealth wouldn't be off the table.

But it took a human being like her to deliver the goods. Computers were getting faster and more powerful with every passing day and artificial intelligence software more and more sophisticated. But trusting AI and an autonomous drone to fly the way she'd piloted the hover angel into the building to spy on Nathan Kurn was still far too risky—at least for now. If it wasn't, she realized, she, and most likely Tye as well, might well have been in prison or even dead by now.

Murnell led the way across the parking lot toward a line of trees, just inside of which stood a dark colored tractor-trailer parked at the edge of the pavement.

"I see you've gone mobile."

"That's right," he said. "We're not the only players on the board, you know."

Whatever that meant. Did she even know how big the board could be?

She decided she better keep her mouth shut from here on in. Just let things play out with Murnell however they were going to play out and hope and pray for the best. Speaking of praying, was it any use praying for Tye or Williamson to come to her aid? Maybe when all was said and done Williamson was somehow working for DHS, too. Maybe she and Tye had been the ones being played for fools all along. Either way, she needed to find a way to get out of here.

They reached the tractor-trailer sitting silent in the darkness. At least four men that she could count, armed with assault rifles, guarded the perimeter around it.

Murnell led her up a set of steps with a railing that led to a door in the side of the trailer, put his hand on some sort of scanner and punched a code into a keypad.

"So what are we doing here, exactly?"

He wrapped his fingers around the door handle. She was about to find out.

26

THE WHITE SEDAN had departed the complex as soon as Tye started to pick his way through the brush and boulders along the edge of the darkened hillside.

He needed to hurry.

But the remaining team of a half dozen agents—if that's what they were—had driven the other two vehicles into the gap between the buildings and, no doubt not wanting to call any more attention to themselves than needed, posted a lookout at the front of the alley.

Tye was at the jumping off point. He'd made it this far without detection, so maybe whatever resources were being employed to track and find them weren't as vast or as formidable as he had feared.

The man posted at the front of the entrance wore a baggy dark sweatsuit, such that he might easily be mistaken for a guy simply out for a late night run. In addition to his gun, Tye had a fighting knife strapped to a sheath inside his boot. No doubt the guard was also well armed, although nothing was visible.

The closest construction vehicle, a small orange pickup truck, stood at the side of the building a mere fifteen yards or so from where Tye crouched behind a tree with the front of the alleyway another forty to fifty yards distant and two more vehicles, one a large bulldozer, in between. The angle of attack didn't look bad, but there was a problem. His new hiding spot was just outside the illuminated area. That fifteen yards would be an eternity once he hit the light.

He had an idea.

Kneeling down on all fours, he felt along the ground in the dark until he found what he was looking for: a rock slightly smaller than a baseball but big enough to make a loud sound when it hit something. His high school pitching days may have been long past him, but with a big enough target he could probably get the job done.

He stretched his arm back and forth like a major league hurler warming up in the bullpen. He eyed his target several yards beyond the man standing guard. There wouldn't be a second chance.

He wound up, reared back, and heaved the rock in a high pop-fly-like arc over the vehicles. He still had a good arm. The rock sailed overhead at the outward edge of the glow from the lights, high enough that the guard failed to spot it. At the far end of the building stood more vehicles and several long metal trailers. The rock landed with a loud clang on the roof of one of them. Bulls-eye.

The guard immediately turned in that direction, drawing a large caliber handgun from beneath his baggy sweatsuit.

It was all the opening Tye needed, sprinting the few steps necessary to make it to the cover of the orange truck. He dropped down and squatted along the fender, still unseen.

He was planning to edge his way from vehicle to vehicle until he got close enough, then hope to take the guard by surprise. But leaning against the truck he spotted something he hadn't been able to see earlier. This side of the vehicle was angled away from the guard's line of sight and the driver's door window was rolled completely down and open to the night air.

The guard crouched lower with his weapon drawn, still

looking in the direction of the sound made by the falling rock but also beginning to scan the rest of his perimeter. He turned and called to someone down the alley. A few seconds later, another agent appeared, with longer hair and not as big, a woman. She also carried a gun holding it with both hands in a shooter's crouch.

Tye stood up and dove in through the open window of the cab, hunkering low in the seat. No shots rang out. No shouts or cries of warning.

He peered over the back corner of the truck's seat at the two agents. They had mag lights and laser sights attached to their barrels and were training them in the opposite direction, slowly advancing toward the noise made by the rock in textbook fashion, one fanning out along the side of the building as they'd been trained to do.

He didn't think he'd be lucky enough to find a key in the ignition, and he was right. But sometimes construction workers left a spare key hidden under a mat or someplace else inconspicuous just in case one of the workers lost the original keys.

Before joining the Army, he'd once watched a guy hot wire a car while out juvenile-delinquenting in Buffalo one night with some of his high school buddies. But that was a long time ago. He hoped if it came down to it, he'd remember how to do it, but he wasn't so sure. He felt around the darkened cab, under the floor mats and inside the seat flaps until his hand came to rest on a small, smooth object. It was a key.

Just as he'd hoped, it slid neatly into the ignition.

At least the truck was an automatic in case he needed to shoot out the window while driving. Easier said than done. This wasn't the movies. He glanced back over his shoulder to see the two guards now nearly the length of a football field away, still training their lights and searching among the trailers.

"All right," he said out loud to himself. "Game on."

27

WITH ONE HAND on the railing, Raina took a long look around the exterior of the tractor-trailer as Murnell started to pull open the door.

Of course it was dark and she could see very little. She wondered if Murnell had a MAV or two—whatever type they were—like the ones he'd had her flying from the sphere keeping a close eye on her at this very moment. The thought sent a chill through her. With a swift prosthetic kick to the groin, she could disable Murnell and, if she was lucky attacking down from the top of the steps, have a shot at relieving the guard nearest them of his rifle.

But where would that get her? She'd still have nearly a half dozen armed agents to contend with.

From the outside the entire rig looked completely normal; it could easily be disguised as any one of a million big trucks plying the roads. But stepping inside the trailer with Murnell, it became clear, even with the lights dimmed inside, that this was no run-of-the-mill commercial vehicle.

The length of the cargo container was honeycombed with bulbous antennas and satellite dishes and some kind of strange composite reflectors and tubing, in the center of which stood a sphere, slightly larger but almost identical to the one she'd worked with at their facility. The wombed cockpit looked pristine, almost antiseptic, and the air around it was permeated with some kind of watery odor.

"What's that smell?"

"Residue from the cooling mixture. We're shielded in here from thermal detection, but I'm sure you can appreciate this mobile unit generates quite a lot of heat."

"Mobile unit. I thought you said the sphere was a prototype."

"I lied," Murnell said. "So shoot me."

He closed the door behind them and stood looking at her in the near darkness. He was beaming.

"What?" she asked.

"Dragonflies."

"Dragonflies? What about them?"

"I was just thinking, that's what they called your old Army helicopter squadron."

"So?"

"Did you know dragonflies are nature's perfect predators?"

She shrugged.

"It's true. Scientists have spent years studying their biology and neural structure. They can even take prey when they're missing an entire wing."

She stared at him for a moment. "So what are you telling me? Is that how you see me?"

"Maybe. I guess we'll know soon enough. Ready to play?"

"I don't get it. You ream me out after apparently crashing one of your super secret drones and then you kidnap me a second time and expect me to just come in here and sit down and work with you."

"I prefer not to think of it as kidnapping. More like rescuing you from your own worst impulses." He continued smiling.

Worst impulses? So, he wanted to play a game of cat-and-mouse. She was tempted to mount an argument, but thought she still better not divulge any more of what she and Tye had been up to. Were these guys the enemy or not? Her gut told her yes, but Murnell remained as charismatic and unpredictable as before. And now here he seemed to want to ratchet up the stakes, seducing her with even more technology. What did he really want from her? There had to be other drone pilots out there.

"I realize this can all seem quite confusing, Raina, and I'm sorry," he said. "But I'm offering you an opportunity a lot of other people would kill for."

"Really." She wanted to send him a message she was unimpressed. "So what, you want me to go to work in one of these trailers for Homeland Security?"

"Maybe. If you pass the test."

"If I pass the test." She snickered, rolling her eyes. "And if I pass this test of yours, what kind of missions would I be undertaking exactly?"

He smiled. "I do apologize. But I'm sure you can understand, information like that has to remain on a need-to-know basis."

"Hmmm."

What she really needed to know was how to get the hell out of here and back to figuring out her mission with Tye.

"And what if I don't want to take this test? Or what if I fail it?"

Murnell sighed. "I don't want to go there with you, Raina. I want to be on your side."

If Homeland were trying to pull a major bad cop/good cop with this guy they were doing a pretty good job of it. She wondered for a moment if he'd been somehow trapped in the same manner she now appeared to be.

Murnell had yet to ask her directly about anything to do with Tye or Williamson. That told her he either already knew all he wanted to know about their activities or didn't care, and she doubted the latter.

She wished she could somehow get a message to Tye or Williamson; but of course they'd confiscated her phone along with the other equipment in the van. She took a step forward, looking over the interior of the trailer again and running her hand along the dome of one of the antennas. It felt warm to the touch.

"All right," she said finally. "What do you want me to do?"

28

THE CONSTRUCTION COMPANY pickup wasn't the fastest thing Tye had ever driven. But it was fast enough. After belting in and starting the engine, he threw the truck into gear, turned the wheel and gunned the accelerator to carry the vehicle, which had been facing in the opposite direction, in a tight arc back toward the entrance.

The first sound suppressed rounds from the two guards flew wide of the accelerating cab, but soon one struck the back pillar just aft of Tye's window. He returned fire out the window with his left hand as he came around, not really expecting to hit much of anything, the black weight of the Beretta jumping against his palm. He kept the accelerator to the floor and the tires of the pickup began to lose grip, causing the truck to fishtail, but he corrected with his free hand. All he needed to do was reach the alley.

The male agent broke cover, attempting to make it back to the alley entrance before Tye did. Tye took a firm grip on the gun with as good an aim as he was able to muster with his off hand, and lead the running agent by a step. He squeezed the trigger, putting the guy down with a hit to the neck.

"Lucky shot," he said to himself.

More bullets came whizzing in from the remaining shooter.

One shattered a headlight, another struck the passenger door, and yet another the front fender. He continued to gun the engine and three or four seconds later sailed into the front of the alleyway, swerving around the big construction dumpster.

The alleyway was less than a block long. He crouched as low as he could, peering over the dash to see where he was going and seeing the remaining agents, apparently not expecting to be ambushed and still trying to figure out what was going on, scrambling for cover with few options left to them in the narrowness of the alley than their own vehicles and the van.

More shots rained in on him. A round blew out most of his windshield.

But the speeding truck was the major weapon in play now, which his adversaries had been too slow to appreciate. Tye wrenched the wheel to the right, sideswiping the first of the sedans, catching one of the remaining agents with his front fender, the guy's body bouncing with a sickly thud against the side of the truck.

Another agent stood directly between him and the van, firing off more rounds into the windshield and grill. Gutsy. Tye plowed into him head on and the truck bucked and the wheel was almost jerked from his hand with the impact.

In the next instant he slammed into the back of the van with a loud bang. Bodies flew, there was a crush of metal and glass, and Tye was thrown hard against his belt, the airbag exploding in front of him. Momentarily dazed, he managed to unbuckle himself, wrench open his door and drag himself out onto through the opening. He kept a firm hold on his gun as he tumbled out into a pile of twisted metal and shattered glass and dove toward the pavement.

A bullet kicked up a chuck of concrete and blacktop right in front of him. He raised into a crouch, returning fire in the direction from which the shot had come, the one remaining intact sedan down the alley. Keeping low, he made a quick survey of the wreckage and spotted the bloody remains of an agent who must have been unfortunate to have been trapped between the alley wall and the van. Counting the one they'd sideswiped and the one he'd just plowed through, that meant three more down, which left only two, the one shooting at him from within the alley and the female agent still approaching from outside.

Tye still had more than a half dozen bullets left in the Beretta. The odds may have improved, but they had him in a pincer. One of his two remaining adversaries had to be put down before they could begin to capitalize on their position.

No time like the present. He rose into a shooter's stance, laying down fire and advancing straight toward the remaining sedan. The agent who was hunkered down behind the fender seemed to panic, starting to return fire before diving beneath the bumper, not realizing he was leaving his head exposed as Tye was closing in. Tye simply shot the man dead with a bullet to his skull.

But as if on cue, the female agent appeared, edging up the wall at the end of the alley and firing her weapon. Bullets sprayed around him, one grazing his jacket, and he scrambled over for better cover behind what was left of the wreckage between van and truck.

He soon lost sight of the woman for a moment, but she must not have lost sight of him. The shooting went on for several more seconds with one large caliber bullet coming so close to Tye's ear that the concrete wall exploding behind him sent fragments knifing into the side of his head. Wiping them away, he paused to switch clips.

The shooting stopped for a moment. The woman must have been doing the same.

A moment later, it was her turn to advance. She bent into a

crouch along the wall and moved straight toward him, sending a hail of fire into the wreckage all around him.

Tye didn't flinch. He ignored the bullet strikes and took a bead on her. Pity. His rounds were dead on target.

The woman tried to return fire, but Tye had the angle on her and she was struck in the arm and mid-torso. She crumpled to the pavement, her gun spinning away and clacking to the ground. Tye stood and sprinted forward. Keeping his weapon trained on her as he reached her, he kicked her gun away down the alley.

She was still alive. She'd managed to pull herself up a little, with her upper back braced against the wall, blood already soaking through her clothing.

He leaned over her. "Where'd the other car go?"

She winced in pain, looking up at him with glassy eyes. "What car? I don't know what you're talking about," she said.

"There was another car here earlier, a white sedan. I know because I observed it. I need to know where it was going."

He pointed the gun at her head and fired a bullet into the wall just above the woman's scalp. Dust and concrete splattered all over her. She blinked several times and her eyes teared.

He pointed the gun at her head again.

"No. Wait."

One part of him wanted to pause to consider just where his actions might be leading him, what kind of divine sense of justice all this might be fulfilling—maybe ending with his imprisonment or a life on the run, a deliberate death by lethal injection—but another part still wanted to put a bullet in her brain.

He could see that her wounds weren't necessarily fatal, at least if treated properly. He was also beginning to understand just how closely he'd become tied to Raina, if not yet by love or something akin to it, at least to a shared outlaw sense of morality.

"Where'd the white car go? I won't ask again."

She blinked once more and turned her head to look at the still intact sedan. "Over there," she said. "GPS."

He thought about what she was trying to tell him. "Is the last waypoint, the one where you came from...is that where they're taking her?"

The agent nodded.

Tye lowered his gun and wiped the sweat and grime from his forehead. He could smell the blood and cordite now, the all-too-familiar remnants of battle.

He went over to one of the dead agents and stripped the sweatshirt and pants off of him. He pulled out his knife and cut the cloth into long strips, went over to the woman and began to bind up her wounds.

"I suppose it's too much to ask who you work for."

The woman spat out a sarcastic half cough. "Forget it, dirt-bag."

"You know I could just leave you to die out here."

"Why don't you then?"

"Believe me, I've been seriously considering it. But I don't think you deserve to die. I'm sorry about your friends. Collateral damage."

Minutes later, he was driving along a dark suburban road in the sedan with the official, government-looking plates. Before leaving, he'd pulled the wounded agent to the end of the alley and set fire to what remained of the van to make sure any trace of digital evidence was incinerated. He'd taken a phone from one of the dead agents and used it to make an anonymous 911 call, giving the location of the woman and the fire, before slowing down momentarily to heave the phone out the window into a passing pond.

Tye's own phone went off in his pocket. He took one hand off the wheel, pulled it out and looked at the display. Williamson.

He pushed the button to answer.

"About time."

"Yeah. Sorry. I saw what you did at the construction project. Got there too late to intervene. That fire you set's got every cop and EMS person in the area headed over there."

"What kind of thing are we into? Those men we killed weren't your run of the mill Homeland agents. Not even sure they were Homeland at all."

"Still working on that. We'll talk more about it when we have the chance."

"Wonderful. Have you got a bead on me now?"

"Stay on the phone and I will in a couple of seconds."

"Someone led us right into a set up back at the Kurn kid's frat house. His old man must have been on to us."

"I figured something like that must have happened. Probably the victim's parents' lawyer again."

"What if we just uploaded what we have to *YouTube* or something?"

"It would be taken down in a hurry if it even made it online at all. Plus, from what I gather, you didn't exactly get as positive an ID of the Kurn kid on the film as you'd hoped."

"What about the cops? I talked to this one detective who seemed like a straight arrow."

"We could try, but the chief wouldn't take my call when I tried to reach him again a few minutes ago. Kurn must have gotten to him, too."

"So we're screwed."

"Not exactly. You forget we still have considerable assets and connections. This is going to be a marathon, not a sprint."

"We need to sit down and have a real long talk after we get Raina back."

"Agreed. But right now it looks like you're going to need my help."

"Good," he said. He glanced at the reverse directions on the GPS display in the car's dash, which told him he was less than a than five minute drive from whatever it was he was walking into. "I've got a feeling where I'm headed, I'm going to need everything you've got."

29

RAINA WAS IN the seat of the sphere again, only this time things were different. She found more controls on the armrests, including some marked in red. Still nothing in front of her, so she had a virtually unobstructed, three-hundred-and-sixty degree view in all dimensions. She was a virtual flying creature, as if she were some kind of a drone herself.

"You understand the additional instructions I've given you?" Murnell asked.

"Got it."

"I know you've been in this situation before, but you need to understand the significance of what we're dealing with. You'll be weapons hot from here on out. Practice is over."

"Guess it's a good thing I'm a quick study then." She tried to keep from coming off as too sarcastic. They must really need her on some mission right now, whatever it was. She couldn't think of any other reason why she was still alive and why they'd be going to all this trouble.

"Yes. Well, this time, I'm also staying with you. I'll be right here next to you the whole time if we get into any kind trouble."

She liked the training wheels his presence provided, but another part of her resented his being there. Did they want a pilot or not?

"Ready?" he asked.

She nodded.

Sitting in the chair as the screens came up carrying her into her virtual world, she was struck again by how much she was drawn to the experience. The sphere seemed to have a seductive power all its own.

She'd met a few Air Force fighter pilots in her time, mostly egomaniacs. But one of them, whom she'd actually liked, tried to explain to her once what it was like to perform a high g barrel roll at the speed of sound.

The guy was so excited he almost couldn't put his feeling into words. She'd felt what she knew were somewhat similar notions at times when flying helicopters or even with the hover angels she was flying now, but nothing like what he'd been describing—and nothing like she was feeling inside the sphere. She wondered if all of these images she was seeing could be processed with planes flying at higher speeds.

"Here we go," Murnell said, reaching to push some sort of button behind the chair.

The screens jumped to life. Not Beijing this time, but mountains spread out to all sides of her, instantly recognizable, the Hindu Kush. Raina snickered to herself. It figured they would transport her back to Afghanistan. Maybe the test was to see how unnerved she'd become, if the fevered memories and sweat-laced dreams of the crash and other missions had taken too big a toll on her.

"You know where you are?"

"Oh, please. Of course."

"I told them you would. Everything okay?"

"Why wouldn't it be?"

She'd flown enough missions over Afghanistan to feel comfortable enough. Being in the sphere was much more akin to flying the Kiowa, with an even better view, in fact, and she couldn't help but recognize the lay of the land. Memories clawed at her, but she'd be okay as long as she stayed focused.

"I still don't know what I'm flying except that it must be some kind of MAV," she said.

"Like I said before, better that you don't."

"But you're telling me I have a weapon's payload?"

"Yes. And I can tell you it's comprised of a tiny amount of liquid explosive and blasting cap. It requires an up-close delivery."

"How close?"

"About as close as you got the other day on that street in Beijing."

She tried to wrap her mind around what he was saying. "This whole thing must really be miniscule to be able to get that close without being detected."

"Mmmm. Think of it as a personal land mine. You're also armed with a dart tipped with neurotoxin."

"Assassination tools."

"Precisely. Think of a sniper or any other type of high value target."

"You mean like the head of the Chinese Politburo."

Murnell said nothing.

"You realize the kind of thing we're talking about here, Murnell? I mean, you're a scientist, after all..."

He still said nothing. She tilted her head to look at him, but he avoided making eye contact.

"All right," she said. "Forget it. So I'm flying."

"That you are."

She was over a narrow valley, with a river meandering along its base and peaks on either side and. Ahead, in the distance, stood a small village.

"I take it someone in the town is the target."

"Affirmative."

"Am I killing someone today, Lance?"

It was the first time she'd used his given name, hoping it would shake him out of the obtuse funk which seemed to have frozen him into minimal interaction.

"We'll see," he said in non-answer.

His continued evasiveness didn't exactly give her the warm-fuzzies. Though it was the middle of the night in Northern Virginia and broad daylight in Afghanistan, she was amazed at how crisp and seamless the overall image was.

She had to be commanding a small swarm of MAVs, she guessed, processing information from multiple different angles. The fact that they could do so with minimal delay meant they'd evolved exponentially beyond her hover angels.

She would have loved to get hold of one of whatever it was she was flying, to examine it, tear it apart and see what made it tick. Would she somehow find a piece of her own heart there, the soul on the other end of the drones' all seeing eyes?

Don't be stupid, she thought. *Just keep your focus and see what they want from you for this job.*

"Stay at the same altitude and along the heading you're on now," he said. "You're doing just fine."

"The town looks familiar for some reason."

"Not all that surprising. Maybe you've flown here before."

"Is this another one of Bin Laden's old cronies we're still looking for?"

She figured it had to be some kind of high value target like that.

"You'll see," he said.

The jagged horizon dipped a little as she slid her fingers across the control pad, maneuvering around a cliff outcropping. The village appeared close up on her screen, directly ahead and to the right.

"Keep going?"

"There is a house in the middle of the village, blue tarp covering part of the roof. You see it?"

"Got it."

The village, she could see now, was little more than a cluster of cinderblock and irregularly shaped plaster houses that looked as though they'd somehow mysteriously sprouted from the rugged landscape, like rock flowers blooming from the granite ground.

"Come in on the roof of that structure."

"You want me to land on it?" She was incredulous. She had no idea what she was even piloting—a fixed wing or rotor. Or was it something in between?

"Just move in on the house and hold in position directly above it."

"Someone's bound to spot whatever it is I'm flying."

The Afghanis and the Pakistanis knew what it was to live under the specter of drones.

"Don't worry about it," he said.

"But I'm sure they must have weapons down there."

"Just keep going."

She did as he instructed.

After several seconds, she was hovering in position directly over the blue-roofed house. A mud-splattered soccer ball stood beside a pine crate in what looked like a small courtyard. Otherwise, she saw no signs of movement or life.

Moments later, one edge of the tarp moved as if someone were folding it to the side. Two figures appeared, a man and a small boy. They were both dressed in traditional Pashtun garb of Partoog-Kortehs, a *pakul*, or Pashtun hat for the man, and a smaller *topi* for the boy. They stooped to bend over something on the ground. Raina couldn't see their faces.

"Recognize them?"

"No. Am I supposed to?"

"Patience. Hold on."

In the corner of her eye, she noticed Murnell watching her closely. The Afghan man in the sphere's image stood to his full height, and, shielding his eyes against the glare from the sun, turned to directly face her. He made no sudden movements or sign of recognition, simply looked directly at her cameras, and she could clearly see the discoloration along the side of one cheek.

"I don't believe it," she said.

"Recognize him now?"

She nodded.

It was the same man with the brown-bearded donkey beyond the stone wall she'd seen years before from the cockpit of her Kiowa brutally beating his own daughter, the man who'd waved at her so callously she'd wanted to kill him. She and Skyles had written him up in their reports.

"One of the two red buttons on your left sends in the package. The one on top for explosive, the bottom one for neurotoxin."

"But the boy...." Her hand wavered over the two buttons.

"Use the dart," Murnell said. "The boy shouldn't be harmed."

30

RAINA HESITATED.

"What are you waiting for?"

The Afghani scene flickered for a moment and her pilot's chair shuddered as a loud bang sounded just outside the trailer, followed by the rapid bark of automatic weapons. A speaker inside the trailer sounded an alarm and Murnell grabbed her wrist and tried to reach across the chair, but she used her free arm to elbow him in the eye socket.

Pushing up from the chair, she ducked away from the punch he swung at her face, catching only a glancing blow, and used her good heel to mash down hard on one of his open-toed shoes, and stepping away from him. He yelped in pain and crumpled to the floor, but not for long.

"You're making it hard for me to keeping liking you, Raina."

Limping, he tried to charge at her. Though her prosthetic wasn't built to be used as a weapon, she threw all her weight on her other foot and turned to throw a kick, the carbon fiber appendage catching him square on the chin, the force of her own blow knocking her to the ground. This time he went down for good.

"How do you like *that?*" she said.

More explosions and gunfire rocked the trailer. Wisps of

smoke appeared from somewhere and the dim light continued to flicker. She pulled herself to her feet to climb out of the sphere, but the sight that greeted her stopped her cold.

The sphere was still operational. The screens no longer formed a composite multi-dimensional view of the mountains in Afghanistan. Instead, she was looking at several images at once, real time CCD camera and thermal images from outside the very trailer where she was sitting, figures running in the dark, charges detonating, and tracers flying. Of course, whatever kind of micro drones she'd just been piloting half across the globe would also be part of the defenses here.

The images dipped and moved and seemed to come from every possible angle and vantage point; you could manage an entire combat encounter, a whole army even, with such a tool, and she couldn't help but watch for a moment, fascinated. Until her eyes came to rest on one lower portion of the screen. A shock of fear ran through her, for in this part of the battle at least, the images were like looking in a mirror—they were all looking down from different angles with cameras aimed at her.

Raina threw herself through the sphere hatchway and crawled along the floor of the dimly-lit trailer. Reaching the door to the outside, she stood and pushed it open.

The scene that greeted her might as well have been in Torah-Bora or Fallujah—night combat, a full-on mini battle.

A larger, not-too-distant explosion rocked the air. She looked for signs of Tye or Williamson, but it was impossible to tell just exactly who was attacking whom. The fight was no longer half-way across the world, she realized. The battle was coming home.

She ducked low, stumbling down the trailer steps and charging into the darkness, while another blast ripped in close and the concussive whumps of incoming fire bloomed all around.

END OF PART 1

PART 2
"FLOCK OF ANGELS"

1

Four Weeks Earlier — Mexico

MANNY PAID NO attention to the man in the white linen suit across the square. He had other things on his mind at the moment, like trying to figure out how he and Lucy, hemmed in by the cheering crowd near the Rio Lerma, were going to find a better position to shoot photos of Mexican State Governor Alberto Martinez, who was about to take the stage.

"These people are delirious!" Lucy hollered. In all the excitement, she was more beautiful than ever. She was beaming.

Manny nodded.

Martinez was a genuine caudillo. The man had risen to power on an anti-drug cartel platform and was growing in popularity with the people. Even to the point of being rumored as a contender in the next presidential election, only a few short years away.

Manny estimated three, maybe four thousand partisans packed the space between the buildings. Young and old, retail clerks and factory workers, families with children, most dressed casually but there were even a few men and women in business suits. Strolling street musicians and a mariachi band, apparently brought in especially for the event, had spent the better part of the last hour whipping everyone into a heightened state of anticipation.

Security was tight. Police and armed personnel ringed the plaza. Manny even spotted soldiers manning the surrounding rooftops, no doubt to keep a wary eye out for snipers or other threats. But down in the square, a ring of Fresno trees provided shade from the heat of the sun. Everyone looked happy, comfortable, and expectant.

Maybe Lucy couldn't help but be swept up in the mood of the crowd, but with his press pass and Nikon strung around his neck Manny had a job to do. Despite Martinez's superstar status, rumors of infidelities and other improprieties still swirled about him, and as a rookie correspondent for the popular website Info Nation, Manny sensed a scoop.

"I've got an idea," he said in Lucy's ear.

Fifty yards distant, the white-suited man in a matching fedora sat by himself at a table in an outdoor café. Deeply tanned beneath graying white hair, trim but not overly fit for his age and puffing on a thin cigar, he could have easily been taken as a middle class expatriate living high on his American money, come to the square for his lunch.

But if Manny had taken the time to look, he might have also recognized the unassuming look of an experienced operator staring into the screen of a laptop on the table in front of him, the man's fingers dancing across the keyboard like they were manipulating air.

"More coffee, señor?"

The waiter spoke impeccable English. But English was hardly needed. Jon Ripley was fluent in Spanish as well as nine other languages, not to mention a couple of obscure Himalayan dialects he'd picked up years before while living in Asia.

"No, gracias. Me he hartado."

"Muy bien, señor."

The waiter had assumed the man was another journalist, a stringer perhaps, or even a reporter from one of the big American news organizations. What the waiter couldn't see was that Ripley's laptop was equipped with a special filter so that no one around him could make out the slightest hint of what he was staring at on his screen. Or that the innocent-looking sunglasses the gringo wore—so common in this sun-drenched part of the world—were anything but normal glasses.

Jostled by the teeming crowd, Manny gripped his camera and held it high over his head. He towed Lucy behind him with his other hand and began shouldering his way through the thick mass of celebrants.

Lucy protested at first but laughed when she saw where they were headed, the elevated base of a concrete statue of a lion that had just been vacated by a swarm of mischievous boys. How appropriate for a politician many in the crowd were already beginning to refer to as "El Leon de Juarez—The Lion of Juarez," in reference to Martinez's upbringing in the burgeoning Mexican border city next to El Paso, Texas.

Manny let go of Lucy's hand, swung the camera round to his hip, and made a leap onto the concrete statue base, grabbing one of the lion's paws and hoisting himself up before reaching back to pull Lucy up beside him.

"You're insane!" She laughed, her eyes bright with excitement.

"Yes, I am."

She reached up to push an unruly lock of his floppy hair off of his forehead and he bent down to kiss her on the lips.

"Best seat on la plaza!" Lucy shouted to no one in particular, clutching the lion's neck as she might a bareback bronco. But the cheers and chants from the crowd drowned her voice out.

Camera in hand, Manny turned to looked out over the assembled throng. Someone from within the crowd started another deeper chant and the noise swelled. Could this be what they'd all been anxiously awaiting?

Manny raised his Nikon to his eye just in time. At precisely that moment Martinez emerged from the side of the stage to thunderous cheers and applause. Manny had to work to steady his hands, engaging the auto-shoot and digital focus. He watched through the viewfinder as the camera clicked image after image.

Meanwhile, across the square, Ripley remained intent on his screen, his fingers flitting across the track pad, apparently unaffected by the politician's grand entrance.

Martinez was as photogenic as they came. No big surprise there. The leader was tall for a Mexican, well over six feet, with perfectly coiffed dark hair. His white teeth seemed to flash in the sun as he smiled and his dark eyes swept over the frenzied crowd. He paused to wave for a moment, pointing and smiling at individual supporters. Just like back home, Manny thought. Politicians were the same everywhere.

Many in the square waved Mexican flags and several hoisted small children into the air to get a better look at their new salvador. Blue-and-white balloons were everywhere, bobbing up and down in rhythm to the deafening music. The waving and cheers of the partisans went on for a few more moments, until Martinez turned to stride toward the podium.

The fat man who had just finished introducing him—some local official no doubt—reached out to shake the great man's hand in preparation for handing over the microphone.

What happened next would soon become the subject of fevered news coverage all over the globe.

Martinez was about to grasp the fat politician's hand when he paused. He raised his arm and swung his hand around to the back of his neck instead. The star of the show's bright smile disappeared. His countenance darkened and he toppled forward as if a bolt of lightening had struck him.

Several things occurred at once.

Screams erupted from those closest to the stage. Police, soldiers, and security rushed forward to come to Martinez's aid. Some were trampled as a wave of uncertainty and panic rippled through the crowd.

"Oh, my god, Manny!"

Lucy clutched at his arm as, perched on the statue, he kept shooting photos. All he knew was he'd just stumbled into the biggest story of his brand new career. His instincts told him to just let the camera do its thing and sort out the best photos later.

"What just happened?"

"I don't know, babe." His Nikon kept clicking. "He went down like a rock."

No one had heard a gunshot. Martinez didn't even appear to be wounded. Once the initial shock had passed, attempts at resuscitation were begun amidst the growing suspicion that the poor man might have collapsed from a heart attack or heat stroke.

"Did you see that?" he asked.

"See what?" she said.

"Just before he fell…something tiny swirled in behind him. Maybe a bug or something. I saw it with the magnification through my viewfinder."

Manny paused for a second. Had he seen something? Maybe it had just been a piece of confetti or a trick of the light.

"Well, he collapsed like he'd been shot in the head," she said.

"He wasn't shot."

"Is he moving?"

Security and medical personnel were all over the stage now, but Manny could still make out the prostrate figure through his lens. "He doesn't appear to be."

"What if he's dead? What if this was some kind of an attack?"

"That's a big leap, Luce. Martinez is a big guy. Maybe he's got health problems."

"You think anyone else saw what you saw?" she asked.

"I don't know, but I doubt it. We have a different angle from up here than anyone else. The camera's tethered to my smart phone—" He pulled it out of his pocket and looked at the screen. "Photos are already uploading. We'll figure it out later."

He raised the viewfinder to his eye again and took more shots of the emergency personnel huddled around Martinez. Sirens blared nearby.

Across the square, the man in the white linen suit closed the lid of his laptop computer. He hadn't left his table when Martinez went down. But now he stood with everyone else in the café to gape across the plaza at the scene for a moment, before turning to drop a twenty peso note on the table and packing up his things to go.

"We need to get out of here," Lucy said. "I'm scared."

"Just a few more photos."

"Maybe you need to report what you saw."

"Report what? I don't even know for sure if I saw anything."

Two policemen approached the statue. One was pointing at them with a stern look on his face.

"He's telling us to get down."

"All right. All right. I get it," Manny said.

He lowered his camera and sat down on the base of the stature. He levered his legs over the edge of the base, but before making the leap, he popped out the camera's memory card, stuffing it into the front pocket of his jeans.

"Be careful," Lucy warned.

Up on the stage an ambulance had been brought around in front of the rostrum. Martinez had a clear plastic oxygen mask over his face and was being lowered onto a stretcher.

Manny jumped off of the statue and helped Lucy down after him. The cops turned away from them to deal with the rest of the crowd. Which was good because the last thing Manny wanted was to fall into the hands of one of the *magistrados* before he and Lucy even had an idea of what they might be dealing with.

He joined hands with her and did his best to blend in with the suddenly silent and somber partisans, many of whom were in tears, making their way out of the square.

All were in shock. With no evidence to the contrary, the assumption seemed to be that Martinez had fallen victim to some sort of health issue, although someone ventured openly in Spanish that maybe the man had been poisoned. The cartels had been known to do far worse to those who dared oppose them.

As soon as they cleared the square, he steered Lucy down a little used alleyway he remembered was in the general direction of where they'd parked their car. It was much darker here between the narrow walls. A bad odor, maybe from a cracked sewer pipe assaulted their nostrils. The few other people using the cut-through seemed to hurry their steps along with them.

"I hope you know where you're going." Lucy said.

Manny said nothing. He tightened his grip on her hand and sped up their pace. Weeks later, he would remember his heightened state of agitation, wondering if it had been some sort of harbinger of doom he'd failed to see.

At the end of the alleyway they came to a smaller square. This one was used primarily for parking motorcycles and other vehicles. They were surrounded on all sides by ancient apartment windows, a number of them obviously vacant and devoid of life.

Manny hesitated as he considered which of the two cutout side streets ahead they should take.

Out of the corner of his eye, he noticed three men entering the square to his right. One wore the black tactical uniform of the *policia federal* with the green, white, and red Mexican flag emblazoned on his sleeve. He also had a black riot helmet and carried a large automatic weapon. The other two were gringos wearing dark business suits.

What was this? He didn't like the looks of it. The three headed straight for him and Lucy.

"Manny Romero," one of the gringos called out as they approached.

Trouble. Manny felt Lucy's hand tighten in his as they stopped in their tracks.

"Yes?" He had no idea who these guys were, but he needed to tread carefully. This was Mexico, after all. His press pass would only get him so far.

"We need you to come with us."

"What?"

They were getting closer—barely thirty paces away.

"Let's not make a scene," the gringo said.

Run.

Pulling Lucy with him, he spun to the side and ducked his head down between parked cars.

"Stop where you are!"

Manny wasn't listening.

"What are you doing?" Lucy said.

"Stay down," he told her. "This isn't good."

He needed to find a way out of the square. Once they

reached the relative darkness of the alley they'd have a better chance.

He could sense the men searching for them among the parked vehicles. Lucy kept quiet. Whoever these guys were, she must have had the same sixth sense about them as he.

Seconds later they stumbled back into the darkness of the alley and began sprinting down the narrow street. If they could make it back to where some of the main groups where still fanning out through the town, they might be able to blend in again and escape.

They ran. No sign of pursuit behind them, at least for now.

Further on, the sounds of the murmuring crowd grew louder. The pungent odor of cooking oil and pampas filled the alley, mingling with the foul smell.

A block later, they came to a fork between buildings. An arched doorway to one side led up a flight of stone stairs. At the top of the stairs was a street where a crowd of people still milled about, men and women talking heatedly in Spanish with animated gestures, no doubt about what had just transpired in the square.

He reached into his pocket to pull out the memory card from his camera and turned to Lucy.

"Here, take this."

"What are you talking about?" She looked at him with wide eyes.

"I can draw them off."

"Who are those men? Why are we running from them?"

"I don't know, but they already know my name. I'm not going with anybody until we get a look at the photos ourselves. Hide the card in your clothes, head up these stairs, and jump in with the crowd. You'll be safe there. Your Spanish is good. I'll make sure we've really lost these guys and circle back around to meet you in ten or fifteen minutes. We can be in touch by text."

"I'm not sure that's such a good idea. What if they catch you?"

"I'll be fine." He glanced down the alley. "But we don't have much time. Trust me and go."

He pressed the card into Lucy's hand. She looked at him for a moment before kissing him on the cheek and disappearing up the stairs.

Manny took the other fork down the alley. Still no sign of the men. He moved swiftly but with a little more care, wary of coming across them by surprise.

After a minute, he reached another cross street, this one a somewhat broader thoroughfare crisscrossed by dozens of clotheslines draped with colorful garments hanging limply in the still air. Below a row of bed sheets, an old woman with a broom looked up at him from down the alleyway for a moment. She turned and went back to her sweeping.

He wondered why the soldier hadn't shot at them when they ran. Could it be because the men in suits didn't want any attention drawn to themselves?

He hoped he wasn't endangering Lucy unnecessarily. His gut told him it was him the men in suits were after.

Either way, if all went according to plan, an hour from now he and Lucy would be miles away, either checked into a hotel room where they could take a good look at the photos he'd shot, or sitting in some out-of-the-way cantina sipping on *Dos Equis*.

He still had his camera slung around his shoulder and his smart phone in his pocket. He thought of pulling the phone out to get a better sense of where he was but decided he better not risk stopping again.

The street made a sharp curve to the right. He came around the bend to find he'd unexpectedly reached the end of the line. He was confronted by a high stone wall where the alley dead-ended into a steep, rock-strewn hillside that looked as unstable as he felt. Heavy traffic swooshed past somewhere above, probably an expressway. But from where Manny stood, he might as well have been invisible. Worse, he hadn't been paying attention to the type of buildings he'd been passing for the past several cross streets. They were commercial and not residential, and since it was Cinco de Mayo all the offices were closed.

The first bullet grazed his leg before striking the building behind him.

No!

It stung like a hornet and popped a chunk of brick off the wall.

He glanced back over his shoulder to see the soldier advancing on him and the men in the suits pointing large handguns in his direction. There was nowhere left to run.

Without thinking he lowered himself into a crouch just as the second bullet ripped into his shoulder, tearing at the flesh like a hungry reptile and knocking the wind out of him.

Was this what it was like to die? The last thing he remembered was the sensation of falling sideways toward the pavement before his head came to rest against the unforgiving ground.

2

RAINA SCAMPERED UPHILL as best she could in the near darkness. It took all of her focus to keep her footing among the bushes and downed trees littering the wooded slope. She only hoped there were no snakes or other wild creatures along her path—that was the last thing she needed.

Behind her, headlights streaked along an interstate connector flowing north. The inky expanse of the Potomac stretched toward the west like some dark liquid blanket.

So they'd brought her across the river. It couldn't have been far, probably somewhere south of Bolling Air Force Base.

A warm front was moving in, bringing with it the threat of rain. The sound of the traffic rose and fell against the backdrop of crickets and other night sounds, punctuated by the occasional growl of a tractor-trailer.

What now? She paused to get her bearings. The humid air smelled of damp loam. She still wore the light jacket she'd had on back in the trailer. Sweat stung her eyes, but at least she was okay and on her own for now.

She wasn't sure who'd been attacking the trailer, but she had a pretty good idea.

Tye. Probably with help from Major Williamson, who must

have driven him across the river and somehow zeroed in on her location.

Where the two of them were now was anybody's guess. They were probably busy making their own escape—she'd noticed the shooting had stopped not long after she managed to flee.

She wondered how Murnell and the others at the scene would explain the gunfire and explosions to whatever local police, media, or other prying eyes showed up to check things out. They'd probably cordon off the area and call it a training excise or something. What were they doing there with the trailer anyway right on the edge of D.C.? All those screens and views she'd seen from inside the sphere…was someone running surveillance on her full time? She peered overhead through a break in the trees. The stars were barely visible, lost in the gathering clouds and lights from the city.

It all looked peaceful enough, but if there was one thing she'd learned, looks can be deceiving. The rumble of a jet taking off shook the night not too far away, so she was right about the air base.

She was proud of herself for one thing. She'd manage to steal Lance Murnell's smart phone from his pocket as she exited the trailer. Leaving it on, she'd tossed it on the roof of a storage shed she passed a quarter mile below the parking lot. Then she'd circled back around to head north, paralleling the interstate connector and the river, hoping the ruse with the phone would keep the bloodhounds off track for a while.

Something vibrated in her jacket pocket.

Oh, no. The original phone Murnell had given her to keep in contact with him.

In all the confusion, she'd forgotten she still carried it. Should she dump it as well and run?

Too late for that now.

She pulled it out of her pocket. The incoming ID message indicated an incoming video call. Whoever it was, maybe she could negotiate or find some way to throw them off her scent.

She huddled down in the darkness between two boulders and pressed the button to answer.

An image appeared on the phone screen, but it wasn't what she was expecting. Instead of Lance Murnell or a command center, she saw a well appointed office. It looked more like a living room than an office actually. Western motif, solid wood furniture, cigar on the desk, thick rugs, lots of leather, and a small bar. In the middle of the room stood a distinctive-looking man pouring a drink into a shot glass.

He turned to face Raina.

"Ah. You answered. Greetings."

She didn't recognize the man although for some reason she thought she should. Ruggedly handsome, despite his parched skin and white hair, his piercing eyes seemed to reach through the cell connection. Not exactly what she'd been expecting.

She said nothing, scanning the sky again for any trace of drones or other surveillance.

The man held up his glass. "If you were here, Chief Sanchez, I'd offer a you a drink. Gran Patron. A fine tequila."

"I don't know you," she said.

"Of course you don't." He lifted his glass and knocked back his shot, keeping an appraising eye on her. "To new acquaintances."

"Are you tracking me?"

"Me?" The man looked disappointed. "No," he said. "I'm much more concerned that you might be trying to track me."

Who was this guy?

"How far do you think you're going to get with only one good foot?" he asked.

"One's as good as the other. Functionally, they're the same."

He smiled. "Isn't that the truth? The same, but not yet the same. To live is to suffer, to survive is to find some meaning in the suffering."

"So says Nietzsche." Somehow she remembered the words from a passage she'd read in high school.

"Why, Miss Sanchez. You are a philosopher."

"And you are not Lance Murnell."

"Ha! Quite true, although we do share many common interests. Dr. Murnell works for me. My name is Jonathan Ripley. My friends call me Jon."

Raina kept silent. She thought she'd rather stick with Ripley.

Setting down his drink, he went to the desk and inserted an unlit cigar into the edge of his mouth. "Again, I apologize. If you were here, I'd offer you one. They are Cuban."

"Of course they are." She waved her hand.

Ripley lit his cigar and appeared to take in her hair, her face and body on whatever screen he was using. "You stand before me a pleasing sight. How may we serve one another?"

"I don't know you. But you seem to know me."

Ripley shrugged. "I know many things."

"Why are you calling me?"

"Well, for one thing, I'd like to find out what you want. Especially after you just managed to almost blow up a billion dollar investment."

Raina scratched her neck. Mosquitos had discovered her in the dark. Just mosquitos? She looked down, tilting the glow from the phone toward the hovering insect to make sure that was indeed all it was. She slapped it dead against her jacket.

"Is everything okay? Are you having a problem?" Ripley asked.

She tilted the phone back toward her face. "I'm fine," she said. "You still haven't told me what you're after."

"You still haven't told me what you're after either. Other than to see that Nathan Kurn finally gets what he deserves,

I imagine—a cause to which I'm sympathetic, by the way, although I'm unable to provide you with any aid in the matter."

"I didn't like what I saw in that trailer," she said.

"Is that all?"

"Where is Murnell?"

"You put him in the hospital."

Ouch. Not exactly a good way to get along with others.

"Why are you trying to run away from, Raina?"

"What you're doing can't be legal."

"I didn't know that in addition to a philosopher you're a constitutional scholar."

"I didn't say that."

"You saw within the TETRA," he said.

"The what?"

He ignored the question. "You're a very special pilot, Sanchez. You've served your country well and might continue to do so. You shouldn't take our overtures toward you lightly."

"What do you mean?" She continued to stare at him.

"You were shot down. You lost your commanding officer and other good men died that day."

She sighed. "What's that got to do with anything?"

"Might your vengeance be more beneficially focused against our mutual enemies?"

"I have no qualms going after terrorists or any other enemies of our country, if that's what you're worried about. But you're talking about something that goes way beyond that."

"You're jumping to a lot of conclusions based on what little you saw."

"I saw enough."

"If you come back in with us, we can talk this through in more detail. You don't have to stay in the dark."

"I like the dark," she said.

"I'll bet you do."

"Okay, that was creepy. I think it's time we ended this conversation."

"Don't go," Ripley said.

"Give me one more reason to keep talking to you."

"I have one," he said. "Since you asked...when was the last time you spoke with your brother?"

"My brother?"

"Yes."

"Manny? What's he got to do with any of this?" A pit was beginning to form in her stomach.

"When's the last time you talked with him."

"I don't know. I guess it's been a couple of months. Maybe more. We're not exactly close."

"So I understand."

"What do you mean? Where are you going with all of this?"

"You might want to check up on your little brother, Raina," Williamson said.

"Manny doesn't need me to check on him."

Ripley shrugged. "All the same, you may want to try to contact him. For both of your sakes."

What was this guy's game?

Whatever it was, her gut told her it came from the shadows, where bad things happen and people can disappear. This didn't sound like the regular military or Homeland Security. If it were, Ripley wouldn't have called her the way he did.

"I'll tell you what," she said. "Why don't you tell me exactly where you are, Mr. Ripley, and I'll just hop right on over there so you can tell me more about why you're bringing my brother into this conversation."

"Ha!" He said. "You know I can't do that right now."

"No, you can't, can you? What was that you told me? Something about staying in the dark?"

Ripley's demeanor turned cold. "You're a patriot who's

served her country and a brilliant pilot, Raina. Working with us will help you fulfill all of your ambitions. Stop your running. It won't end well."

"Let he who is without sin cast the first stone."

"From the gospel of Matthew, isn't it?...the words of Jesus of Nazareth."

"Yes. And my grandmother," she said.

3

RAINA CUT THE connection. She'd seen enough smooth operators in her time. You could never really take people like Ripley at their word. For all she knew, he'd had her on a satellite image or on cam from a hovering drone the whole time they'd been talking.

Fumbling in the dim light, she turned the phone over and pried open the case. She popped the battery out and tossed it and the phone into the woods, as far away from her as she could.

She needed to keep moving. The good news was, if she could manage to avoid detection, she knew exactly where she needed to go. The place was only a few miles away, and she knew exactly how to get there if she could just make it the mile or two on foot to Congress Heights Metro station. She had to pass through a couple of rough neighborhoods along the way, but given the threat of a storm she figured she'd be all right. And if anyone tried to mess with her, she knew how to handle it.

In the meantime, no one would expect a woman walking alone at this time of night to remain in unlighted wooded areas. Which was okay with her. At least there were no security cameras to worry about. And she'd traversed far more rugged terrain growing up in New Mexico.

After another fifteen minutes of walking in the woods, she sat down on a rock and crossed one leg over the other. She pulled up one of her pant legs and reached around to pull off a flattened pouch attached to the back her prosthesis. Her emergency survival kit, she called it. She carried no ID, but the pouch contained cash, a Metro card and bus pass. She stuffed these in her jacket packet and continued on.

Soon, she emerged from the woods next to a school, crossed a street, and entered a neighborhood of low brick townhouses. The homes were all of post WWII construction. The street looked anything but prosperous, but there was also an air of pride evident in the level of care given to many of the postage stamp lawns.

She strode down the sidewalk with purpose, keeping her eyes straight ahead. No one seemed to be outdoors on this sweltering night. Air conditioners purred from windows. A dog barked from behind a fence.

The only other living being she encountered was an elderly black gentleman seated on his porch wearing a red VFW garrison cap, who nodded respectfully to her as she passed by. She remembered one of her flight instructors in Warrant Officer school talking about military bearing. He'd described it as not so much an appearance but an attitude. Maybe she was reading too much into the situation, but the old man seemed to instantly respond to that in her.

After a few blocks, she turned a corner and came along a row of older two and three family dwellings. Their chipped paint and PROPERTY FOR RENT signs caused her to quicken her pace. How much longer before she made it to the Metro?

But a couple of blocks later, whether by sheer luck or the

force of her determination she found herself drawing within sight of the Congress Heights station.

The station wasn't large. A concrete gazebo style structure with heavy metal bars covered the escalator leading down to the trains. A couple of homeless people had set up camp beside the entrance and one tried to speak to her, but she pulled the hood of her jacket up, lowered her head to avoid detection by cameras, and hurried by without stopping.

Minutes later, below ground and safely on the train, she stared out the window and rubbed the top of her knee. She was in good condition but the hike through the woods had been hard.

The train was mostly empty at this hour. A young African American couple sat at one end of the car. Teenagers, they held hands and laughed at something on their smart phones. The only other riders were an elderly Asian man dressed in a janitor's uniform and a middle-aged father and his young son clothed in Washington Nationals gear, apparently on their way home from a late game.

Raina took let go of her knee and stared out the window as the train raced through the dark tunnel. Try as she might, she couldn't help glancing around her from time to time. Was she being watched? What she'd seen inside the trailer's sphere still haunted her.

She'd been lucky earlier—that was all there was to it. Lucky that Murnell's mobile facility had apparently suffered enough damage to knock Murnell's mini-drones offline for a while. She didn't know how many spheres or pilots he and his people had at their disposal or how many more of their stealth MAVs might be out looking for her, but the very idea gave her the creeps. How much longer before her luck ran out?

Come to think of it, he'd never actually shown her what type of MAV she was supposed to be flying from within the sphere. Whatever they were, they must have been state of the art, given the location of the parking lot and the proximity to Joint Base Anacostia Bolling.

JBAB was home to no less than the Defense Intelligence Agency, not to mention the adjacent Naval Research Laboratory. If Williamson was right, and they were all caught up in some kind of clandestine domestic power struggle between different groups, where did Ripley and Murnell fit in? Did they have so much juice with the system that they'd been practicing their drone tricks right under the nose of the military hierarchy?

But she was also lucky on another front. No doubt Ripley was preoccupied at the moment explaining all of those explosions and bullets and maybe even a few dead bodies to the folks from the base, not to mention the media, internet jockeys, and self-appointed news junkies that would have been tipped off about the noise of the brief battle. He wouldn't tell her where he was, which meant he must have been someplace else; that would make managing the situation even more difficult.

A couple stops later, she disembarked from the green line train and switched to the orange line. It was coming on to midnight and the last trains for the night were departing. Her car was busier on the new train, but she found an empty corner seat and managed to keep to herself.

She rode the train under the river into Virginia as far as Ballston, where she got off to walk again.

Some time later, she found herself nearing her destination. She entered the residential neighborhood where she'd spent so much time the past few weeks.

After all that had happened, she hoped it would still be safe. Still, she was wary approaching the single story brick ranch tucked among similar residences where Williamson had housed them for much of their MAV training. The dwellings appeared to blend with one another, distinguished only by their street addresses marked on the curb. Anonymity in numbers, Williamson had told them. Why he'd chosen this particular place she wasn't so sure. Proximity to the city, she supposed, ease of access.

Only a few house lights remained on along the block. The house had a side door under a small porch facing the empty driveway. The neighboring homes on either side were both dark with their shades drawn. In one of the driveways sat an older model minivan.

She scanned the sky and the immediate vicinity for any signs she was being observed but saw nothing. A cooling breeze swept around her and swirled up through the surrounding trees. A rumble of distant thunder heralded the approach of the promised late night rainstorm. She turned into the driveway, and stepped under the porch up to the door.

It was locked, of course. There was no window either. A deadbolt also helped to keep out potential intruders, but a small, indistinguishable button built into the side of the wall-mounted mailbox popped open a security panel with a keypad. The mailbox itself was empty, of course, but she made a show of looking inside all the same, as if she were any other homeowner returning late from being out.

She punched in the code she'd memorized. As soon as she hit the last number, she heard the comforting click of the locks disengaging.

Welcome home. Sort of.

At least the training house was someplace familiar. It also put her indoors and, she hoped, still offered her a safe place to crash. The building was outfitted with supplies and weapons and shielded from outside surveillance. Still, her heart pounded in her chest as she stepped inside.

The central air conditioning system cut on with a click,

surprising her with a sudden whoosh of cool air. It had been a while since she'd felt so jumpy. It reminded her of combat.

As far as she could tell, there was no sign of Tye or Major Williamson. Maybe they were still busy themselves covering their tracks and eluding Murnells's people. She wondered if they would make for here as she had done. Regardless, she wasn't waiting around for them. She would have to cross that bridge when she came to it if they didn't show up in the next couple of hours.

Inside the small vestibule a second door required a fingerprint impression. She placed her index finger on the glass screen. A green light came on and this lock released with a smooth whir.

Pushing on the handle gave her a strange feeling of deja vu. There was a light switch on the wall just inside the door. She flipped it on and looked around. The interior of the house looked no different than when they'd last trained here a couple of days before.

She quickly closed the door behind her and paused to let her eyes adjust to the difference in light. Several interior lamps and wall sconces had come on at the flip of the switch, as had a couple of fluorescent fixtures in the kitchen area. At least she wouldn't have any trouble seeing what might be coming at her.

Which was a good thing, because at that moment she noticed the faint, shimmering flutter of a hover angel MAV rising from behind the kitchen counter.

What the...?

The angel wasn't alone. Within seconds, a handful of identical MAVs were in the air and moving around the room, probing the space like a living swarm. Even more unnerving, like tiny gnats, they were often difficult to spot, depending on the angle of the light.

Who was controlling them? Had someone gotten here before she did? Were these MAVs armed?

She had no way of knowing the answers to any of these questions. She could only hope these angels were little more than autonomous sentries triggered by her entrance.

The good news was none flew toward her in an aggressive manner. They hung back as if they were watching and recording her movements, which they almost assuredly were.

Whatever their intentions, Raina wasn't taking any chances. She hurried to the weapons locker in one of the suite's closets. It was a tall metal safe with more electronic locks. Again, she punched in the code from memory and the door to the safe clicked, but she was in for a shock as it swung open.

Nearly all of the guns and ammunition had been removed. All that remained inside was a serviceable Glock 17 with a couple of loaded clips and a stash of 9mm ammo. Okay, one gun was certainly better than nothing.

She grabbed the pistol off the shelf, disengaged the slide, and rammed a clip in place. If any of these angels tried to turn on their mama pilot she'd waste the thing and ask questions later.

Emboldened, she decided to try an experiment waving her hand in front of the nearest drone. It failed to veer at all from its apparently pre-programmed path.

All right. She was dealing with watch-drones then. Which also meant someone knew she was here. As if on cue a mobile phone rang from behind the kitchen counter where the little drone had first appeared. She picked her way among the swirling drones and came around into the kitchen area where the device lay plugged into the wall on top of the counter. She picked it up and answered.

"You made it."

The sound of Tye's voice filled her with relief. She also realized how much she'd been worried about him.

"Where are you?"

"With Williamson."

"Well, that's good. Is it safe to talk on this line?"

"He tells me it's secure."

"Okay. I assume you guys were doing all the shooting back outside the base."

"Affirmative. Who else did you think it might have been?"

"I guess I should thank you then."

"Williamson did tell us this was some kind of war. Those folks who took you must really want you for some reason."

"I guess so. Where are all the weapons and ammo we had stored here? All that's left is a pistol."

"Williamson said he stopped by there earlier and got geared up in case we ran into trouble. Which turned out to be a wise decision."

"Are you on your way here now?"

"Not yet. We're a little bogged down at the moment, but we will be soon."

"Be careful. You won't believe the technology we may be up against."

"More drone voodoo, huh?"

"I've never seen anything like it."

"Well, whatever it is, I think we put a crimp in their style. At least, for now."

"How far away are you?"

"Not far. Should be there in a while."

"What am I supposed to do in the meantime, hang out here with these floating guard-dogs?"

Tye chuckled. "Williamson said he thought you'd like those. Hey, maybe it will help you know better what it feels like to be on the other end of them."

"What's going on, Tye? This has got to about a lot more than just Nathan Kurn and his son."

"Not to worry. Williamson says all will be revealed."

"But don't you think—"

Static crackled through their connection. "Can't talk right now, Rain."

"But—"

"Sit tight. Gotta go."

The line went dead and she was left to stare across the suite at the tiny, swirling MAVs.

Great.

She tossed the phone into the pillows on the couch and sat down in one of the overstuffed chairs. Unless she wanted to start taking pot shots with the Glock, she had no way to reach out or do anything except sit.

She studied the MAVs for a few moments. They were beautiful in their own way, she thought.

Wasn't there something in the Bible about that when it came to humans? 'Fearfully and wonderfully made,' if her memory was accurate. What happens when the machines we build become more like us?

Discovering the drones when she'd walked in hadn't come as a complete shock, of course. She might have expected as much from Major Williamson.

She realized how much of a whirlwind she'd been living these past few weeks. There'd been little time to sit back and consider, to think through the full implications of what they were doing. This entire house had been Raina's covert playground for practicing with the MAVs. Moving in and out of doors, over furniture and through rooms, inside the walls, HVAC, and lighting systems. For the past few weeks she'd been focused on one thing alone. And now she was being recruited, maybe even blackmailed by some shadowy group of apparent insiders to put those skills to use with even more sophisticated technology.

Blackmailed.

Wait a minute. Didn't Tye just tell her this was a secure phone line? What was Manny's number? Maybe Ripley's play had been nothing more than a bluff or a threat to go after her brother. One of the little luxuries Manny's new job provided for him was a satellite phone that was supposed to work anywhere on the planet.

She'd committed the number to memory. She went and dug the phone out from beneath the couch pillows and dialed.

Then she waited. The line went through a series of electronic sounds as it attempted to to complete a connection.

Finally she heard a message. "This number is no longer in service."

What? Could it be?

If Tye said this phone was secure, then maybe she could also use it to search the Internet.

She typed in the web address for the InfoNation website and found their contact information. No phone number listed, but they did offer a chat feature to speak with a customer service representative.

She clicked the box and typed in the message that she was trying to get in touch with one of their reporters, Manny Sanchez.

For a minute or more, there was no response. She was beginning to wonder if her message had even gotten through when an answer suddenly popped on her phone's screen.

WE'RE SORRY. WE HAVE NO REPORTERS BY THAT NAME ON OUR STAFF.

4

SHE TOSSED THE cell phone on the couch and sat back down in the chair.

A big part of the reason Raina had said yes to Tye and Major Williamson in the first place was she still harbored shreds of hope that one day she might get back into the air as a pilot. Flying drones, MAVs, or whatever you wanted to call them, may not have had the same cachet or appeal as strapping into the seat of an attack helicopter, but it seemed like a step in the right direction. What she'd seen in Murnell's sphere had given her a glimpse there might be even more.

If something had happened to Manny, and Ripley had anything to do with it, she'd make the man pay, one way or the other—national security be damned. But things could get complicated.

She thought about Tye, all muscled six-feet-four and tousled hair of him. A guy she'd never expected to see again after Afghanistan. For the first time in a long time, she felt what might be the spark of a real relationship.

She made sure the Glock stayed within reach on the arm of the chair and laid her head back to look at the ceiling.

Not much to see up there, just a couple more of the tiny angel drones floating about like ephemeral beings. She turned toward the kitchen. When was the last time she'd had anything to eat? She suddenly felt famished.

She pushed herself to her feet and went over and checked the refrigerator. To her surprise, she found some fresh cheese, half a six-pack of Mountain Dew (Tye's), and even a strawberry yogurt that had yet to expire. Even better, in the cupboard she discovered some crackers and a jar of peanut butter. She spread everything out on the table and ate some of the food, washing it all down with the tangy sweet soda.

She noticed the drones had stopped swirling. What was going on? She was about to go retrieve the Glock when she realized the drones had all landed by themselves and were now lined up next to one another on the counter across from her like an orderly miniature air force.

How cute. It only made sense, of course. They were all pre-programmed and couldn't run forever without recharging.

"Ten-hut, guys."

She toasted the line of MAVs with her soda can.

The angels remained still.

Figured. Can't even get a rise out of a bunch of flying robots.

She crossed her arms to form a pillow and put her head down on the table. Was she losing her mind?

The next thing she knew she was dreaming. It wasn't a very clear dream. She found herself floating somewhere and reaching for something, like a handhold perhaps, back before losing her foot when she enjoyed rock climbing.

She awoke with a start to the phone's dull electronic ring.

She looked around. The house otherwise remained quiet. The hover angels still stood in their positions on the counter. How long had she been out? It couldn't have been that long.

She remembered the phone on the couch, pushed away from the table, and rushed over to it.

"Hello?"

"We were afraid something happened to you."

It was Williamson.

"Sorry. I'm fine. Must have dozed off."

"Understandable. All right, listen up. We're only a few minutes out from your location. You need to pack up everything you can find left in the suite, any equipment, MAVs, ammunition. We're clearing out of there."

"Right now?"

"Yes, now."

"Shouldn't be too hard. There isn't a whole lot left here except for the furniture, a little bit of food, and your little guard dog drones."

"Check all the closets and storage areas for anything I might have missed. Control devices and ancillary equipment like power cords, data cards, anything."

"Why the hurry?"

"Just hit the news," he said. She could hear the sounds of him driving in the background. "Derek Kurn was found dead tonight in his room at the fraternity."

"What? Are you kidding me?" She felt her stomach clench. "How can that be?"

"We can talk about it when we get there," he said. "Time to saddle up."

5

MURNELL STIFFENED AS his escort, a fresh-faced marine in camos, entered the room. Wincing as he touched his chin, he didn't want to guess how bad the bruise on his face would look the next day. It felt bad enough already.

Three hours at Bethesda Naval Medical Center outside D.C. had not been his idea of how to spend the remainder of a productive summer night. His promising new pilot Raina Sanchez had turned into a nightmare. She'd left him with more than just bruises and a bad headache. Losing her stoked doubts about the mission and doubt was something he could ill afford.

At least his CT scan looked okay. The diagnosis was a minor concussion, and there'd apparently been no permanent damage. Still, even pulling on his socks required more than the usual effort.

"You may have headaches for a few days. Possibly longer," the doctor said. He'd given Murnell some pills and told him to take it easy for a while.

Like that was ever going to happen.

To the scientist in him, any kind of hindrance at such a critical juncture of his project was just about the worst thing that could have happened. No matter how much sympathy he might have felt over Sanchez's predicament, he wouldn't make the mistake of letting her get the drop on him again.

The soldier stood in the doorway waiting. "The chopper's ready, sir."

"Thank you. Tell them I'll be there in a minute."

"My orders are to escort you to the helipad."

"At-ease. I'm not some three-star general."

"Yes, sir." The marine remained at a respectful distance, standing at parade rest just inside the door.

One of the things Murnell had always appreciated about his own time in the military was the discipline and adherence to protocol. But now that he was a civilian, sometimes it could be a pain in the ass.

"All right. All right," he said. "I'm coming."

He finished putting on his socks and shoes. Trying to ignore his dizziness, he followed the marine out the door.

The hospital corridors were quiet. They saw no one until passing a night shift worker dressed in white who walked behind a machine that was polishing the floor. Murnell felt a little better as he walked. Maybe getting out into the fresh air would be good for him, too.

Which would help because he wasn't looking forward to explaining his lack of situational awareness to his boss. If there was one thing Jon Ripley didn't abide it was incompetence.

Even if the numbnut power-jockeys in the DHS bureaucracy failed to understand the real mission Ripley and a few other forward thinkers like Murnell had undertaken, his boss was going to stay on task. No doubt he was going to make sure Murnell, his prize scientist, kept his focus where it belonged, too.

Ripley was a legend in the intelligence community. He was also a classic Renaissance man, an outside consultant who'd earned that right the hard way.

On unofficial, unspecified assignment with Homeland

Security, his boss was also a charismatic leader, notorious gambler and womanizer with clandestine connections all over the planet. Not to mention a willingness to color outside the lines when he deemed it necessary.

Perhaps the best testament to Ripley's prowess was that many in the CIA and NSA mistakenly believed he was no longer among the living. A persistent rumor held that he'd perished in the flaming wreckage of a C-130 off of the coast of northern China a couple of years before.

Rounding a corner, they came face to face with a working hospital drone. It was, to Murnell's eyes, an antique—a quaint looking quadcopter that flew across their path down a perpendicular passage and appeared to be transporting medications or other vital supplies in a secure compartment.

"Those buggers still creep me out sometimes," the soldier muttered under his breath.

"I know how you feel." Murnell couldn't help but smile.

He was beginning to wonder sometimes if he and Ripley were going too far. Their goal was simple enough: if they didn't get out front of and secure control of the world's most top-secret drone technology for the benefit of those in power then the world risked falling into either tyranny or anarchy—take your pick.

Evolving stealth technology and MAVs were the cutting edge. But the sword was wielded by Murnell's sphere interfaces that melded an operator's awareness and capabilities with the drones themselves. Artificially intelligent, outward-looking sensors channeled through responsive biofeedback loops—known as the TETRA—were going to change the world in ways most could scarcely begin to imagine.

But Murnell could. He could do more than imagine.

His doctoral dissertation at Stanford on potential pathways for human/artificial intelligence interface may have been groundbreaking in its own right. But he was beginning to understand, in retrospect, just how crude his initial understanding had been.

They reached the exit that led to the helipad. The helicopter was waiting on the pad, its rotors already spinning.

As the doors swished open to admit them to the night, a wave of cool humid air rushed up to greet them. The pavement was still wet from what must have been an earlier downpour and the sky above was still shrouded by clouds. But the low ceiling wouldn't be of much concern where he was flying. It wasn't far.

He followed the soldier to the chopper. Another marine was holding the door open for him.

Once inside, he sat down and strapped in, slipping on his headset as the hatch was secured behind him.

"Welcome aboard, sir," he heard in his earphones.

"Thanks," he said into his mike. "Let's go."

6

"I THOUGHT WE WERE going someplace safe."
Raina stared through the front passenger window of the Dodge SUV Major Williamson was driving. Car lights shone through the glass, stinging her eyes. They were headed back along the I-495 beltway with Tye hunkered down in the back seat. Though traffic was light in the wee hours of the new day, a few big trucks and other vehicles still plied the highway.

"Change of plan," the major told her. "Got another job for you."

"Another job?" She glanced back at Tye before looking again at Williamson. "You can't be serious."

"You want to find out what happened to Derek Kurn, don't you?"

"Well, yeah, but—"

"Best way I know how is to go back into the frat house while the scene's still hot, only this time without anybody knowing you're there."

"You're insane."

"Maybe. But I've got a portable system with a laptop in the back for you. You'll be using the same kind of MAVs."

"But I haven't trained with a different system."

"Don't worry. It's similar to what you've been using. You'll be fine."

She looked over the seat at Tye. "You on board with this?"

He shrugged. "I'm game if you're game."

"You're both insane."

"Probably," Tye said.

"You said all would be revealed."

"At the right time and place. With this news about Derek Kurn, you want to try to get into everything here?"

She looked back at Williamson. "Yes, I do want get into everything here."

"Fair enough," the major said. "Let's trade."

"What do you mean?"

He kept his eyes on the road. "Why don't you tell us about whatever you saw in that trailer and who you were working with, and I'll give you whatever information you need."

"How about you go first? I got into this whole thing because of Nathan Kurn and because I wanted a way to start flying again. But now that Kurn's son is dead, I don't see why any of us need to keep going. Why not let the police handle it?"

They'd pulled off the exit ramp a couple of miles from the college. A large office building and parking lot filled the space to their right. It must have been some kind of all-night facility; even in the wee hours the lot was nearly full.

Williamson wheeled the Dodge into an empty space among one of the outer row of cars. He cut the engine and turned to face her.

"Okay, look," he said. "There is a lot at stake here. You think it was just some kind of accident you were kidnapped—twice by the way—and ended up in that trailer?"

"Of course not." The truth was she still felt torn. Although her gut told her she was right to run away, she still felt a pull toward the technology Murnell was offering her.

"What were you doing in there, Raina? What did you see?" She hesitated. "I have a strong suspicion you already know." "Humor me. Please." Williamson stared at her.

She wondered how much information she should share. Her gut told her Lance Murnell, despite his appeal and supposedly government-sanctioned ways, wasn't to be fully trusted. But she still had doubts about Williamson, too. Why all the mystery? What was he really after?

"Okay." She described for them in detail most of what she'd seen and done, leaving out the part about being asked to kill the man at the end.

Williamson didn't look very surprised. "Who was your trainer?" he asked.

"He says his name is Murnell. Dr. Lance Murnell. He's some kind of scientist."

"Hmmm. Probably told you he's with Homeland as well."

"I wondered about that. But they said I was being guarded by marines."

"Oh, I'm sure your Dr. Murnell has at least a loose affiliation with DHS. Just not any part that's open to scrutiny, even from those in the chain of command."

"Some kind of domestic black op?"

"Trust me when I tell you, guys…we're way beyond a black op here."

"Great," Tye said. "What kind of suicide mission have you gotten us into, Major?"

"I told you up front it might be dangerous."

"Danger I can take. But I'm not sure I want my name planted on some federal watch list."

"Especially with the way you guys lit up the sky earlier," Raina added.

Tye shot her a look. "Hey, we got you out of there, didn't we?"

"Hold on, guys," Williamson said. "What happened back

there at the parking lot and earlier in the alley was regrettable. The blood of people who thought they were on our side was spilled and that's never good."

"What do you mean they thought they were on our side?"

"I mean what you've been seeing so far and what we're about to talk about is completely compartmentalized information, known only to a few."

"So the guys I just killed thought they were the good guys, just like us," Tye said.

"More or less."

Tye shook his head. "That's messed up, man."

"I know. A lot of what I'm about to tell you is going to sound that way. None of us have to worry about ending up on an official kill list."

"Right. Just an unofficial one."

"True. But the last thing the people running the show want is publicity or more scrutiny of their activities. Believe me, they'll find a way to take whatever happened back there across the river and scrub it clean."

"Spoken like a true spook."

"Former," Williamson said. "And it takes one to know one."

"So why not just expose whatever's happening?" Raina said. "This is still a free country with a free press."

"Huh." Williamson pulled back a smile. "It sure looks that way most of the time, doesn't it?"

"Are you trying to tell us the whole system's messed up?"

"I'm saying that with the resources and connections people like Dr. Murnell have at their disposal, that's a lot easier said than done."

"What about the other guy I talked to?" she asked.

"Oh?" Williamson raised any eyebrow. "Who would that be?"

"After I got away on foot I had to make my way to the

Metro and I was stupid. I forgot I was still carrying the phone Murnell gave me."

"And?"

"I didn't get very far before it rang."

"Murnell?"

"No. It was someone else. And it was a video call."

"Who was it?"

"He said his name was Ripley."

Williamson showed no reaction. "Go on," he said.

"He told me he was Murnell's boss."

"What did Ripley want?"

"He said he wanted to find a way to convince me to come back and join whatever it is they're doing. He said I was a talented pilot. But he also said they wouldn't come after me."

"That's a lie," Williamson said.

"How do you know?" Raina asked.

"Trust me."

"You know this guy Ripley?" Tye asked. He was leaning over Raina's seat. She could still smell the sweat on him.

"I used to work with him," Williamson said. "That's part of the reason we're here."

Raina looked at Tye. He shrugged and raised his eyebrows at her as if to show this was news to him as well.

She looked back at Williamson. "Great. Is the fact you used to work with this guy supposed to make us more or less comfortable?"

"I'll let you be the judge of that," he said.

"Don't worry. I will. Especially since Ripley said something completely unexpected."

"That would be like him. What did he say?"

"He brought up my brother," she said.

7

THE LAST TIME Raina had seen her brother Manny in person was at Christmas time the year before. Full of life that day, he was excited about his new job as reporter for some big website. Raina, on the other hand, had just been glad her younger brother had found what could best be described as a real job.

Since graduating from college Manny seemed to have been spending most of his time as an activist for one cause or another. Earning a living was never high on his list of priorities. As long she could remember, he'd moved from city to city, crashing with one group of friends or another along the way. Raina was never quite sure where he was or exactly what he was doing. Obsessed with computers and video games since he was a kid, his hacking prowess appeared to give him an 'in' almost anywhere he went. Overseas assignment as a globetrotting correspondent was a long way from where she and her brother had grown up outside Santa Fe.

"Your brother?" Tye leaned forward in his seat. "You never said anything about having a brother."

She shrugged.

"What did Ripley say about him, Raina?" Williamson asked.

"He hinted, not so subtly, there might be something wrong with Manny. He told me I should try to get in touch with him."

"That doesn't sound good," Tye said.

Williamson sighed, the first time he'd shown any kind of reaction. The major obviously knew something he wasn't telling her.

"What?" Raina had a sick feeling in the pit of her stomach.

"I need to show you something," he said. "I was saving this for later, but you might as well see it now."

"About Manny?"

"Yes."

A coldness ran down the back of her neck. What if her brother was dead?

Williamson looked around the car. "We can't stay here," he said. "It's private, but they're bound to have security cameras. Tye, you and I need to switch places. You drive. I need to get at a compartment under your seat."

He opened his door and climbed out.

Tye did the same and a moment later Tye was behind the wheel with Williamson seated behind him. They backed out of the parking space and were soon headed back out onto the beltway.

"Just drive for a few minutes while we talk," Williamson said. "We'll circle back around toward the college."

Tye nodded. Williamson reached across the back where he was now sitting and pulled on some sort of hidden tab to lift up the cushion of that part of the seat. Underneath was a document-sized door with a combination lock. He spun the knob to the correct numbers, swung open the door, and extracted a manila envelope. From the envelope he pulled out a stack of blown-up photographs. He handed them over the seat to Raina.

"These photos are a few weeks old. I just came into possession of them," he said.

She wasn't sure what she was supposed to be looking for. The first few photos showed a crowd gathered around some kind of a stage and a speaker's platform. In the background stood office buildings, some modern but many of an older style. Then she caught sight of a face in the crowd circled in black ink.

It couldn't be.

"You recognize the man pictured in the crowd?"

She was so absorbed by the images she didn't say anything for a moment.

Tye glanced over the back of the seat before turning his eyes back to the road. "Who is he?" he asked.

"His name is Manny Sanchez," Williamson said.

"He's my brother," Raina said.

"How come you never mentioned him before?" Tye said.

"To say Manny and I aren't close would be an understatement. I mean I've tried to be a good big sister. I've tried to be friends with him…but Manny and I are just different…." She choked on her words.

She scanned through the other photos. Time stamps showed them to be in sequential order ten to twenty seconds apart.

"Where were these pictures taken?" she asked.

"Outside Mexico City," Williamson told her. "They're satellite images."

"But how did you—?"

"Don't ask me how I got them."

Raina looked more closely at the date. "This happened four weeks ago."

"Yes."

"That was about the time you approached Tye and me to start this mission."

"That's right. But I just received these now. When was the last time you spoke with your brother?"

She felt suddenly defensive, like she had to apologize for not getting along with her younger sibling. "I don't know…

maybe a couple of months ago. He called from New York. I don't really remember when it was."

"Is that unusual, I mean, for you two to be out of contact for that long?"

Raina shrugged. "Not really. Like I said, we're not exactly sympatico. Do you know what Manny does?"

"I do now." Williamson crossed his arms. "After I received these, I started looking into him. He's a freelance online journalist. An ambitious and inventive one who's been trying to make a name for himself by exposing government secrets."

As she dug deeper into the stack of photos, things began to come into focus. Manny continued to be highlighted, but in the background you could clearly see the speaker on stage, a middle-aged man dressed in a business suit. Then something happened. The speaker could be seen collapsing on stage. In the next series of photos there is a great deal of commotion as the crowd starts to panic and security personnel react."

"What happened here?"

"A politician died. A potential Mexican presidential candidate," Williamson said.

"I think I read something about that online. What was his name again?"

"Martinez. Alberto Martinez."

"Right. Weren't there rumors he was assassinated? Some kind of poison?"

"That's been alleged, yes. But there's been no conclusive evidence."

In the next few photos Manny seems to be caught up in the maelstrom and he's holding someone's hand—a girl."

"That's his girlfriend Lucy with him," Raina said. "What was she doing there?"

"I don't know," Williamson said. "You tell me. Keep going to the last few photos."

In the next few images the venue changed. Now Manny and Lucy had become separated from the crowd and were headed down a narrow alleyway. Then they parted ways. In the last picture where they were together, Manny appeared to be handing something to Lucy.

But the final two images made Raina pull up short.

"Oh, my god." She felt sick to her stomach. In the first of the final photos, Manny was running but appeared to be throwing his arms out as if hit by something. In the final image he was lying face down on the pavement while a pair of men in suits approached.

"What happened to him?"

"We think he was shot."

"What?" Raina shook her head in disbelief. She wiped a tear from below her eye. For all of the disagreements and fights she'd had with her brother over the years, starting with the separation of their parents, she still loved him. "Is he…is he?"

"The source who provided me with the photos said they think he's still alive," Williamson said.

She examined the final frames more closely. Though the photos had been taken from such a distance, Manny's face was clear enough. He lay face up on the pavement with a clump of his dark hair matted over part of his forehead and a pair of hulking figures bent over him.

"He could be anywhere by now," she said. "Are the people who shot him from one of the drug cartels?"

"No, I don't think so. I think the people you just escaped from in that trailer have something to do with it."

"But how can that be? What are they, some kind of rogue group within our government?"

"You might give them that label. But these people are more than just a group," he said. "And the technology they're about to wield is far more dangerous."

8

WHEN JONATHAN RIPLEY had first approached him about connecting MAVs to human operators, Lance Murnell was intrigued. And when Ripley got to the part about designing and building an artificially intelligent MAV operating system patterned after the brains of actual pilots, Murnell was even more intrigued. It was Ripley who'd pulled the strings to get Murnell his official cover job with DHS. It was also Ripley, operating through several layers of surrogates and the fronts of several smaller defense contractors, who continued to supply the funding for his work.

Ripley was at the hub of a growing network of drone believers—people in positions of power and authority, both private and public, who'd become convinced the control and exploitation of future UAV and MAV technology was critical, even vital, to the future. Since global markets had begun their steady but apparently inexorable decline the year before, the world was becoming an increasingly unstable place. Despite all best efforts to salvage some semblance of democracy and freedom, power and control might one day soon be all that was left.

All of Murnell's work was classified as top secret, of course. Everyone involved operated on a strictly need-to-know basis, including Murnell himself. He knew from experience that those further up the chain of command at DHS could, for the most part, be kept in the dark about what was happening in his lab. And Ripley seemed to possess unlimited resources. But Murnell was beginning to worry about who had ultimate authority and what their aims might be.

And that wasn't even his biggest concern. How far was Ripley—indeed, how far was he, Murnell—willing to go to protect, some would say cover-up, Empyrean's secrets and some of the problems they were experiencing?

He thought about all of these things as his Sikorsky Seahawk flew at less than six hundred feet over Washington, D.C.

Outside his window, the sky had turned as gloomy as he felt. A gust of wind buffeted the chopper and drizzle streaked the glass. The guys up front were no doubt only interested in powering him the short distance to his destination as quickly as possible, before the bad weather broke.

Murnell looked down at his hands. Not as powerful as they used to be when he was working out regularly. But they were still dependable. They were still hands he could rely on to work a keyboard, a joystick, or touch screen controls. In his experience, problems with almost any system almost always came down to the people involved. The X factor with Empyrean was always going to be the operators, not the breakthroughs in software and micro circuitry that made what they were doing possible.

His prized new pilot Raina Sanchez was, at the moment, problem number one. Or maybe she was tied for first place with the aborted effort they'd made in the case of Derek Kurn. The fact of the matter was even with the most advanced autonomous systems he could imagine and build, the computer's capabilities were always enhanced, and in most cases, multiplied by orders of magnitude when coupled with a human partner. And no one—no one sane, at any rate—wanted to consider weaponizing any drone without humans in control.

It took humans to see the nuances and make the judgment calls, but more than that, it crossed a barrier he and most of the scientists with whom he kept in touch were unwilling to cross. Even a completely autonomous drone had to have a program and someone had to build and design it. Swarming models based on insect behavior had their potential, but they only went so far.

Humans, on the other hand, properly vetted through chain-of-command, could act almost anywhere on the planet, in any conditions, day or night, under the proper authority. This had long been the case using conventional planes, ships, and satellites. Micro Air Vehicles expanded the field of operations far beyond previous capabilities to the most intimate level possible. No venue was impenetrable. A conventional electronic air defense shield was useless against tiny, low-flying MAVs.

Of course, with such capacity for stealth the potential for mischief, illicit espionage, and outright breaches of human rights, not to mention violations of constitutionally protected freedoms, grew exponentially. His team had come so far, but they weren't the only ones seeking to exploit such ideas.

Murnell was neither arrogant nor naive enough to think he had a corner on the market of advanced neural electronic interfaces. The Chinese, Russians, Israelis, Japanese, Germans, and French, among others, could only be so far behind. All were part of this race to the top—or was it the bottom?—of MAV and AI capabilities. The goal was undetectable flying platforms for gathering intelligence and enforcement of order.

Would the very idea of the state and independent nations eventually cease to exist in the face of such technology? Would any freedom be safe? But there was no putting the genie back in the bottle, and no one understood that better than his boss.

Still, Murnell was beginning to dread his encounters with Ripley—and that wasn't even considering what had just happened with Sanchez. Ripley seemed to be growing more and more evasive the closer the TETRA came to being operational. Murnell appreciated the need for compartmentalization and the critical need for operational security, but he was beginning to resent a growing marginalization as the ring of control grew ever smaller.

Whatever had caused the psychological problems exhibited by some of his operators—it wasn't getting any better. For all Murnell knew, the same thing might be in the process of happening to all of his drone drivers, and where would that leave them or the entire program?

Ripley's only concern seemed to be keeping a lid on things, even if that meant resorting to extreme measures. Kidnapping, extortion, and beyond in the most extreme cases like Derek Kurn's—no potential action had been deemed off the table.

Derek Kurn had never been one of Murnell's better prospects. He might have actually been the worst, although his gaming skills had caused him to at least show some promise. If it hadn't been for the insistence of his powerful father, the younger Kurn would have never been in Murnell's program at all. He would still be playing football, living the high college life, and maybe never would have turned out to be the extreme problem he'd become.

Murnell was beginning to worry that the TETRA opened up a window into an operator's basest instincts, one that might be impossible to close. Then again, if it hadn't been the TETRA, something else might have just as easily brought out the potential rapist lurking inside Derek Kurn. Who was he to say?

Thinking about the fallout from tonight's events gave him an even bigger headache than the one Raina Sanchez had left him with.

9

"WHAT EXACTLY ARE we talking about, boss?" Tye said from behind the wheel.

They were still cruising along the capital beltway. At a certain point, Raina figured, they'd have to turn around, but they seemed safe enough for the time being.

"It's called Project Empyrean," Williamson told them. "The technology they're working to bring online is part of what's known as the TETRA."

"Murnell's boss mentioned that word on the phone," she said. "What is it?"

"Sound's like you've already experienced it—part of it, at any rate. From what I've been able to figure out so far, the TETRA's not like anything anyone's ever seen before. It takes a whole new generation of MAVs and melds them with powerful computer networks and a whole new generation of AI-augmented display technology."

"That sounds like what I saw in the sphere."

A tangle of ideas swirled through her mind, but her thoughts were drawn back to Manny.

What had he been doing on the Rio de la Puerta at that political rally? How could this exotic new technology and what Williamson was telling them have anything to do with her brother? He was clearly injured, at the very least. Had he been kidnapped? Or worse? He was her brother, after all. She loved him despite their differences.

"What else do you know about what happened the day these photos were taken?" she asked.

Williamson shook his head. "Only a little so far. The investigation of Martinez's death is still ongoing. Even after the autopsy, no one's quite sure how it happened. They ruled out a heart attack or other natural cases and no shots were fired."

"But why would anyone shoot Manny?"

"I think he may have seen something certain people didn't want him to see."

"So where is my brother now?"

"The people who provided me with the photos have no idea," he said.

"He could be dead for all you know then."

"It's possible," Williamson admitted. "But I'd take what Ripley said to you as a hopeful sign."

"You think Ripley has Manny?"

"From the sounds of it. Or at the very least he may know where your brother is. Why else would he bait you like he did?"

Raina said nothing. She took in a deep breath and let it out.

Tye spoke again. "What about that guy back by the building yesterday afternoon? Was he with these Empyrean guys? Who took him out like that?"

"That was me," Williamson said. "Sniper drone. The guy on your tail worked for Ripley. Not a good dude, and he would have either taken you out or called in help to do it if I hadn't intervened."

"Can you teach me how to use that sniper drone thing?"

"Yes. All in good time. It isn't as sexy as the TETRA, but sometimes even more effective."

"What else can you tell us about this TETRA technology and Empyrean?" she asked.

Williamson looked at his watch. "Okay," he said. "Why don't I break out the laptop control unit you're about to use, and I'll give you a capsule summary while I'm getting it set up."

They watched and waited as he pulled the laptop and touchpad from their bag along with a case of small MAVs.

"The name TETRA comes from the Greek word representing all four points of the compass," he continued, pausing for a moment to eye the few cars flowing along the beltway around them to make sure they weren't being observed. "The Empyrean project began as an outgrowth of the widespread successful use of early drones like the Predator and Reaper UAVs in Iraq and Afghanistan and elsewhere, and increasingly rapid breakthroughs in drone and micro drone technology. It was supposed to have been discontinued when DARPA funding took a hit in the budget cuts a few years back, but that's when Ripley took it over and brought in the TETRA."

"Who actually invented the TETRA?"

"Unclear. I think it's more of a team effort, but your man Murnell has had a lot to do with it. He has a PhD and his background and research all revolve around flight and artificial intelligence."

"So Ripley is actually in charge of Empyrean?"

"Yes. He's either at the top, or very near the top, and the fact he reached out to you tells me how much they value you."

"But why would they want to recruit me?"

"You tell me. I can think of a lot of reasons, one of which may have something to do with your brother."

"How big is this Empyrean thing?" Tye asked.

"Again, that's somewhat unclear. Empyrean has a lot of tentacles and layers of secrecy," Williamson said. "There are people and elements sprinkled across all different layers of government, from law enforcement to DHS, to the CIA, the NSA, and the military. Even up as far as some members of the chiefs of staff or beyond, from what I can tell."

"We talked about this before," Raina said, "But do the President and his advisors know about Empyrean?"

Williamson shook his head. "It's impossible to say. That's why blowing the whistle, even with proof, might bring the weight of the world down on our heads."

"But I don't get it," Tye said. "What's so great about this technology? What are these people trying to achieve?"

"All I can tell you without being here all night is that Empyrean has far-reaching cultural and societal consequences, arguably beyond that of even the Manhattan Project."

"So you're saying this thing is more powerful than nuclear weapons?"

"In many ways, the answer is yes, but it's different. Empyrean is about intimate surveillance and control, micro-targeted killing. The MAVs and the TETRA are only a means to an end and part of an even bigger picture. You combine them with existing satellite and high altitude piloted reconnaissance aircraft and you have the ability to flood a target, any target, anywhere in the world, with undetected, all-encompassing surveillance, close-up video and audio, and most important, potentially untraceable killing power."

"Wait a minute," Tye said. "You think that's what happened to the politician dude down in Mexico?"

"It's possible. And as the technology advances, the costs and scale of production decrease substantially, to the point where routine, wide spread deployment becomes feasible."

"Sounds like if you knew what you were doing you could control the whole world with this thing," Raina said.

Williamson shrugged. "As I said, like the Manhattan Project. Except this is a 21st century version. Empyrean doesn't require the same massive amount of human resources and raw materials the atom bomb required."

"Which makes it easier to keep secret."

"Exactly."

"How far away is the TETRA from being operational on a large scale?" Raina asked.

Williamson rubbed at the stubble on his chin. "The short answer is I don't know. That's the reason we're here. But one thing I do know for certain is that it's not completely or fully operational yet. "

"How is that?"

"Because I'm still here, living and breathing and talking to the two of you."

"Oh, great," Tye said. "That sounds encouraging." The car swerved a little.

"Just keep your eyes on the road and stay away from the express lanes," Williamson cautioned. "We don't need any more cameras."

"Right. Not that we're probably safe from observation anywhere if what you're telling us is true." He glanced overhead through the windshield as he drove.

"Tye's right. How do we know we're not being tracked?" Raina said. "Those people knew enough to be able to kidnap me from the apartment in Fairfax. And they showed up at the van where I was working when we were trying to get the confession out of Derek Kurn."

"Yes." Williamson nodded. "That was because they were able to track the MAVs you were using. The ones I've given you are early prototypes of what Empyrean has. They emit a signature signal so Empyrean can keep track of them." He held up the small case of MAVs. "But I've reprogrammed these to a different frequency. Have to stay a step ahead of Empyrean. They're not happy they lost them."

"What, you stole these things?"

"More or less. But the important thing is your brother may have been on to something I don't know about. We need to find him so we can find out what that is."

Raina waited. She glanced up at Tye, who seemed to be listening with rapt attention but wasn't asking any more questions for the moment.

"I still don't understand how Nathan Kurn and his son tie into all of this," she said. "We know about what happened with Kurn and his Afghanistan cover up, but what does any of that have to do with Empyrean?"

"Nathan Kurn is connected with Empyrean in other ways. He chairs an industry study group on the use of drone technology for newsgathering and we know he's invested in some of the technology for use by one or more of his media companies. I know he met officially with the leadership of Homeland Security. He most likely knows a lot more than makes some people comfortable, which is most likely the reason the word went out even to members of Congress to go easy on him and look the other way about that battle incident in Afghanistan."

"So the fact that his son was a date rapist was just a means for us to try to get close to Kurn?"

"Yes and no. I suspect there is more than meets the eye with what happened to Derek Kurn."

"That's seems pretty obvious," Tye said. "The guy's dead, and I sure as hell didn't do it."

"There's something more about Derek I didn't tell you," Williamson said. "He was in ROTC."

"Derek Kurn was in ROTC?" Raina could hardly believe her ears.

"That's right. But he only lasted a couple of semesters before dropping out."

"Must have been a stick-a-middle-finger-in-the-old-man's-face sort of thing," Tye said.

"Maybe." Williamson ran a hand along the side of his face and scratched the back of his neck. "But I think there may have been more to it than that."

"Something to do with his father? Or this Empyrean thing?"

"Possibly. That's what I've been hoping you two can help us piece together."

"What else does Nathan Kurn have that Empyrean wants?" Raina asked.

"Money," Williamson said. "Millions, and the ability to raise billions."

"What do you mean?"

"I said before Empyrean doesn't require as much personnel or materials as the Manhattan Project. But one thing it might need even more of is cash. Empyrean needs a mountain of it to keep going. The project doesn't even officially exist. And even as a black op, they can only get so much from government sources. So I think Ripley's gone after outside money."

"Nathan Kurn's become an investor in Empyrean."

"Correct, and he's apparently been bundling it together from others. That's what I've been trying to tell you and why we need to keep the focus on Kurn."

"All of Kurn's money doesn't seem to have kept his son alive," Raina said.

"True."

"Even if the kid was a scumbag like his old man, he didn't deserve to die. Ten to twenty in the state pen would have been more like it. Why would Empyrean want him dead?"

"It's hard to say. But I find it interesting he was about the same age as your brother Manny."

"Why would Nathan Kurn want to put so much money into something like Empyrean?" Tye asked.

"It's pretty simple actually," Williamson said. "You know he already controls a large media empire through his networks, satellites and affiliates, along with several TV stations, newspapers, and radio outlets. Not to mention websites and Internet content."

"So?"

"Ever heard of a company called Oculum?"

"No."

"Not surprising. Most people never have.

Oculum is a tech company begun a few years ago with venture capital out of Silicon Valley and elsewhere to develop and manufacture drone technology for defense and media applications. The company has apparently been making some major leaps forward, but they don't have a lot of revenue to report yet, and unlike most of their fledgling competitors, Oculum has been keeping most of its work completely under wraps. They're completely private."

"Which means less scrutiny of what the company is doing," Raina said. "Okay. So what about them?"

"Nathan Kurn is also a major investor in Oculum. And he is about to make a move to try to take over the company."

"You mean the merger he was talking about when he was talking with Tye?"

"Exactly."

"What's Kurn want with a drone company?"

"Potential audio and video access on an unprecedented scale. If Kurn gains control of Oculum, some in the industry fear he'll have way too much power and exclusive access to drone-acquired information, video, and live news feeds before anybody else. The FTC, not to mention Wall Street and many others, are paying close attention."

"The rich get richer," Tye said under his breath.

"This isn't about riches. It's about power."

"But why are you so focused on Nathan Kurn?" Raina asked. "Why not just go directly after Empyrean?"

"I decided some time ago that trying to expose Empyrean and Jon Ripley directly would be extremely difficult if not impossible. It would only make me and whoever is working with me a giant target. We'd all end up dead, discredited, or in prison.

Kurn and what happened to his son are the best hope we have for bringing all this to light. Nathan Kurn's a softer target. He's not officially employed by the government, and he doesn't maintain nearly as much security."

"But Kurn has lots of connections," she said.

"You bet he does. And not just with Ripley and Empyrean. He may be a softer target, but Nathan Kurn's not someone to be taken lightly. His influence goes high enough that the word came down to lay off him about what happened during the war. But even with all of that, if I had to lay money on it, I'd guess his son was murdered. I'd also bet that whoever did it is linked to Empyrean."

"Which means Kurn must be in a panic over more than just losing his son."

"Exactly," Williamson said. "Which is why we need to get back in that fraternity house tonight to see if we can find anything new about what just happened."

Raina looked again at Tye, who nodded.

The Major reached under the back of the driver's seat and lifted out a duffel bag. He unzipped it and pulled out three sets of gray overalls and hooded baseball caps.

"Here," he said, handing a set to each of them. "Put these on over your regular clothes.

"What are they?" Tye said. "Invisibility cloaks?"

"Close. This clothing is made of a special synthetic material that blocks most of your body heat and makes you much harder to spot in the dark with infrared cameras."

"Perfect," Raina said. "What's next? Magic wands?"

10

THE PARTY WAS long since over and the frat house looked quiet at four a.m. Except for a quartet of police cruisers lining the driveway and a pair of media vans kept at bay down the block.

It seemed surreal that Derek Kurn had died only a few hours before. Raina couldn't help but wonder how much, in deference to Derek's powerful father, was being shielded from public view.

She yawned as she stared into her optical head-mounted display. They'd set themselves up on a hillside street with an unobstructed view of the neighborhood, not that she could see anything except through her screen. Hidden in the back of the SUV wasn't exactly her favorite way to work, but she'd have to make do.

"Com check." She spoke softly into her headset microphone.

"Com is good." Tye's voice came through her earphones. "I have eyes on the target. Launching hover angel."

"Roger that."

With her dragonfly's night vision camera already flown to its rooftop perch, she kept a bird's eye view on the scene while piping the video feed to Williamson, who sat up front in the cab of the SUV watching though his own eyeglasses display.

She peered past her glasses display at the spot down the hill where Tye crouched, hidden within a thick stand of bushes in the dark. Williamson had been right about the clothing. Even with the dragonfly's infrared, if she hadn't known were to look on her screen, she wouldn't have been able tell he was there.

They'd argued over whether to send Tye down the hill at all. But in the end it was decided, if they were able to infiltrate the frat house with the MAV, someone had to be stationed closer to the house in case things went wrong.

"Maybe we should wait and come back later after the cops are gone." Tye sounded wary. He'd no doubt spotted the line of patrol cars.

"And miss your chance for glory? I'm surprised at you," she said.

"Yeah? Well, you try sitting like some peeping tom staring down a bunch of people who'd no doubt be more than happy to slap some handcuffs on you."

"I'm doing that, too, aren't I?"

"Up there safe with your computer."

"You think you're a suspect?"

"People saw me going into his room, didn't they?"

"Good point. They do say criminals often return to the scenes of their crimes."

"Very funny." Tye wasn't laughing.

"What do you think, Major?"

"I don't see a forensics van. Which tells me they're not necessarily considering this a crime scene," he said.

"That's weird."

"Not really. Could be he overdosed, or it was self-inflicted."

"Suicide?"

"Maybe."

For the first time, she felt a sliver of sympathy for Derek Kurn. At least they didn't have to worry about sneaking Tye into the frat this time around. That was all up to her and her minuscule hover angel. All she needed to do was find a way to get inside the house again and take a look around. Those inside would be on high alert this time around.

"Keep a sharp eye out for officers," Williamson cautioned. The last thing any of them needed was an encounter with the cops.

She let the hover angel climb for a couple of minutes, then drove it straight toward the rear of the house.

"I think I see an opening. I'm going under a gap in the doorjamb leading from the back porch."

"Sounds like a plan," Tye said.

"I'll stay low to the floor and try not to get stepped on. Anybody sees me, hopefully all they're going to think is that I'm a mosquito."

"You are so much more than a pest," Tye said.

"I'll take that as compliment."

"Let's cut the chatter, people," Williamson said.

"Right," she said. "All I need is a fraction of an inch."

There followed a long period of silence as she maneuvered the drone beneath the back door and onto a checkered linoleum floor. She was in the kitchen. So far so good.

No sign of anyone in the house, either. Not yet, anyway.

She buzzed the angel along the overhang of a line of under-counter kitchen cabinets, looking for anything out of the ordinary. When she turned the camera to peer out, there wasn't much to see. A few empty beer bottles lined the counter opposite along with dishes and scatterings of unfinished food. Dirty dishes were piled high in the sink.

It looked like exactly what you'd expect of the aftermath of a big party. She came to the end of the counter and rounded a door jam. Just down the hallway stood two uniformed police officers. They were talking with a couple of male students, although she couldn't make out what they were saying.

"Not good," she whispered. "Can't go that way."

"Looks like there's a closed door to your left with a gap at the bottom," Williamson said.

"I see it. Probably just a closet."

"Maybe," he said. "But let's take a look, anyway."

She did as the major suggested and flew the MAV under the door. Instantly, her screen was enveloped in darkness.

"Switching to infrared."

As soon as the camera changed, the shadowy green outlines of the interior of a small space came into focus. Shelves overflowed with a hodgepodge of cereal boxes and other foodstuffs. A mop had been propped next to a cleaning bucket in one corner.

"Nothing," she said. "Just storage."

"Right."

Switching the camera view back to normal vision, she spun the MAV around and flew back under the door. She hovered in place for a minute, turning to take in the entire room, searching for another way past the hallway where the cops blocked the way.

Something caught her eye on the far wall across the floor: another door. She pushed the MAV forward, speeding low and silent across the kitchen.

"Going to check this door out, too."

"Roger that," Williamson said.

"I see a light switch on the wall next to the doorframe. Looks like it's been flipped to the ON position."

"Sounds more promising than the closet."

It was more promising.

As she flew under the door, Raina found herself with a view of a lighted stairwell going down.

"Basement," Williamson said.

"Sure looks like it."

She angled the MAV down and descended the stairs. Almost as soon as she did, she began to pick up a faint sound. A voice—someone was speaking below.

"Got more people here."

"I hear that," Williamson said. "Can you tell who it is?"

She tried to listen more closely. "Not yet. Let me get a little closer."

She moved the drone deeper into the basement.

"Careful," he cautioned.

She continued slowly down. The exposed underside beams of the old house soon came into view, as did an open area that appeared to be used mostly for storage. There was no sign of anyone.

But behind her position to the left, a newer, concrete wall appeared to have been added to the old, subterranean floor. It had a metal door that hung slightly ajar.

The voice was coming from beyond the door.

Raina brought the MAV to a halt. "Hold up. I think I recognize who's speaking."

"Me, too."

"It's Nathan Kurn."

"Yes, indeed."

"Great," Tye, who couldn't see or hear what they were watching, interjected under his breath.

"What's he doing down here?" Raina wondered aloud.

They listened for a while longer.

"Sounds like a one way conversation," she said.

"He must be on the phone," Williamson said. "See if you can get any closer."

She moved the MAV up to the crack in the door, keeping

it low to the ground. All at once, Kurn's voice came into clear range.

"But this is my son we're talking about." The man seemed to be choking back tears. "Don't tell me you don't know what happened to him."

Kurn fell silent as he listened to whomever he was talking to on the other end of the phone. Raina was thinking she'd love to get closer, but she didn't dare go too far. Then Kurn said: "I don't care about national security. I want to know why my son is dead."

She nudged the MAV further through the crack in the door to see what was happening.

As the room came into view, she was surprised to see Kurn, dressed in a dark business suit, seated in front of a bank of computer screens. She counted several screens, in fact, all dark. On a console in front of Kurn were scattered multiple different joysticks, hand pieces, and various types of video display goggles.

What was this place?

"Looks like some kind of control room," Williamson said.

"It might be for gaming," she speculated. "Look at some of the boxes."

Sure enough, several boxes and DVDs for popular video games were stacked along the base of the screens. Kurn was still sitting and listening to the phone pressed to his ear.

"So some of the guys in the fraternity are video game junkies. Not much of a shocker there," Tye said. "Kurn's kid must have had an unlimited budget."

"Could be. But this looks like more than a high tech gamer's setup," Williamson said.

Kurn picked up one of the controllers, a handheld device the likes of which Raina had never seen before—not that she was any kind of expert. They listened as he spoke into the phone again.

"No, I don't know what's going to happen with the board vote. Look, my son is dead. This was my only son…do you understand what I'm trying to say?…." He paused to brush back a tear from the side of his face. "Your 'sorrys' just aren't going to cut it anymore."

Kurn fell silent again, listening.

Raina stared into her optical display, trying to make sense of the scene. There was something about the room that reminded her of Murnell's sphere. She flexed her shoulders to ease the tension. Maybe it was just her imagination.

Kurn leaned forward in his chair. "That's it," he said. "This thing either performs or it doesn't. Do you know how much money I have at stake here? I can't go into any more of this right now. My son is dead and the police are here waiting to talk with me again."

The man jabbed a finger on his phone screen and ended the conversation. He looked up for a moment, staring into the bank of screens on the wall. Then he shoved the phone in his suit coat pocket and rose from his chair.

Before Raina could react, he was striding toward the door. What if he caught a glimpse of the angel and realized someone had been eavesdropping?

Her first instinct was to move, but then she realized that might draw Kurn's attention to her tiny drone. She held at hover as Kurn's dark polished shoes grew ever larger in her view.

Right up until the moment the feed was lost and the image went blank.

11

I T TOOK BARELY five minutes for the Seahawk, which had switched to quiet rotors, to cover the ten or so miles to Murnell's lab.

Murnell didn't need to be told what awaited him: a severely pissed-off Ripley. And more questions about what was needed to overcome the problems with the TETRA. They were questions he was in no condition at the moment to fully address.

No doubt Ripley was still dealing with the fallout from his screw-up. That was how the old spymaster would choose to label it, no doubt.

But how else could it be described? Even leaving aside what had happened with Derek Kurn, other personnel on the ground, good agents, had died tonight. To top it off, a mini firefight had erupted not that far from a major military installation.

Murnell was the one responsible for setting in motion the whole chain of events. He'd abducted Sanchez again and brought her into the trailer, parked where it was to conduct some testing in close proximity to Bolling and some of the base's electronic resources. Why had he done it? To prove something to Sanchez? Then, to top it off, he'd let her get away.

Empyrean's operations people had been tracking her since

she'd left his lab. He knew she was involved with people who might be targeting Kurn and going after his son to expose them. Murnell could have tried to head things off sooner, but he'd waited, and in the end he'd simply acted on impulse.

From the moment he read her file, Chief Warrant Officer Raina Sanchez had been near the top of his draft list. The fact that she looked like a knockout hadn't hurt either. Had he allowed his attraction for her to cloud his judgment? Maybe.

Come on, Murnell, aren't you getting a little too old to let your balls do the thinking instead of your head?

He'd misjudged Sanchez and the miscalculation was bound to be costly—not just in dollars and cents. They had to find a way to clean up the Kurn mess and get her back or deal with the consequences.

He consoled himself he was still integral to the project. He'd designed most of the interfaces for the gem of a cockpit and virtual extension world to which he'd introduced Raina Sanchez. There was much more to the TETRA than what Murnell had shown Sanchez, of course. A fact she would come to learn soon enough, one way or the other.

In the meantime, appeasing Ripley was his most immediate problem.

The chopper touched down on an empty helipad surrounded by dark woods. While it might have been wilderness, they were still barely a twenty-minute car ride from Capitol Hill. Hiding in plain sight, as Ripley liked to say.

Glassmanor, an abandoned federal psychiatric facility, had proven the perfect cover for Murnell's work. More than a mile and a half from the main highway, thick woods shielded the grounds of the old hospital. All that remained above ground were the boarded up shells and remnants of buildings that made up the old psychiatric hospital, some dating back to before the

Civil War. What kind of ghosts, Murnell sometimes wondered, stalked their walls?

From the outside, the only hint of what lay below and in the bowels of some of the old buildings were the presence of armed DHS security guards at the front and back gates, who themselves had no idea what they were really guarding.

No sooner had the chopper's wheels touched pavement than a trio of dark-colored, electric-powered ATVs, bristling with equipment and soldiers carrying automatic weapons, appeared like ghostly apparitions themselves from different directions.

These were no mere sentries. Their dark green camouflage-painted faces under floppy hats and camo uniforms emblazoned with both the American flag and the history-rich "Don't Tread On Me" insignia marked them as Navy Seals. An officer in command of the small detachment stepped from the nearest of the ATVs and greeted Murnell with a handshake. No salute this time.

They waited for a moment for the chopper to clear the trees, its stealth departure accomplished as quietly and efficiently as its arrival.

"Need a retinal scan and a DNA swab," the officer said.

"Wouldn't dare try to get into this party without it."

Murnell cracked a smile, but the officer didn't seem to be in a joking mood. Maybe word of his screw-up and the events over at Bolling had already rippled through the ranks. He wondered how much this guy knew or didn't know, but of course protocol demanded he keep such a curiosity to himself.

Entering the byzantine, surreal world of the Project Empyrean facility wasn't exactly like leaving planet Earth, although some had compared it to such an experience. Most often, those few who had dedicated their professional and personal lives to toil within its ultra secret confines compared it to working at Los Alamos during World War II. Nowadays, you could accomplish so much more with far fewer personnel. The people, it seemed, were becoming secondary to the machines.

With his biological crosschecks completed, Murnell hopped into the empty front seat of the ATV next to the officer, and they roared off into the dark. As usual, he could barely see where they were going. The headlights from the ATVs had been shrouded to the point of being virtually useless and he noticed the Spec Ops soldiers behind the wheel of each vehicle were utilizing night vision goggles to drive.

Nothing like barreling silently at thirty miles an hour into darkness. A bit like some of the things his MAV pilots had to face.

A couple of bone-jarring minutes later, they arrived outside the old main hospital building. A small swarm of MAVs appeared, as if from nowhere in the dim light, and Murnell remembered that they'd probably been tracking them from the moment he'd left the chopper. The facial characteristics and identities, even the breathing patterns, of Murnell and each of the soldiers, had already been thoroughly vetted and analyzed.

These new MAVs were virtually invisible, especially in darkness or low light. Still, Murnell, who knew what to look for, could sense a number of them about him now—their miniscule traces spinning like imperceptible dust mites in a scatter-and-protect formation. These MAVs were still experimental, not quite as stealthy as some others; but they had the ability to patrol autonomously and were put to good use here at Glassmanor.

"End of the line, sir," the officer in command of the Seals told him.

"Right." Murnell must have been lost in thought. He scrambled out of the ATV.

These guys weren't too big on chitchat. The scientist in him wondered if there was some kind of brain wave pattern analysis or psychological testing that could predict what kind of candidates might make it through the hyper-rigorous elimination process used to pick Navy Seals. The government could save a lot of time and money if there were.

But the non-scientist side of him hoped there never would be. Murnell had sold his soul to science. These Seals, he knew, had sold out their own to an ideal and a code, one he couldn't help but admire. Even if he sometimes wondered what they might think if they understood the full extent of the type of work he'd undertaken.

Without another word from the officer, the three ATVs spun U-turns and sped off into the night.

No sooner had they disappeared than a portion of the old hospital exterior wall began to slide open, revealing a door about the size of a small truck. Just inside the opening stood a pair of soldiers, dressed in the fatigues and black berets of the USAF Special Forces. Next to them was Jonathan Ripley.

"Welcome back, Dr. Murnell. Glad to see you're still in one piece."

Welcome, my ass.

Ripley looked anything but pleased.

12

THE VACANT ROOM was on the first floor of a popular chain hotel. It was designed for someone in a wheelchair and had a back entrance that opened to a small handicapped lot protected by bushes.

Williamson told them the manager was an old friend. He'd arranged for them to use the room to regroup while they made arrangements to travel someplace more secure. Outside, the sun would be coming up soon. They needed to be on the move again before dawn.

The three of them sat across from one another at the unit's small kitchenette table. Raina sipped at a warm cup of coffee. Despite the fact the night had cooled, they were all soaked in sweat. None of them had said much in the rush to get away from the frat house after losing the angel. They hoped Nathan Kurn had stepped on the MAV, crushing it inadvertently, without ever realizing it had been there.

"So that was pretty wild back there with Kurn," Tye said.

Williamson shrugged. "Could have been worse. I don't think we were spotted."

Raina pulled her short hair together behind her head. "So you still think Kurn was talking to Ripley?"

"Either Ripley or someone working with him. And if I'm right, then what happened to Derek Kurn was definitely no accident, no matter what his father may have just been told on the phone."

"Kurn said he had a lot of money at risk."

"That he did."

"All I know is that was some kind of game room those frat boys had back there," Tye said.

"Maybe it was more than a game room," Raina said. "Maybe he was training or something."

"What? You mean like we've been doing? You think the Kurn kid was messing with MAVs or something, too?"

"Could be."

"Derek Kurn was probably just relaxing and playing Halo games against guys in Japan or Germany like a lot of college guys with too much time on their hands. Not everything has to do with drones, you know."

"Maybe," she said.

She looked at Williamson. She could tell he was still considering what she'd said.

"Why'd you quit working with this Ripley character?" she asked.

Williamson finished his last sip of coffee and set his cup back down on the table. "Let's just say...it didn't end well. We worked together in Iraq and Kuwait after 9/11. During the early days of the War on Terror we started building the first crude prototypes for what would become Project Empyrean. That was long before things were consolidated years later here in the states."

"So you left Ripley on bad terms?"

"Yes."

"What, you have some kind of personnel vendetta against the guy?"

"You might say that. You might also say I'm trying to get to the bottom of something much bigger than just Jonathan Ripley."

She thought of her time in the sphere, the street in Beijing and the village in Afghanistan with Murnell demanding she kill the abusive Pashtun.

Williamson went on. "What I know of Ripley tells me there is a lot more going on with Project Empyrean these days than anyone is aware of. People have died, like that politician in Mexico. Others have disappeared, like your brother. I'm betting major problems have developed with whatever Ripley may have up his sleeve. Not that they would be admitted to, even if those in the chain of command knew about them."

"How many people overall know about what Ripley's doing?"

"Not many." Williamson glanced across the room at a clock on the wall before looking back at Raina. "A good number may know bits and pieces. As to the whole picture, I doubt that it may go much beyond Ripley himself. That would be his M.O. That's how he's managed to survive for so long."

"So what are you saying? He's gone rogue? Not just doing his part for Uncle Sam anymore?"

Williamson smiled. "I'm not sure Jon Ripley's ever been just about doing his part for Uncle Sam. Although that's a really effective excuse when he needs it."

"You think whatever happened to Manny down in Mexico may have something to do with all this, too?"

"Yes, I do. Let me ask you a question. Did they want you to kill someone when you were flying inside that sphere?"

"How do you know to ask that?"

"Because I'm convinced that's what happened to the politician down in Mexico. I think it was practice. The man was an expendable target. While posing as a reformer, he was actually in bed with the cartels. Everybody in the intelligence community knew it."

"So Manny may have known it, too," she said.

"Probably. If he had any good sources."

"So maybe the Mexican guy deserved what he got," Tye said.

"Whether he did or not, Raina's little brother and his girlfriend may have evidence of an assassination."

"What evidence?" Raina said.

"Some of the close-up digital photos he was taking."

"Where are they now?"

"I don't know. That's part of what we need to find out."

"So now you want me to help you because you know I want to find my brother."

Williamson stared at her. "I'm sorry, Raina," he said. "I know it doesn't seem fair."

She looked at both men, considering the ramifications.

"I have another question," she said.

"Name it."

"How did you know about the rape with Kurn's son?"

"Easy. I got a tip. The Air Force Two Star whom Kurn first contacted privately about his son is an old friend of mine. The general was upset when he learned of the rape, of course, but Kurn also told him he had some kind of involvement with Jon Ripley and Empyrean. The general knew I used to work with Ripley and that I was concerned about what Ripley had been up to these past couple of years, so he got in touch with me.

After that, it was simply a matter of putting the pieces together. The general said he'd serve as a reference for whoever I sent in, which turned out to be you two."

"So we are all going to report back in to this anonymous two-star general?"

"No. Not right now. He's out of it. He said he has his own concerns over Ripley and what he might be up to, but he can't make any moves right now due to politics. Both Homeland Security and the Air Force are starved for money in the current climate."

"So he wouldn't care if Nathan Kurn were cozying up to Ripley and that they might have developed some sort of financial entanglement?"

"Sure he'd care. There are pretty strict rules about government programs and private contractors. But my guy says he's not in a position to try to stir up a hornet's nest right now. And remember, Ripley's not military. He's beyond military."

"Which means he probably knows where all the bodies are buried," Tye said.

"Something like that."

"Great. Maybe he knows where Jimmy Hoffa is, too."

"So tell me something else..." Raina kept her focus on Williamson. "Why'd Kurn reach out to this general friend of yours in the first place?"

The major offered another shrug. "The general said Kurn told him it was because of his advocacy and involvement with the issue of soldiers suffering from PTSD."

PTSD.

Raina bristled at the term. She knew she probably suffered from it, but she hated putting any kind of a label on how she felt.

"What does PTSD have to do with Derek Kurn raping a coed?" she asked.

"I don't really know just yet if it has anything to do with it."

"You said Derek was ROTC."

"Yes."

"But he washed out, right?"

"That's correct."

"Did something traumatic happen to him during ROTC?"

"I talked to the head of his program at the university. According to him, nothing happened to Derek Kurn during ROTC that doesn't happen to thousands of others. The kid just washed out, he said. Told everybody the Air Force and the military weren't for him."

"He was Air Force ROTC?"

"That's right."

Raina thought for a moment. "So then Derek Kurn ends up raping a coed, and his old man wants to blame the brief time Derek was signed up with the military," she said.

"Something like that," Williamson said.

"I don't buy it," Raina said.

"Me either. Which is another reason I've been leaning hard after Nathan Kurn besides the fact he's a lot easier to get to than Ripley. There's a big connection missing. Kurn wouldn't tell the general how he found out about the rape his son had committed."

"Yeah," Tye said. "He played dodge ball on that point with me, too."

"So we think Kurn's been investing big money in Empyrean," Raina said. She needed some sleep and more time to think things through.

"That's right," Williamson said. "Not everyone inside Empyrean is on board with everything that's going on there. Stuff leaks out."

"So where is this top secret project headquartered? They must have some kind of clandestine lab or something."

"You would think so, wouldn't you?" Williamson said.

"What do you mean?"

"I still haven't been able to pin down where it is."

"You mean after all this time you're still not even sure about their base of operations?"

"I have my suspicions. And hopefully, thanks to you, we'll soon have a much better idea exactly where it is."

"Thanks to me? What are you talking about?"

"In that little firestorm we created near Bolling, your friend Mr. Palmer here was able to slip in close and fire a sticky gun loaded with a microscopic tracker. He put it right on the mark attached to that trailer they had you in."

"But they'll be sweeping it for bugs and anything else after what happened."

"Sure they will. But they won't find this one. I designed and built it myself. In fact, I'm hoping we might be able to deliver ones just like it with some of our modified MAVs. You two will be training on doing just that over the next day or two."

"Has there been any movement on the tracker?"

"Not yet. But I don't think they'll leave that trailer in the parking lot any longer than they have to. I expect it to be moving today."

"How do you hide a big lab and base of operations along the lines of what you've been talking about with Empyrean?"

"Good question." He and Raina stared at one another.

"I was there, wasn't I?" she said. "With the sphere and everything. When those guys first drugged me and took me in."

Williamson crossed his arms. "So it appears."

"I went back another time, you know. On my own."

"I wondered if you did."

"They didn't drug me, but they hooded me and drove me in a car."

"For how long?"

"Not that long. It couldn't have been more than half an hour from the apartment in Fairfax."

"Interesting. Which means we're still talking about somewhere in the greater D.C. area. Not an easy place to hide something as big as Empyrean, but it' also in line with my suspicions."

"And what are those suspicions, Major?" Tye asked.

Williamson smiled. "That's all they are—suspicions, people. At least for the time being. Let's see if our little tracker helps turn them into truth."

13

"HEY. IT'S GOING to be okay," Raina said.

Tye didn't answer. She was worried about him. Williamson had left the room, saying he'd be back in a few minutes, when they'd be shoving off again for who knew where. It was the first time she'd had a chance to be alone with Tye since everything had happened and instead of confiding in her he'd clamped up tighter than a drum. His brow curled together to form a deep crease in the center of his forehead. Dark shadows half-mooned below his eyes. In any kind of gunfight she would stack him up against anyone, but all bets were off if he was incapacitated by lack of sleep.

"When was the last time you caught some shut-eye?"

He held up hands in a half shrug. "Can't remember," he said, his gaze still on her. She could tell his mind was elsewhere.

They were a long way from where they started, a long way from Afghanistan.

"C'mon," she said. "Talk to me."

He pursed his lips and turned his head, stretching his neck. "This whole thing sucks, you know? First, I find out you were bugging out on me without even saying anything to me about going off to fly some new crazy ass drones. Then, we didn't even know if you were going to make it out of that trailer alive."

So there it was—finally out in the open. He cared for her and he was hurt.

"I'm sorry," she said. "I should have told you back when they first took me."

"Yes," he said. "You should have."

"But how'd you find out where I was after they got me from the van?"

"I went back to the alley where you were supposed to be. I saw them load you into a vehicle and drive off. Didn't exactly look like you were going voluntarily, so I had to do something. And, like I said earlier, I managed to commandeer their other car and Williamson helped do the rest."

"That's when people died then. Back in the alley."

"Yes. I had to get the car. There wasn't any other way."

"You still trust him? Williamson, I mean."

"I think so."

"I'm not so sure."

"He helped pull your butt out of there when the shit was flying, didn't he?"

"True."

"And even if only half of what he says about this whole Empyrean thing is true, then I, for one, want to try to help get to the bottom of it."

"Not to mention get my brother back."

"Speaking of which, why didn't you ever say anything about him before this?"

She sighed. What could she say? "He hates us."

"What do you mean, he hates us?"

"He hates U.S. soldiers. Thinks we're all a bunch of criminals."

"Oh. One of those types, huh."

"Yes. One of those types."

"But you're his big sister, right? I mean—that has to count for something."

Raina ran a finger through her hair. "I don't know. It just seems like…well, I'm not really sure we can be completely certain anybody is who they say they are anymore, or at least what their agenda is."

"Well, all I know is we've got to pick a side to be on, and this one is ours."

"And if it turns out to be the wrong side?"

"Then as soon as we find out, we're gone."

"Mmmm…I suppose…" she said.

"You look tired, too."

"Huh. Wouldn't you be? After getting drugged, kidnapped, shot at, kidnapped again, and oh, by the way, trained on some kind of sci-fi, enemy-of-the-state wacko machine by some Brad Pitt-looking PhD all in the space of forty eight hours."

"Don't forget seduced. You did suggest the guy tried to seduce you," he said with a smile.

"Shut up, Mr. Hero."

She wanted to slap him, but it was good to see he was still able to joke. She looked down at the floor. She still felt ashamed for not sharing everything with him sooner about Murnell and Homeland Security.

"I really want to apologize to you again," she said. "I mean, for not being totally straight with you."

He waved a hand at her.

"Forget it," he said.

He stood up and before she could move, leaned across the table, and kissed her on the forehead. Then he pulled back.

She was too surprised to speak.

"What else have we got besides each other?" he said.

14

"Y OU'RE LOOKING A little peaked, wouldn't you say, Captain Murnell?"

A hundred feet below the surface in a well-appointed office within the Empyrean complex, Murnell turned to face Jon Ripley. They hadn't talked much in the elevator on the way down. No doubt his boss had been saving any tirade until now.

For the most part, Ripley managed to inspire equal parts fear and respect among those within his circle. In contrast to the soldiers, he was dressed in a stylish mock turtleneck and gaberdine trousers. Even in the chilly depths of a top-secret homeland security lab, Ripley looked every bit the part of the high level international operator he was, the definition of an old hand.

Murnell felt ill, but he didn't think it was anything physical. A creeping anxiety seemed to have invaded his spirit, and facing Ripley wasn't helping matters. He'd felt fine on the chopper, but as soon as they'd descended into Empyrean, the anxiety returned. Dressed in the same kind of civilian clothes he normally wore these days—blue jeans with a collared shirt and a dark blue traveling jacket—he couldn't even remember the last time he'd donned his Air Force uniform.

"No one's called me captain in quite some time."

"You don't mind, do you?"

"Not really."

"The U.S. taxpayer helped fund a big portion of your education, after all."

The older man was one to talk. Whatever the sources of Ripley's apparently considerable power and private fortune, Murnell had no doubt that both had been obtained as a result of the man's affiliation with various governments, including his own. He also felt certain, without even asking, that looking for Ripley's name within any kind of budget or government accountability report would be a waste of time.

Ripley appraised him for a moment, perhaps expecting him to respond. Murnell said nothing.

"So now we have another problem. With this Sanchez woman."

"Yes, sir."

"Quite a stunner, isn't she?"

He shrugged and nodded.

"For a gimpy chopper pilot, I mean…You like classical music?"

By now, Murnell was used to Ripley's sometimes abrupt redirections.

"Sorry." He shook his head. "Not my cup of tea."

"Pity. I prefer it over almost any other type of music. Even jazz. The variations and modulations help me focus."

Murnell stayed quiet. He was always struck by the transcendental quality of his boss's demeanor, the calmness of his eyes and the steadiness of his movements.

Ripley produced a small remote control from somewhere and pressed a button on the keypad. A few seconds later, the sounds of orchestral music drifted softly through the room. Ripley closed his eyes for a moment, his hand sweeping the air, conductor-like.

"I talked to her, you know," Ripley said.

"Who? Sanchez?"

"Yes. On the phone. Right after she escaped. She failed to dispose of the phone you gave her, at least until I called."

"Did you track where she went?"

"For a little while."

"What did she say to you?"

"I believe she was freaked out by what she saw of the TETRA."

"Can't say as I blame her. Do you?"

"No, Dr. Murnell." Ripley opened his eyes, suddenly back to business. He turned his gaze back on Murnell. "I blame you. For failing to adequately prepare her."

Murnell started to speak but stopped himself. What could he say in his defense? Nothing that made any sense.

"Tell me more about her skills as a pilot," Ripley said.

"She's good," Murnell admitted. No sense denying the fact.

"How good?"

"Among the best pilots I've seen. Maybe the best. Even learning a new control interface. She's a natural when it comes to flying drones."

"A natural, huh? You think it's because of her previous flying experience?"

"Not really," he said. "We've had F-16 pilots experienced in night landings on the rolling deck of an aircraft carrier in high seas who haven't performed as well."

"It might be worth it then."

"What's that, sir?"

"Doing whatever we have to do to bring her back into the fold. We already know what she wants."

"To find her brother."

"Precisely."

Murnell rubbed a hand across the back of his neck. He badly needed some rest.

"Let's both sit down, Captain. You're making me nervous."

Ripley gestured toward a small grouping of rich-looking club chairs in the center of the room.

He hadn't even realized he was still standing, but now that he did he also noticed he'd been tapping one toe, a nervous tic leftover from a fidgety childhood.

"Sorry," he said.

Ripley's office suite, the intellectual and visionary nerve center of the complex, may not have been as gee-whiz, high-tech impressive as the rest of the vast underground MAV proving ground, but you knew when you sat in one of Ripley's chairs you were as close as you could get to the seat of true power—maybe even closer than the Oval Office.

Murnell followed Empyrean's secretive director to the grouping of chairs and sat in one across from him.

Ripley leaned forward with his hands spread across the tops of his thighs. "What is the critical path here?"

"The first priority is the Kurn situation."

"I agree. What have you done to contain the problem?"

"A clean termination. Our MAV was able to exit the area undetected."

"What about removing the implant?"

"Not possible, under the circumstances. The house was filled with other undergrads and Kurn's father was moments away from entering the premises, not to mention the small wound the arthroscopic extraction would leave in his skull."

"Autopsy?"

"No doubt the cops will want one and Kurn Senior will demand they perform it."

"Find out who's doing it and if we can get to them."

"I've already started the wheels in motion."

"Good. We knew this young man had become a problem for us. You should have eliminated him earlier when you had the chance."

"But his father—"

"His father be damned. You let me deal with Nathan Kurn. This mess with our drone operators needs to be contained."

Murnell swallowed hard. "But that hasn't been our approach. We agreed we have to deal with the training pilots who experienced symptoms on a case-by-case basis."

Ripley paused, pursing his lips. "Maybe it's time we reassessed that approach," he said. "Before things really get out of hand. You and I have talked about this. Our mission is going to have major ramifications, not just for our own country, but for all of civilization. Would you rather someone else be waging this battle? We you rather we be having this conversation with the People's Liberation Army maybe, or the gangsters in the Kremlin?"

"No." It was hard to argue with his boss when the old man got going.

"I admit, it's unfortunate there have to be casualties. But we have to be able to judge the difference between acceptable and unacceptable losses. If the full story of our efforts goes public and we get shut down, then what? Before we have a chance to fully develop defenses and countermeasures our own creations will be stolen and turned against us. Count on it. Not a single one of our leaders will be safe, to say nothing of the rest of us."

"But the problems—"

"The problems are being addressed, aren't they?"

"Yes, sir. They are, but—"

"Do you think the people who fought World War II and built nuclear weapons weren't without their problems? You think they didn't lose some personnel as well?"

"No, sir."

"Well, that's the kind of situation we're dealing with here. We've got a world spinning out of control. Anyone with vision can see that. Things are going from bad to worse, especially overseas, and we've got a real chance to get out ahead of the curve here with our technology. And if we're not careful, it may be the last chance we get. Do you understand what I'm saying?"

Murnell nodded.

"Now, where are we with Williamson?"

Murnell winced. "Nowhere at the moment. He's slipped away. Major Williamson and his friends are a big pain in our ass. He managed to recruit Sanchez and he's brought in some muscle with this guy Palmer."

"Palmer's the one who just took out a couple of our people."

"Yes, sir. We can get them all branded as terrorists."

"No. That won't work. It would only call attention to us. Speaking of which, I've just been on the phone with Kurn trying to clean up the media side of the mess you made up at Bolling. What were you thinking bringing one of our trailers up there?"

"I thought it'd be a good place to do some training, to give Sanchez some more experience."

"Well, you thought wrong. Where are the trailer and the sphere now?"

"I've been in touch with operations. It's being assessed for damage and any kind of infiltration. We'll tow it back here as soon as possible. Unfortunately, Williamson hit us pretty hard."

"Yes. Well, he would know what to shoot at, wouldn't he? Remember, Captain, this is not some gee-whiz laboratory experiment we're running here. You should know that better than anyone."

"I do."

"Then we have to do everything we can to protect it until it's fully developed and operational. Not everyone's going to be happy with what we're doing…Back to what's happening with Williamson. It's high time we dealt with him more severely. He knows way too much about Empyrean."

"But, sir, he's—"

"I know who he is. He's got a lot of old friends in the agency and elsewhere, but so do I. Since Sanchez got the jump on you, we have to assume she's joining back up with Williamson and Palmer."

"I wouldn't be so fast to make that assumption, sir."

"What makes you say that?"

"I think she fell in love with our technology and it's capabilities."

"Good. The flying part, you mean."

"Yes."

"It is somewhat addicting, isn't it?"

"It can be."

"Do you think Sanchez suspects she's walking around with an implant?"

"I don't think so. Not yet."

"Good. Then that's an edge we may be able to use to bring her back on board. I only wish we could track her whereabouts."

"That won't work."

"I know, I know. You think she'll reach out to you again?"

"I think she might," Murnell said, although a big part of him wondered if she ever would after what happened in the trailer.

"Let's hope she does, Captain. For all of our sakes," Ripley said. "Otherwise, we have to move her to the top of the kill list along with Williamson and Palmer. She can't be that great a pilot. Just like she's not the only beautiful woman on the planet, she's not the only good flyer in the world."

15

"W E'LL HEAD FOR the woods."
Williamson's demeanor seemed to change as soon as their small passenger jet touched down. It had been a short flight from the private airfield in College Park. The jet was taxiing along the deserted runway of the tiny, rural airstrip.

They'd hitched an undocumented ride under the anonymous cover of a privately-registered tail number courtesy of yet another of Williamson's friends. Outside, it was still mostly dark, though the sky above the surrounding mountains had begun to brighten.

"Keep your heads down, and make sure you keep those Mylar hats on I gave you. Our landing might have been observed on satellite. Get ready to move down the stairs just as soon as they drop them for us. The pilot's going to keep moving, pausing just long enough for us to jump out before moving on to the hanger to pick up fuel."

"Who's flying this thing?" Raina asked.

"A couple of former Air Force pilots I know. It's better for them and for all of us if we keep them out of all this."

She nodded. To anyone who might be keeping a tab on the area through overhead imaging, this would look like just a routine refueling stop. If they kept their profiles low, their presence on the runway would go undetected and the cover of the woods would supply the rest.

Raina felt for the holstered .45 she'd been given. Not that Williamson was expecting any trouble. Tye also carted an M4 and had geared up with a full Army Ranger load just in case.

She felt the plane begin to turn and lurch to a stop. Williamson pulled the safety lever and the pilots did the rest, dropping the stairway door.

"Time to go, people!"

Seconds later, she was on the tarmac following Williamson with Tye right behind. Cold air enveloped them. The jet angled away, its stairs retracting.

Tall trees, their outlines becoming visible against the brightening sky, surrounded the airstrip. The drop in temperature change felt like a punch to the stomach after the warmth of D.C, and Raina was glad she'd changed into a jacket and jeans. She'd also switched to a blade prosthesis for her foot she'd retrieved from the closet at the safe house.

Tired or not, she wasn't about to be slowed down.

Ahead of them loomed a thick grove of tall pines. They left the runway, crossed a drainage culvert, and climbed an embankment to bring them under the cover of the trees. They kept moving a couple of hundred yards into the woods, until the airstrip was well out of sight.

Williamson held up his hand for them to stop.

"I think we're good. Everybody okay?"

She and Tye nodded. She scanned the area around them. It felt peaceful. She'd always liked the soft quiet of a pine forest floor.

"What now?" she asked.

"Now. We walk."

"Where are we exactly?"

"Looks like Pennsylvania," Tye said.

"Not a bad guess. West Virginia," Williamson said. "This is part of a massive tract that used to belong to a big paper corporation. Company went belly up. Now the bankers are fighting back and forth over it. Not much to see out here, except where we're going. It's about ten clicks from here."

Ten clicks, Raina thought. More than six miles. At least she'd been able to grab a catnap on the plane.

"I'm good to go," she said. "Although leaping tall buildings in a single bound is definitely out."

Williamson smiled. "Don't worry. No buildings out here."

Tye took an exaggerated deep breath. "I don't know about you guys, but I could get used to living in a place like this. A little romantic cabin in the woods, maybe. What do say, Rain?"

"Don't get too excited, lover boy."

They both laughed.

"Which way are we headed?" Tye asked.

"We travel through this forest for a couple of clicks, then up into the hollows between the mountains," Williamson said.

"Sounds good."

"Okay. Let's get a move on then."

They walked for more than an hour. The terrain was steep from time to time, but Williamson seemed to be following some sort of trail that made their hike easier as they wound their way between high ridges. In many places, the shadows formed by the mountains and trees were so deep they might as well have been walking in darkness, though the rising sun was burning off any remaining night fog and clearing the sky overhead.

Lowering their packs, they stopped briefly along the side of the trail to drink from their canteens. They were all sweating again despite the cooler temperature.

"Air still feels cold," Tye said, taking a long pull on his water.

"That's right," Williamson told him. "It's the elevation."

"Roger that. You hear that, Rain? Cool in the summer, too, I bet. See what I'm saying about that cabin?"

She said nothing. But she did let a smile creep across her face at the pleasant distraction.

"All right, people. We need to keep moving," Williamson said. He shouldered his pack, preparing to go.

At that moment, a rumbling buzz, like a giant, low-flying insect split the air.

"Get down!" he hissed.

They scrambled to hunker low among the brush and rocks besides the trail. Raina found herself next to Tye, with him almost on top of her.

The buzzing grew into an aerial engine throb. Not deafening, but certainly loud enough to get their attention. An instant later, a large shadow passed swiftly over top of them, moving on until the engine sound faded over top of a ridge.

"What the hell was that?" Tye asked.

Williamson pulled himself out from beneath the crook of a boulder. "New kind of drone," he said. "The military and DHS have been testing them out up here in the mountains. They're usually higher up, but this one must have been flying nap of the earth."

They all stood and brushed themselves off.

"Looking for us?" Raina asked.

"Let's hope not."

They watched and waited for a minute or two, but heard nothing more.

"All right. Let's get going. We've still got some ground to cover. Be careful of your footing and keep a watchful eye out for snakes."

"Oh, that's comforting," Tye whispered under his breath. "Forget what I said about that cabin."

"Dark mountains and snakes," Raina said. "What's not to like?"

They climbed a long slope until reaching a forested plateau, walking along it for half a mile before descending into a small valley filled with younger-growth trees. Every now and then, they'd encounter a deer, sometimes more than one. Raina always found them beautiful to look at. At one point, they even heard the distant hooting of an owl, no doubt finishing its night of hunting.

She was just beginning to wonder how much longer they were going to have to hike when Williamson held up his hand again, bringing their little column to a halt.

At first glance, nothing looked any different through the woods ahead—just trees and undergrowth, with a few large rocks here and there.

But then a different kind of shape appeared in Raina's line of sight. Unnatural in its regularity and geometric lines, a structure of some kind, built into the side of the mountain, fronted by a small terrace of land.

Mostly underground, apparently, it had been constructed in such a way as to be swallowed up by the ridge and woods. Had they not walked right into it, she might have easily mistaken it for just another rock outcropping, one among the thousands of rocks and boulders deposited in these mountains by some receding glacier eons ago.

"What is this, Jack London's secret lair?" she asked.

"Hardly," Williamson told her.

"Who's Jack London?" Tye teased, grinning.

Raina rolled her eyes. She kicked out with her blade foot, missing the back of his leg on purpose, but not by much.

"I like it," she said. She righted herself and folded an arm across her hip, raising her other hand to her chin. "But I don't know...I think it needs a little something. Who's your decorator, Major?"

"Very funny, guys," Williamson said. "The entrance is down here along the ridge."

16

THE DOOR WAS nearly invisible behind tall weeds and forest undergrowth. They entered through a heavy, reinforced hatchway that opened via a double set of electronic combination locks.

Impressive, Raina thought. You'd either need the code or a good charge of explosives just to get inside.

The entrance opened into a straightforward passage through the soil and rock, reinforced with heavy timbers, concrete, and stone. The place had been built to withstand things—similar to a fallout shelter. Which, apparently, was exactly how Williamson wanted it.

"Expecting to be attacked up here, boss?" Tye asked.

"Not anytime soon, I hope," he said. "But I'd rather be ready if that day comes."

At the end of the short passage, the main rooms of the underground structure were nothing special to look at. A phalanx of outdated entertainment equipment, an old console TV, bookshelves, and other paraphernalia flanked other modest furnishings. In all, the place had the feeling of a comfortable, if not cozy, bunker or wartime headquarters. Anyone who somehow managed to break in here would think it belonged to preppers expecting the end of the world.

Raina let her pack and canteen slip from her shoulders and took off her holster and gun. A wave of weariness washed over her. Her leg was beginning to throb.

"I don't know about you guys, but I wouldn't mind a little more sleep. Where's the bunk room?"

"Down the back passage," Williamson told her. "But how about some food first?"

"Okay," she said, although she wasn't particularly hungry.

She looked at Tye, who nodded in agreement. He was still checking out the space, admiring the handiwork perhaps.

They ate at the modest kitchen table, savoring thawed bread and warm scrambled eggs Williamson produced a few minutes later. The breakfast wasn't half bad. Of course to Raina, who'd eaten nothing in the past 24 hours except what she'd managed to scrounge at the safe house, anything would have tasted good.

Her eyes soon grew heavy with fatigue, however, and she retired down the hallway to the small "guest" room, as Williamson called it, that held a pair of bunk beds across from one another on either wall. There was a small bathroom further down the hall, which she used before sitting on a low wooden stool to remove her blade prosthesis and wipe it down. Then she lay on one of the lower bunks, leaving the light on. She pulled a blanket over her and closed her eyes.

Tye walked in a moment later.

"Sorry. Didn't mean to wake you," he said. "I was going to crawl into the other bunk."

"It's okay. I just lay down."

He set his stuff down on the floor and lowered himself onto the bunk across from her. He lay on his back, with his hands behind his head, staring into the bottom of the bunk above. "You believe this place?" he said. "I'm pretty good at recon, but I'd have a hard time finding it again."

"It won't be on any map, that's for sure. What I'm having

a hard time about is seeing how any of this is going to help me find Manny. And why didn't Williamson tell me about him sooner?"

"You hear what he said. He just got the satellite photos."

"But how did he make the connection Manny was my brother?"

Tye shrugged. "I don't know. But there must be some logical explanation."

"There better be. Because it sounds like you and I have signed up to take on a pack of insiders with a lot of official assets at their disposal."

Tye shrugged. "Well, one thing's for sure. If and when they do come after us, no one's going to be hearing about it on the evening news."

They were silent for a few moments and Raina was about to close her eyes again.

Tye chuckled to himself. "Worse comes to worst, from the way Williamson was talking about this place, wouldn't surprise me if the man's got a few Stinger missiles, maybe even a SAM missile battery packed into this hillside."

"Oh, great." She couldn't help but laugh, too. "He does seem to be on some sort of crusade, that's for sure."

"Remember that movie Conspiracy Theory with…. Who was the actor who played the crazy guy?"

"Mel Gibson," she said.

"Right. Mel Gibson. His character's name was Jerry. Doesn't this all sort of remind you of that story?"

"Maybe. A little," she said, yawning.

"You remember what happened at the end of the story, don't you?"

"Vaguely." She was too tired to think about movies.

"Well, I remember," Tye said. "It turned out Jerry was right in the end."

17

RAINA MUST HAVE slept for three or four hours. She was thirsty when she awoke and her lips were dry and pasty. Tye was snoring softly in the bunk across from her.

The lights were still on in the small room, so she swung her legs out of bed. Careful not to make too much noise, she reattached the blade to the bottom of her leg. Then she pushed up from the bunk and stepped quietly out of the room.

She found Williamson out in the main room of the bunker, wearing reading glasses and doing some work on a field-grade laptop computer.

"How'd you sleep?" he asked without looking up from his screen.

"All right." There was a sink with some glasses on a shelf in the corner. "Is it okay to drink this water?"

"Have all you want. The well goes down six hundred feet, taps into a spring at the base of the ridge."

She went to the sink, filled a glass of water, and drank it. It was cold and tasted clean.

"Can I talk to you about something?" he asked.

"Of course."

"I want to go over more about what I think might have happened down in Mexico."

"Okay."

"Here, come look at my computer screen."

She pulled up a chair and sat next to him.

A minute later they were looking at an even larger sequence of satellite photos taken from the event where Manny had disappeared. There were several closeups of the candidate on the stage from various angles. Then, a series of photos in which the speaker reached up to touch his neck, a look of pain on his face, before collapsing to the ground.

"Not a pretty sight," Raina said.

"No," Williamson said. "Let's zoom in for an even closer look."

He pulled up one of the last series of photos and zoomed into where the politician grabbed at the back of his neck. It was difficult to make out on the grainy image, but from one angle it appeared as if something small and almost ethereal hovered there.

Raina realized at once what might have happened to Manny. "The speaker was assassinated by a MAV."

"That's what I think, too. An undetectable drone."

"Undetectable. I don't like the sounds of that."

"That would explain why no one saw anything and why the cause of Martinez death is still an open question."

"But that doesn't tell us why Manny was taken."

"Well, I've been looking into some things. Empyrean's new MAVs may not be completely undetectable after all."

"What do you mean?"

"They may not be visible to the naked eye most of the time, but there may be other ways of detecting their presence. I think your brother may have uncovered a vulnerability."

"How do you know that?"

"You see the way the victim is clutching at the back of his neck?" He pointed at the screen. "If the MAV was still hovering there at the moment he raised his hand, he may have struck it in such a way to render its stealth technology inoperable. At least for a brief moment and from the right angle."

"And Manny may have seen it."

"Not only seen it. He may have snapped some digital photos of it, too."

"But nothing shows up in the photos we're looking at here."

"Remember, these were taken from miles overhead. Manny's camera would have produced far better pictures."

Raina was beginning to further understand some of the implications of the TETRA sphere and what Murnell had been showing her. Not only did she have far more precise control, the MAVs she'd been flying from the sphere couldn't be seen. No wonder she'd been able to approach the Chinese politburo member on the street in full view of both his family and security detail.

"You mentioned there are other ways of detecting Empyrean's new drones."

"Countermeasures, yes. Highly sensitive motion detectors. Motion microscopes. There are some deployed around this property and out to a perimeter of several hundred yards."

"Do they work?"

"They should. But I haven't exactly been able to conduct laboratory testing to verify that fact."

"So now you're trying to tell me our government is secretly assassinating foreign leaders. You're starting to sound like my little brother."

"Only an element of the government—known to just a few. And it's still experimental, as far as I can tell. But you're the one who has been inside the TETRA. What do you think?"

She didn't know what to think anymore. She wanted to fly again and she wanted to serve her country. Why did it have to be so hard? How had it become so complicated all of a sudden?

"Wait a minute," she said. "If these people have Manny and

they got his camera, why couldn't they just destroy the evidence and get rid of him?"

"I don't think they've been able to do that. Because a friend of mine inside DHS sent men an encrypted message indicating your brother was using a camera tethered to a portable computing device to upload pictures to the cloud. All the photojournalists are using them these days. Which means all of Manny's images may still be out there somewhere."

"You're saying the photos might be stored somewhere on some server."

"Yes. And knowing your brother's background, maybe even protected by encryption. Only Manny would know how to access them. Your little brother may be a lot of things, but he's apparently no dummy when it comes to the Internet."

"What about Lucy, his girlfriend. What's happened to her?"

Williamson shook his head. "I've got nothing on her so far. If she got away, maybe she's gone into hiding."

Raina didn't know Lucy all that well. The one time she'd met her the year before she'd liked her. But it was only a brief encounter at a coffee shop in D.C.

Lucy was from southern California, a Stanford grad, and Raina remembered thinking—as messed up as her brother seemed to be—he must have been doing something right to attract a girl like that.

"Okay," she said. "Thanks for telling me about all this."

"It's still only educated speculation. I can't guarantee anything when it comes to your brother."

"Tell me about it. How did you know he was my brother, by the way?"

Williamson stared at her. "Do you even have to ask? If you know the right people, you can find out almost anything about anybody these days. The company has had a file on Manny for a few years now."

"The CIA?"

"Yes. Manny's spent a fair amount of time overseas, hasn't he?"

It was true. She needed some more rest and time to think. "Yes," she told him. "Thanks again. I'm going back to bed. I'll let you know if I think of anything else that might be helpful."

"I'd appreciate that."

She was turning to go when her gaze came to rest on a small framed photo hanging in a corner of the back wall. It was a picture of a woman and child.

"Is that your family in the photo on the wall?"

Williamson stopped what he was doing and turned to look back at the image with her. "Yes, it is."

"Where are they?" she asked.

He paused for a moment. "They're dead," he said.

"Oh, no," she said. "I'm so sorry."

His face grew softer. "Thank you for saying that. It was quite a few years ago. I wasn't there when it happened."

"Was it some sort of accident?"

He paused, long enough for her to sense his conflict about revealing more.

"You don't have to tell me more if you don't want to," she said.

"Let's just say, it looked very much like an accident," he said.

"What do you mean?"

"All I can tell you is they were killed by mistake along with several others in a coalition airstrike on an apartment complex in an Arab country."

"How did it happen?"

"Supposedly, they were someplace they shouldn't have been. Which wasn't true."

"Was that why you left the CIA?"

"Partly," he said. "But there's something even more important I haven't told you."

"What's that?"

They stared at one another for a moment. "The airstrike was ordered by Jonathan Ripley," he said.

18

"BACK TO WORK today?"

One of his lab assistants greeted Murnell in the hall as he left the secure entrance to Ripley's office suite. Murnell was coming from yet another meeting with his boss.

"Not if I can help it."

The assistant looked at his face. "I heard you got a shiner."

"You should see the other guy."

The man chuckled and headed off in the opposite direction.

At least Murnell was back on familiar ground. It had been a mistake to take one of the trailers off site before they were fully ready to go operational. A mistake he wouldn't make again. He felt a renewed surge of confidence being back in his lab.

The underground complex beneath D.C. wasn't overly large. But what it lacked in size it more than made up for in sophistication and high tech wizardry. Underground, Empyrean essentially amounted to an extensive augmented reality testing ground, where pilots could fly invisible drones in dozens of simulated scenarios and a select number of real outside situations and environments. But it was the pilots themselves who were really being tested. It was their responses to each and every flying situation that were methodically being recorded and added to Empyrean's vast AI database.

But most exciting of all, the information exchange had become a two-way street. The more the pilots experienced the TETRA, the faster and better their responses became. And the more the supercomputers interacted with the pilots, the stronger the TETRA itself grew. It was the exact type of symbiotic human/machine interface Murnell had envisioned while working on his doctorate, and now it was becoming a reality.

Further down the hall, a pair of Air Force officers in fatigues, one male and one female, greeted him. They escorted him into an elevator encased in a thick column of steel and stone. Each officer and Murnell in turn subjected themselves to a fingerprint and retinal scan on a recessed panel in the wall before the elevator doors closed behind them.

After that, it was a rapid descent to the research level 190 feet below. Murnell felt the momentary vertigo he always felt when dropping the equivalent of several stories underground.

The doors soon swished open, revealing an empty corridor about fifty-feet long and twenty-feet wide. The entire length of the passage was saturated by a dim red light.

Exiting the elevator, Murnell immediately had the sense he was being watched. Not just watched in the way he'd been kept under surveillance via the security cameras and initial wave of small drones he'd encountered above ground, but surveyed in a much more intimate way.

Maybe he knew too much for his own good.

The dozens if not hundreds of tiny drones that swarmed about him now were completely invisible. If he reached out to try to touch one, he might have succeeded and rendered it momentarily visible. But after what had happened in Mexico, the TETRA was beginning to adjust. The artificial intelligence had already begun employing evasive maneuvers to try to avoid any type of physical encounter by its MAVs with a warm-blooded human being that might upset the MAVs delicate electronic balance.

Maintaining such a balance was critical to the convergence of advancements in miniaturization and metamaterials that created the ability to bend light waves around their tiny surfaces. Which, in turn, created the MAVs cloaking effect.

Impressive as it might have been, such technology came at an exorbitant cost. Empyrean's official black ops budget, if you could even call it that, had long ago been spent. More and more money was required to continue the work toward full operational deployment of the TETRA.

But somehow, the cash kept flowing in. Ripley encouraged him not to worry about that.

Speaking of Ripley, the old man was upset again because Murnell's logistics people still hadn't brought the trailer back down to Empyrean. It turned out the sphere had been more severely damaged than originally thought. Some critical hardware repairs were required before trying to move the trailer, unless they wanted to risk flushing a year's worth of work down the drain. Ripley had reluctantly okayed the delay and Murnell had been out to the site again himself yesterday to check on things.

But he'd received word a little while ago that the repairs were almost complete. They should have the trailer back in his lab by that afternoon.

He and the two officers reached the lab door, where a similar but slightly different ID procedure was repeated before the locks would disengage.

"Have a nice day with your toys, sir," the woman said with a smile as she and the other officer turned to leave him alone.

Toys indeed.

He wondered how much the officers really knew about Empyrean, how far in depth their briefings went. Murnell had never found the female officer particularly attractive, but she did have nice teeth.

He lifted his hand part way in a mock salute.

"Don't worry. I intend to," he said.

19

TWO DAYS HAD passed. Raina left the shelter with Tye each morning to train with MAVs in the woods and returned each afternoon.

She wasn't happy about waiting. She couldn't understand why they weren't moving more quickly to find her brother. But Williamson convinced her she needed more tools and more preparation. Maybe he was right.

At least it was nice to be outdoors for a change. The solitude and quiet of the mountains gave her more time to reflect on their situation.

She and Tye worked with various attachments for the MAVs—Williamson had a number of different tools in his inventory—some capable of doing more than just taking video or feeding audio. There were instruments that could deliver small objects, for example, placing stationary cameras or monitoring equipment. They could attach minute tracking devices, similar to the one he said he'd attached to the trailer, to surfaces. Or infrared beacons that transmitted light invisible to the naked eye but seen with night vision.

Such markers had been used for years by larger drones in Afghanistan and elsewhere to kill terrorists after spies or paid informants marked their locations. Raina had never really stopped to consider their civilian and domestic applications.

At Williamson's urging, Tye even started taking the first steps toward learning to fly the MAVs. Williamson also promised to eventually show him how to operate the sniper drone he'd used on Ripley's man.

But Raina had more immediate reasons for wanting Tye to acquire some flying skills.

"What if something happens to me in the middle of an action? You might need to take over," she told him.

"That wouldn't be very pretty," Tye said.

But he'd watched and listened, and when it came his turn to try his hand at the controls you could see he at least had some potential.

"It's like a video game."

"Sort of…not exactly." She watched as he struggled to keep a tiny MAV from flying into a tree branch and failed.

"Forget it," he said. "Just give me an M-16 and you fly these little critters."

"You'll get used to it," she'd assured him.

The sun was rising over the ridge directly behind them, just beginning to burn through the morning fog and cold. They'd set up a bivouac along the upper tree line of a large clearing, with the hill sloping away from them so they could keep a better eye on the drones.

Staring into her laptop screen, she was glad for the bit of warmth her Army jacket offered. She blew on her fingers and rubbed her arms together, placing her hands back on the controls. She peered through a cloud of her own breath.

"Too bad these little drones don't come with a heater," Tye said.

"Yeah." She smiled. "We should put in a request."

"We'll have to get you a pair of shooter's gloves. They're thin enough you can still feel the controls. But they might help with the cold."

"Sure. I'll just put in a requisition."

"How are things going?"

A few seconds before, they'd launched an entire little squadron of MAVs into the forest. From what she could see on her split screen display keeping tabs on all six of them, a couple of her charges had already risen above the tree tops.

"Not too bad," she said.

She had barely finished speaking when an enormous black bear and her cubs ambled into a clearing about a hundred yards below their position.

Raina froze. Tye had seen them, too.

Wouldn't it be the height of irony if, despite all of their high tech wizardry, they were taken out by some kind of natural predator? She knew black bears weren't generally too dangerous or aggressive, but it was still a good idea to give them a wide berth. And it was never a good idea to be seen as threatening to a mother bear with her cubs.

The mama bear had probably already picked up their scent, which was why she had the cubs on the move here in the daylight.

"I think we need to sit tight for a couple of minutes," she whispered.

"No argument from me." Tye kept his voice low, too. "What's that old joke about one guy being able to outrun the other when facing a bear?"

"Very funny."

The bears continued moving as if they hadn't noticed the human intruders, disappearing further on into the woods.

Raina shifted her attention back to her laptop screen.

"There they go." Two of the MAVs had the bears on camera, moving steadily away down the mountain.

"Great. At least we'll have fair warning when we're about to be eaten," he said.

She punched him playfully in the arm. "You know, I've been thinking things over," she said.

"Uh-oh. Whenever a woman tells me she's been thinking things over I know I'm in trouble."

"Just listen, will you? No matter what Williamson says, we're outnumbered and outgunned against this Empyrean thing, right?"

"Can't argue with that."

"And these people want to recruit me. They went to enough trouble to drug me and kidnap me twice."

"Okay. So what's your point?"

"I need to turn myself back into them."

"What? Are you nuts? After we went to so much trouble to get you out of there?"

"I know you did and I appreciate that. But doesn't it make sense for me, knowing what I know now, to try to get back in there as a spy?"

"No way can that be safe for you."

"Neither of us is safe, regardless."

He took a deep breath and stared at her for a long moment. "I still don't think it's such a good idea. The way this looks to me, there's something much bigger going on here than any of us may realize. Something where more and more people are ending up dead."

"But how else am I going to find out what happened to my brother? Look at all the assets Ripley and Murnell have at their disposal."

"Are you sure this doesn't have anything to do with that suave scientist you've been talking about?"

She shook her head no. But a part of her wondered if he might be right. Was she being seduced, not just by her love of flying, but by the attention of Lance Murnell and his movie star eyes?

The drones were all in a stable hover for the moment, awaiting her next command. Without thinking, she suddenly turned away from her screen, leaned over and grabbed Tye by the jacket, pulling him into a kiss.

It was easier than she'd expected. Like flying.

For his part, Tye quickly recovered from the initial surprise and seemed to be enjoying it, too.

But the crackle of their walkie-talkie broke the spell.

"Base to Sanchez and Palmer. Hey, are you two finished your training yet? I need you back here on the double."

It was Williamson.

She broke away from Tye's embrace and they stood looking into one another's eyes. He had to know she was right about what she was proposing. Without taking his gaze off of her, he reached over and picked up the radio.

"Roger that. We're done here. Pulling in the MAVs and we'll be on our way."

20

"WHAT'S UP, MAJOR?"

She and Tye lowered themselves into chairs on either side of Williamson in front of a map projected on a large computer screen.

"The trailer you were in that I've been tracking...," he said. "It's been on the move."

"What am I looking at?" she asked.

"This is the greater Washington, D.C. area." He indicated a bright red dot on the monitor. "And that is your trailer. I've been watching it for more than twenty minutes."

"Where are they headed with it?"

"Exactly where I thought they would go. And, if my guess is correct, it looks like they've almost made it to their destination."

"Where would that be?"

"Downriver a little ways into Maryland. If I'm correct, they'll end up at a location off Indian Head Highway. Less than ten miles south of the capital."

"What's down there?"

"The place I've been keeping an eye on. It's a decommissioned federal psychiatric institute.

The old hospital, called Glassmanor, dates back more than a century and was closed after the 1970s, but the Department of Homeland Security took over control of the property more than ten years ago. It also just so happens to sit in the middle of a thousand acres of sheltered and closely guarded forest terrain."

"What did DHS want with the place?"

"According to the official record, the hospital facility and land have been earmarked for quote, 'future expansion,' unquote."

"Let me guess," she said. "Nothing's been officially done with it so far."

"You got it. As far as anybody knows publicly, DHS is just sitting on the place."

"What about the old hospital buildings?"

"Outwardly, nothing has changed. From aerial views, the central structure looks like something out of One Flew Over The Cuckoo's Nest. Except that it's all shuttered up. The only visible activity comes from DHS and Marine guards patrolling the perimeter, and the occasional car or truck going in and out. There's also a helipad in the middle of the woods. Hardly ever used, but you wouldn't know it from the way it looks to be maintained."

"So where's big bad Empyrean?" Tye asked. "This place sounds just like a lot of old federal facilities the government hangs on to."

"It's underground," Raina said.

No one spoke for a moment. Williamson turned to face her. "That's exactly what I was about to say. How did you know that?"

"I'm not sure," she said. "I was either drugged or blindfolded until I got inside, but when I was there, I just had the feeling we weren't above ground."

"Did you see any windows or skylights and catch any glimpses of the outdoors?"

"No." Raina shook her head. "Nothing like that."

"But why go to all the trouble and expense of building underground if you've already secured the surrounding area?" Tye asked.

"Because that's part of the concept behind Empyrean, the way Ripley and I originally conceived of it. The full extent of its operations are only supposed to be known to a very few."

"Okay. If we know where they might be, why don't we just call up the Washington Post and blow the whistle on the whole operation?"

"Believe me, I've thought about doing just that. But for one thing, that dot on the screen you're looking at is the first potentially conclusive evidence I've had, and even that's still circumstantial. Even if does go away when it gets to Glassmanor, DHS could be maintaining an underground warehouse there or some other type of facility. What if Empyrean's main lab is somewhere else? What if they're developing multiple facilities? All of those were possibilities in the original planning."

"Yeah. I see what you're saying."

"That's not even the worst part. Think about what we're dealing with here. So what if we did find a reporter, maybe even a congressman or two, willing to do some digging? Whatever they might find out, the government would just deny it. There are many ways to discredit reporters and legislators. Jonathan Ripley has done more of that kind of thing to more powerful individuals than anyone else in the business. He's so effective, very few people even know he exists. And if Project Empyrean is capable of even a fraction of what I think it might be capable, he's got more tools at his disposal than ever."

"So what are we supposed to do then?"

"Exactly what we're doing now. Like I told you in the beginning, this is a secret war."

"Seems like more of a small insurrection if you ask me,"

Raina said. "No offense, Major. But what do you and your friends and contacts have compared to the TETRA?"

"Never underestimate the power of a small but determined force."

"What do you think Ripley's really after with Empyrean? He must have some objective."

Williamson sat back and folded his arms while the dot continued to move on the screen. "Can't say for sure. But if I had to guess, given his track record, it's something political. A lot of things are happening in the world. Here in D.C. we've got another presidential election coming up soon. Anytime there's a potential shift in power, people like Ripley are moving well in advance behind the scenes."

"More like in the shadows."

"You got it."

"You think he's aligned with some political figure?"

"Maybe. Too soon to say."

"So what's your strategy to stop him?"

"Like I've been telling you," Williamson said. "We try not to take on Empyrean directly, at least for now. We pursue Nathan Kurn as far as that thread will take us. And we see what we can do about helping you get Manny back in one piece."

She rubbed a hand along the back of her neck. "You think Manny's being held at this Glassmanor place?"

"It's difficult to say."

"If you're right about this old hospital, they must have lots of layers of security."

"No doubt."

"Have you actually been to this place?" Tye asked.

"I've driven around it a couple of times. All you can see from the road are the guards at the two entrances, front and back."

"But you really think this might be the place, huh?"

"Well, Mr. Palmer. We should have a much better idea in just a minute." He leaned into his computer screen again. "If I'm right, and Raina's intuition is correct, we should lose the signal when the trailer goes subterranean. And it looks like our trailer's about to enter Glassmanor."

They watched the screen together and waited.

Willamson zoomed in the map so the red dot could be seen leaving the last marked highway and entering the unmarked Glassmanor property. The dot kept moving, although at a slower pace. It seemed to take forever, but eventually it reached the point in the property where the old hospital buildings were located.

Then it happened—just as Williamson predicted.

Raina glanced at Tye, who glanced back. They each turned to look again at the screen. The red dot had disappeared.

21

MANNY SANCHEZ SAT up in the cot to which he was chained. The peeling wallpaper he leaned against felt worse than sandpaper against his back. The soup they'd brought him to eat tasted like watered-down garbage. He took another spoonful, forcing himself to eat it anyway.

He felt like little more than a piece of trash himself— tossed away and forgotten. Somehow, for reasons he was yet to understand, he'd gone from high-flying tech master to a barbarically imprisoned shell of what he'd been just a few weeks before.

For the first time in his life he felt some sympathy for soldiers who had to risk not only death but capture and maybe torture. Manny, too, was a soldier. Not like his big sister Raina, with her Purple Heart and all of her commendations. Manny was a soldier of a different type.

He hadn't sworn allegiance to Uncle Sam or any other nation or creed, but to the truth. At least, whatever portion of the truth he could find. And he was finding the cold reality to be more than he'd ever imagined.

At least these people, whoever they were, had provided him with medical care. His shoulder still ached from the bullet wound and the surgery they performed on him, but after five weeks, it was healing nicely. The last bandage had finally been removed, and a nurse checked on his progress every other day.

The nurse, a sandy-haired man with a Mid-Western affect, was obviously American, as were the rest of his captors. The first few days after his surgery, when he was brought to the broken down house that would serve as his prison, were merely fuzzy memories now. Wounded and drugged after what happened in Mexico, he barely remembered how he ended up here.

He didn't even know where "here" was exactly, although he'd figured out pretty quickly he was no longer south of the border. All he knew was that he was in the woods, someplace in Maryland maybe, or the Midwest, judging by the air temperature this time of year and the little bit of weather he could see through the dirty window. On days it rained, a cold dampness invaded his unheated prison bedroom. He'd been given nothing to read, not even a Bible or newspaper, no music or electronics of any kind. At least the plumbing worked and the open toilet next to his cot he was forced to use didn't smell as awful as it otherwise might. He was allowed to stand up and exercise twenty minutes a day, but that was it. His captors had little patience for complaints.

Speaking of his captors, he thought he'd begun to understand them a little. Military? It sure felt like it, but none of them, including the nurse, wore uniforms, so he couldn't say for sure. Two of his guards were white and one was black. Clearly Jarheads. Do your job and don't-ask-too-many-questions types.

Maybe they were special operations. But if so, why would they be keeping him here? All attempts at meaningful conversation, even with the nurse, had been rebuffed or deflected. He played mental games to keep himself sharp and tried doing as much stretching as he could while being chained to the bed, but he ended up sleeping much of the time.

He must have been asleep when the white haired man in the dressy blue jeans and hunting jacket entered the room. The man was seated in a hardback chair looking at him from across the narrow room.

Manny awoke with a start.

"What the f—"

An uncomfortable surge of adrenaline shot through him. He was irritated and scared.

"Not to worry, Mr. Sanchez," the man said. "I'm not here to hurt you."

He was an older man but lean, with chiseled features and icy blue eyes that seemed to cut right through Manny.

"Who are you?" Manny asked.

"Who I am is not important. Who you are—now that seems to be the question."

"I don't know what you're talking about."

"You don't?"

"You just called me by my name. You people are obviously American and I'm an American citizen. Why am I being held here against my will? This is a clear violation of my civil rights."

The man smiled. "I always find it fascinating how those who work so diligently to tear down America are often the first to invoke the name of the country they demean at the first hint of any perceived loss of their rights."

Really? This guy was a trip.

"Being chained up like an animal is a lot more than a hint, if you ask me."

The man nodded. "I'm glad to see you haven't lost your mind. But I urge you to reflect on how well you've been treated, compared to how much worse it could yet become."

It couldn't get any worse than it already was, could it? What good would ending up dead in a ditch somewhere do him? This dude didn't seem like the type to make idle threats.

"What do you people want from me?" Manny asked.

The man cupped his hand and examined his fingernails. "It's not all that complicated, actually," he said. "We want you to come work for us."

22

A N ALARM TONE was reverberating through the walls of the bunkroom.

Raina awoke with a start. What time was it? She'd been grabbing a much-needed nap. At some point, half asleep, she remembered hearing Tye step into the room to climb into the bunk above her.

A glowing digital clock on the wall told her it was past five p.m. The harsh noise ended as abruptly as it'd begun.

"Any idea what that was?" She fumbled for a light.

"Don't know." Tye was already scrambling down from above. "But I guess we need to check it out."

In the main room, they found Williamson standing to one side, clutching an overstuffed notebook thick with papers.

"Sorry about the alarm, folks. But the satellite's overhead and our target is coming into range," he told hem.

Satellite? Target? "What are you talking about?" she said.

"I may not have all of Empyrean's capabilities, but I do have a few tricks up my sleeve. Mr. Palmer, would you mind stepping away from that wall to your left?"

Tye shrugged and did as he asked.

She looked at the wooden beams framing the space behind him. They looked pretty solid to her, but Williamson punched in a sequence of codes on his phone, and a few seconds later, part of the wall began to slide away. Behind the wall stood a desktop console with a trio of workstation chairs, including keyboards, joysticks, and a half dozen wall-mounted digital displays.

"You've been holding out on us," Tye said.

"Somewhat," Williamson said.

"What's this, your backwoods version of NASA?"

"Not exactly." He sat down in the center chair and began typing in commands as the screens came on line. "Have a seat, folks," he said. "This is where the fun begins."

They were soon looking at a long sidewalk from above through a video feed. The walkway snaked through a park surrounded by trees. It was a middle class residential neighborhood. There were children playing and running through a playground, parents seated on benches, and cars lining the streets all around.

"What is this place?" she asked.

"Northern Virginia. Not far from where we've been working."

A man appeared on the sidewalk. But instead of continuing along it, he started walking across the grass toward the middle of the park.

"Bingo," Williamson whispered under his breath.

"That's Nathan Kurn."

"Indeed, it is."

In the middle of the park stood a thickly wooded area, the view from above obscured by leaves. The man looked to be heading directly toward the trees.

At that moment, another man appeared on the sidewalk at the far side of the park. He, too, veered from the walkway toward the wooded area.

She focused on the second man. He appeared to be up in years but fit for his age and relaxed with white hair.

"That's Ripley."

"I know." Williamson toggled the image in for a better view of the two men before they could disappear beneath the leafy canopy.

"How'd you know they would be meeting here?"

Williamson smiled. "I have my sources," he said.

"You think that was Ripley himself on the other end of the phone with Kurn back there at the fraternity?"

"Probably."

"Kurn's son dying must have somehow upped the ante on whatever they're doing with Empyrean."

"Well, whatever's going on, it must be something urgent for them to be meeting face to face. Ripley's not usually one for taking chances."

The men appeared to be walking on an intersecting course. They were heading straight toward one another, but at the last second before reaching the trees each veered off in a different direction.

"What just happened?" Tye asked. "Why'd they split up?"

"I don't know," Williamson said. He tried making adjustments to the image to see if they could get a better look.

"Did they pass anything between them?"

"Not that I saw."

A second later, the screen went blank.

"Oh, no," Raina said. "What just happened?"

"We've been jammed," Williamson said. "The feed's being blocked. They must have somehow figured out they were being watched."

"Can they trace it back to us?"

"No." Williamson said. "I've got this feed routed through a couple of dozen different shadow servers. We'd see them coming a mile away. All they managed to do just now was close the back door. Obviously someone got word to Ripley, who chose to abort the meeting."

"Can you get the picture back?"

"Not easily. And not before those two have long since left the area."

"Great," Tye said. "All this James Bond garbage is just fabulous when it works…" He linked his hands together behind his head. "…but when it doesn't…we're screwed. We're blind and we're screwed."

"Not exactly," Raina said.

"What do you mean?"

She turned to Williamson. "We may still be able to track one of them." She'd been watching the screen closely as Williamson manipulated the satellite image to zoom in on the two men. "Did you see what Kurn was wearing?"

Williamson scrolled backward through the digital recording of the video until he found a close-up frame of Kurn.

He stared at the image until a smile crept across his face. "I see what you mean. Nathan Kurn doesn't know tradecraft. That's a problem for Ripley."

Tye scratched at the stubble on his face. "What are you two talking about?"

She pointed at the image frozen on the screen. "If I'm right, Nathan Kurn's staying someplace where they keep horses. Those are riding boots he's wearing on his feet."

23

NATHAN KURN USUALLY split his time among properties he owned in Florida, California, Europe, and Hong Kong. But whenever he was in Washington, D.C., the media mogul kept residence at his five-million-dollar condo overlooking the Potomac.

Since his son's death Kurn was reported to be in seclusion at some undisclosed location. A spokesman said he was "in mourning" and "spending time with his family." Kurn had lots of friends and associates in the Washington area. One of his closest friends and business partners, however, was a foreign financier who owned an expansive, heavily guarded estate in Loudon County an hour west of the city. Judging from the riding boots, Sanchez and Williamson figured Kurn had to be holding up there.

The story of Derek Kurn's tragic death had hit the news a couple of days before. So far, there'd been no mention of Tye, although authorities were quoted as saying they were still looking for any witnesses. It went without saying, if they talked to the detective from the car and the girl who'd been in Derek's room, Tye should at least be considered a person of interest if not a suspect. Of course, that would depend in part on how Derek died.

For now, no one seemed to be saying too much, and Derek's sudden and shocking demise was receiving a surprisingly respectful, muted treatment in the press.

The narrative was familiar enough. Another rich college kid—in this case scion of the rich and famous—gone off the rails. The story was easy to swallow as it was instantly broadcast, Facebooked, Tweeted, and on and on, around the globe.

The usual assumption was drugs. So what if the father happened to be a big media guy? Just another sad tale of woe to be quickly lost and forgotten among the daily tsunami of similarly sad or far more horrific stories.

Could Derek Kurn have committed suicide under the threat of being exposed as a rapist? The possibility couldn't be discounted. But usually in the case of a suicide, especially a high profile suicide, word leaks out. Nothing of the sort had been mentioned in Derek Kurn's case. According to Williamson, even his best source in law enforcement had told him information surrounding the case was being sequestered to protect "the privacy" of the family.

The good news was it was less than two hours by car from Williamson's wilderness bunker to Loudon County. They'd made the relatively short drive packed together in the cab of a rattly pickup truck emblazoned with the name of a fictitious landscaping and lawn care service.

It was well past dark by the time they arrived. They didn't expect too much security, but they weren't taking any chances. Recent aerial surveillance of the area pointed them to a spot where she and Ty could be dropped off—on the shoulder of a lightly traveled side road less than a mile from the main house of the estate.

"Okay. You're good to go," Williamson told them. "It's a bit of a long shot, but let's hope Nathan Kurn is there."

"Will you be wired in?"

"Not this time. There's something else I need to do. But I won't be that far away. Call me if you need me."

"And if there's trouble?" Raina asked.

"Improvise," he said.

The pickup crept slowly away into the darkness.

She and Tye slipped on their gear. In addition to a secure phone, she was outfitted with a sidearm, night vision goggles, and binoculars—not to mention the remote drone backpack with which they'd been training. Tye was similarly equipped but also carried his M-1 on the off chance they found themselves caught in the middle of a shit storm.

"Once more into the breach," he whispered as they moved together into the cover of the woods.

Raina smiled in spite of herself. She hadn't spoken to him about their wilderness encounter earlier and how it had made her feel. They'd both had too much to do.

He walked on ahead. She moved quietly behind him along the edge of a mown field. They were careful not to stray from the protective cover of the trees. For all they knew, Murnell and Ripley could have a swarm of drones watching over the place where Kurn was staying.

"I make the fence line about fifty meters ahead," he said after a couple of minutes.

They stopped and looked around. She notice a small rise to to her right that, while still within the trees, offered sight lines in all directions.

"Let's head over here."

"Whatever you say, my lady."

They surveyed the small hill and she picked out a pair of large boulders that would provide cover from the direction of the estate. Tye stood beside her, sweeping the area for threats, his gaze remaining focused through the night scope of the M-1.

Crouching behind the rock, she took out the night vision

binoculars. He trained his scope over the top of the stone, and together they looked out over top of the fence through scattered trees and open grass toward the well-lit compound in the distance.

The main house was a stately colonial affair, built along the side of a ridge to maximize the views over the countryside. The landscaping around the main driveway was Disney theme park immaculate. From this angle, no vehicles of any kind were visible in front of or to the side of the main building.

"All clear," Tye said.

"Let's hope it stays that way."

Directly behind them, she found a good-sized tree stump that rose a couple of feet above the ground. She brushed debris and leaves off the top, slipped her backup off her shoulders and took out the laptop and mobile control pad. She fired up the computer and quickly closed it to operate in clamshell mode, slipping on her optical viewing glasses to see the screen.

TETRA or no TETRA, the advantage of sending operators in on the ground was the ability to launch the drones up close and personal, to get a firsthand human impression of the environment before committing MAVs. Remote operators were sometimes prone to tunnel vision, losing sight of the overall mission domain. While the TETRA seemed capable of overcoming this obstacle, she wondered if even its advanced capabilities were an acceptable substitute for actual on-the-ground intelligence.

She handed the MAVs to Tye. "Ready to launch?"

"Thought you'd never ask."

The sky was clear and windless, with only a sliver of a moon, and for that she was thankful. She watched as he lifted the tiny drones in turn, tossing them gently into the air as he might throw a minuscule paper airplane. The new and improved MAVs Williamson had had them training on were programmed for auto-takeoff and landing, even in the darkness of the woods. All but silent, the two of them were instantly lost to sight.

Raina's optical screen came alive in split screen mode, with multiple views of the estate and surrounding terrain from above. The drones were set to hover at fifty feet until she took control of them. Infrared and thermal imaging gave her a much better appreciation of the size of the estate. It also alerted her to the presence of at least a half dozen security guards and a small fleet of Land Rovers deployed around the property that had not been visible from their position. Although not exactly on high alert, the guards looked to be keeping a vigilant watch over the main house and the perimeter. What worried Raina was the security they couldn't see.

"Looks more intimidating from the air. Some security guards and vehicles."

"What are you going to do, fly down a ventilation shaft or up some drain pipe like you did before?"

"Not exactly."

On the screen projected through her glasses, she watched as a car pulled into the driveway. It drove around to the front of the house. She turned her attention to her flying controls for a second, allowing one of the angels to continue its hover as over-watch and pushing the other angel toward the house.

"In fact..." She eased the image toggle forward until the drone's camera gave her a close-up of the car. She paused for a moment as a woman and a small child exited the vehicle. The child was a girl about four years of age—one of Nathan Kurn's grandchildren perhaps. "I'm wondering if one of these people might just be our express ticket into this little fortress."

"Man or a woman?"

"Neither," she said. "A little girl."

24

SHE MANEUVERED THE angel to drop behind the child. The night overshadowed the dim light from the house and provided the MAV cover. Raina moved in closer. The back of the girl grew larger in the screen.

They were committed now. She let the drone descend to the back of the sweater the little girl was wearing.

"Done."

"Don't tell me you're hitching a ride," Tye said.

"You have a better idea?"

"Not really. And you're right. No one's going to frisk a little kid."

And they didn't.

Raina plugged an ear bud into one ear to check her audio before shifting the angel's position to burrow ever so slightly into the garment, an invisible hitchhiker. There was no reaction from the girl. Neither the child nor anyone else showed the slightest indication they were aware of the tiny drone.

"Everything okay?"

"Worked like a charm," she said.

"That's definitely a new technique."

"Williamson did say to improvise."

She turned up the microphone with her control pad and,

via the other angel's camera hovering further off in the distance, watched as the woman and the girl entered the back of the house. They passed through what appeared to be a metal detector without incident. Most such devices were looking for guns or knives, something larger than the minuscule hover angel.

"They're inside," she said.

"Okay, but you better get off that kid's back soon. Otherwise you'll be flying blind."

Tye had a point. What if the angel popped out from the mesh of the girl's garment into a well-lit setting within close-up view of the mother? Raina could hear but not see on her screen what was happening. Other than audio clues, she would have no idea what she was flying the MAV into when it emerged.

"We're here to see my father," she heard the woman say.

So she'd guessed right. Derek Kurn must have had an older sister, and a niece to boot.

"Yes, ma'am. He's in the den. Right this way." This sounded like a secretary.

"Thank you."

"Can I get you or the little girl something to eat?"

"No. Thank you. We've already eaten. Dad's expecting us. We'll be at the funeral the day after tomorrow, naturally, but I just wanted to check on him to see if he needs anything."

"Very good, ma'am."

Even if Raina couldn't see what was taking place, the MAV provided them with a tiny mobile bugging device. Her instincts told her to sit tight.

Through her earbud came the sound of a soft knock on a door. This was followed a few moments later by the murmur of low voices. No doubt the secretary announcing Kurn's daughter and granddaughter's arrival.

Even without an image, Raina felt as if she were living in some sort of time warp, as if she'd actually been metaphysically transported into the room itself. She remembered Kurn's face in the basement of the frat house. She could almost see the long, fallow expression of the formerly cocky mega-mogul, now humbled and withdrawn, the dutifully concerned daughter, the uncomprehending innocence of the child.

"Nice to see you, Katherine."

"Nice to see you, too, Dad."

Nathan Kurn's formality with his daughter at such a time and place said more about their relationship than any snooping drone ever could. The hover angel was just the means to affect the grand unveiling, the daughter's broken expectations, and the last flickering vestiges of the supposedly great man's heart.

"I can't believe Derek's dead."

Her father said nothing, and in the silence that followed his daughter might have read the truth, that Nathan Kurn was at least partly at fault, or, in his negligence, wholly responsible for what had befallen his son.

"What happened, Dad?"

"I don't know," Kurn told her.

Raina was struck by the fact that though she'd never actually met Nathan Kurn in person, these seemed like the most truthful words she'd so far heard him say.

They struck an emotional chord with her as well. Wasn't she in a similar position to Kurn's daughter, wondering what had happened to her own brother Manny? Was Manny already dead like Derek Kurn?

At least Kurn's daughter already knew her brother's fate, as horrible as it might have been. She just didn't know the why.

Raina had even less information to go on than that. What about Kurn's granddaughter?

She made a split-second decision. Tweaking the controls to launch the hover angel into the air, she quickly banked away from the little girl. Instantly, the video feed's image box went from an unrecognizable blur of dark color to a view of the mahogany walls and soft lighting inside Nathan Kurn's private study. Raina hoped she hadn't been spotted.

"I see you've brought Stephanie with you...Come on over here little one," Kurn said.

Why isn't the little girl saying anything? Raina wondered. *Maybe she's intimidated.* Did she even know her grandfather?

Raina turned the angel toward the relative safety of a bookshelf lined with hardbacks and decorative bookends. Landing the MAV on the edge of one of the books, she was able to spin around and bring the whole length of the room into focus.

The elder Kurn slumped in a thickly upholstered club chair. Raina had been right. Gone was the swaggering figure he'd projected a couple of days before.

In its place sat a hollowed-out man—his tie loosened with rolled-up shirtsleeves and hair disheveled, in the dimmed light looking every bit his age and more. Resting on a coaster in the center of a small table beside him was a half empty tumbler of clear brown liquid. No doubt a brand of fine Scotch. As reprehensible as he may have been, the man had lost his only son, and Raina almost felt sorry for him.

Kurn's granddaughter hesitated, put off perhaps by her grandfather's appearance. No doubt she'd been told something about her uncle's death but was probably too young to understand all that it meant.

"It's okay, little one. Grandpa's just tired, that's all." Kurn reached an arm out to the little girl and she moved toward him.

But she didn't climb up into his lap. Instead, she went and stood next to him.

He gave her an awkward hug. He turned to look at her. "You've gotten much bigger, I see."

"Yes, Grandpa."

Raina wondered how long it had been since Nathan Kurn had seen his granddaughter.

"Mommy promised me a new toy," the girl said to Kurn.

"Oh, she did, did she?" The volume of the old man's voice rose in mock surprise.

"Honey, why don't you and I go practice your piano in the living room for a little while? Grandpa has a meeting," Katherine interjected.

"I don't want to practice piano," Stephanie said. "I hate piano."

"You can just play then. Maybe there's a new toy or two we can find for you."

"Sure," Kurn said. "Check with Helen in the kitchen. She can get you all set up."

"Can I get you anything?" his daughter asked.

"No. Thank you."

She moved toward the little girl. "Come on, Stefee. Let's go see what Helen has to play with."

The little girl's mood seemed to brighten at the prospect of playing.

"Bye, Grandpa."

"Bye," Kurn said.

They headed from the room, the mother holding her daughter's hand.

Nathan Kurn sat motionless, staring into the crackling fire. His hand reached out for another taste of the whiskey. As he picked his glass up, Raina noticed a cell phone sitting on the table behind it. Kurn finished his sip and put down the glass before picking up the phone. He pushed a number displayed on the screen and put the phone to his ear.

"Tell him I'm ready for him now."

A few seconds later, there was another knock at the door.

"Come in."

The door opened and a short, balding man, wearing

eyeglasses and dressed in a blue blazer, entered the room. The man carried a briefcase. Kurn didn't bother looking up.

"Have a seat." Kurn gestured toward the club chair opposite his by the fire.

"I'm terribly sorry for your loss, Nathan."

Kurn nodded.

"I brought the numbers you asked for." The man sat down in the second chair, pulled the briefcase onto his lap, and opened it. He took out a manila folder and handed it across to Kurn.

But Kurn didn't open the folder right away.

"What do you think I should do, Harvey?"

The man hesitated before speaking. "Well," he began, "I've been a corporate financial attorney and your CFO for more than ten years. If you remember, I told you I thought this was a mistake from the beginning. Although I never in a million years imagined it might come down to this—I mean what just happened to Derek."

"You were right," Kurn said. "I should have listened to you."

The bald man said nothing.

"How much money are we talking about?"

The man blew out a breath and shook his head. "That's hard to say, under the circumstances. At least a couple hundred million of your own, plus all the money you've packaged from others. It could be well above a half billion."

Kurn whistled and put his hands behind his head. He leaned back and stared up at the ceiling. "Jesus, what an idiot I've been."

"You're far from an idiot, Nathan. You have the shrewdest business mind I've ever known. But this is…this whole thing goes way beyond business."

Kurn put his arms back down and looked across at the man. "That it does, my friend. And we still may be able to salvage some things out of this situation, but right now I need to bury my son."

The bald man folded his hands on top of his briefcase. "Understood, sir. You should take as long as you need."

"I'm concerned about those files on the isolated server at Oculum," Kurn said. "That information could really come back to haunt us."

"Agreed."

"How secure are they?"

"Extremely secure. Protected by the best encryption available and physically inaccessible to anyone but us. The company officers there don't even have a code key to access that room in the building. They lease the property from us."

"Good. But I'd still like those files disposed of. Do whatever you have to do. Burn down the whole goddamn place if you have to."

"Understood. It's not quite that simple. May take me a couple of days, but I'll take care of it."

Kurn set the manila folder on his lap, took a pair of reading glasses out of his pocket and put them on. He picked up the folder, opened it, and began reading.

The man waited.

Kurn finished reading and closed the folder. He took off his glasses and slipped them back into his jacket pocket. Then he stood from his chair and walked over to the fireplace with the folder. He stood looking into the flames for a moment before tossing the folder in on top of the logs. Kurn stood and his CFO remained seated as they both watched the manila folder go up in flames.

"Will that be all for now, Nathan?"

"Yes. Leave the other file you brought there on the table. I have an important meeting later tonight. Thank you for coming on such short notice."

"Of course." The bald man opened his briefcase again and took out a second file. He stood to go, laying it down on the side table. "And again, I'm very sorry for your loss. Please express my condolences to the rest of your family."

"Thank you for your years of loyalty and service. I know I pay you a lot of money, but I probably don't say that enough."

"I appreciate you saying that, sir."

Kurn turned to look at his CFO. "And don't let me down on getting rid of those digital records, Harvey."

"Yes, sir. I will make it so."

25

TWO THOUSAND MILES to the south, an ocean breeze pushed up against the heat-filled air to the twelfth-floor balcony of the Royal Sonesta Hotel in Puerto Vallarta. It swirled Lucy's thin swim cover up, exposing her tanned, bikini-clad back. A shiver ran through her body, and not just because of the wind.

Behind her, just inside the sliding glass doorway to the hotel bedroom, the thirty-something businessman/banker, who had stripped down to his boxers and a bathrobe, stood talking on the phone to his wife.

"Yeah, that's right. Just put all the charges on the room," he said. "Enjoy the spa, baby. I'll be down in a little bit."

Baby. What a creep.

The businessman was hideous, Lucy thought, if not physically unattractive. With gluttonous blue eyes and sandy blonde hair, six feet tall and well muscled, his was the kind of semi-drunken, Ivy League lechery that made Lucy's skin crawl.

He ended the call and, a moment later, had slid up behind her, pressing himself into her. She could already feel his excitement growing. Forcing herself to smile, she took a deep breath, and turned into his arms.

"When I saw you in the lobby and you spoke to me," he whispered, "I couldn't believe it. I had no idea...why me?"

He tried to kiss her, but Lucy placed a gentle finger on his lips. This was going to be easier than she'd thought.

She took him by the hand, and guided him back through the doorway and into the darkened bedroom. Reaching the bed, she undid the tie to her cover up and let it drop to the floor.

Beside himself with lust, the man laid his cell phone on the bedside table and began to move in.

"Uh, uh." Lucy grinned, pushing him away. "Safety first."

"What? Oh, yeah. Right. Of course."

The man turned away to hurry to the bathroom where he'd left his wallet on the floor, crumpled in the pocket of his summer khakis. Lucy grabbed his cell phone and hit redial, before putting it back on the table.

In a flash the man was back, tossing a condom pack on the bed. Lucy pulled him down on top of the bedspread and mounted him.

"You want me?"

"Oh, yeah, baby," he said.

In the hotel spa several floors below, the man's wife, an attractive brunette, saw the call was from her husband and picked up her phone. She heard a woman speaking followed by her husband.

"Tell me how much you want it."

"Oh, I want it. I really want it. I want to feel you..."

"Take me, baby," Lucy said. "Now...Oh...yes!"

The wife's face turned red with rage.

Back upstairs, the man pulled at Lucy and tried to kiss her again. She pushed him back down. He got more aggressive and she flung her long hair back.

"Come on!"

"Wait," she said. "Wait just one second. I've really got to pee."

"What?" The man pouted.

"Be back in a flash." She kissed him coyly on the forehead, and hopped off the bed. Stumbling on purpose, as if in her haste, she swept her hand over the bedside table, knocking the phone off the table, and pranced into the bathroom, closing the door behind her.

Hopefully, the phone call had done the trick. She felt sorry for the man's wife, whose make-up kit and implements were arranged neatly next to the sink and whose own bikini hung drying on the back of the bathroom door. It should only take a minute or two for the elevator to reach their floor.

"Hurry up," the man called impatiently from the bedroom.

"Coming!"

She flushed the toilet and waited for a few more seconds before throwing open the door and returning to the man in bed.

Her stomach turned to ice. The man in the bed was holding his expensive smart phone.

"Did you touch my phone?" he demanded.

"What? No." Lucy gave him her best seductive walk and danced onto the mattress next to him. "Tell me again how much you want it."

"I'm done talking," the banker said, tossing the phone on the pillow. He grabbed Lucy roughly by the arm, pulling her down on top of the bed, using his height and strength to straddle her.

"Stop...no..." This was getting serious.

BAM

Just in time, the man's attention was averted as the hotel room door flew open, banging hard against the entryway wall.

"You son-of-a-bitch!"

The man's wife stalked into the room, still wearing her spa robe and clutching her phone and purse.

The banker leapt off of Lucy. "What are you...no...honey, it's not what you think."

His wife flung her purse and phone to the floor and charged into her husband, punching and slapping at him.

"I hate you!"

"Wait! I can explain!" He tried to block her punches, looking faintly ridiculous, his erection still showing through his boxers.

Lucy seized the opportunity to jump off the bed and scoop up her swim robe, backpack, and the woman's purse, before bolting out the door.

It only took a couple of seconds to reach the bank of elevators.

"Come back, you little whore!"

The elevator doors closed just in time.

Ten minutes later, she burst into a small women's restroom at a beachside cantina several blocks down the street. The room was relatively clean and empty, thank god. She locked the door behind her, and, still shaking and breathing hard, set her bags on the tiled floor. Choking back a sob, she looked at herself in the mirror.

Sweat dripped from her nose and the heavy eye makeup she'd put on was beginning to trickle down her cheeks.

That had been close. Too close. What had she been thinking? What if the wife hadn't showed up when she did?

Disgusted, she ran the cold water and splashed it where he'd touched her on her face, arms, and legs. After drying herself off with paper towels, she dug into her backpack and pulled on shorts and a shirt. Then she checked the concealed compartment inside the backpack to make sure the memory disk Manny had given her was still where she'd hidden it.

Being constantly on the run in the four weeks since he'd been kidnapped was beginning to take a toll, so when she saw the opportunity to make a bold move with the banker and his wife she took it. Like falling off a cliff, she'd simply gone with her gut and some of her acquired acting skills from her short-lived time doing summer theater. Even looking at the pictures from the disk on an Internet café computer, she still wasn't completely sure what they contained, but she felt fairly certain they were the only thing that might be keeping Manny alive.

She'd remained in the region for the first couple of weeks, using up most of her and Manny's cash reserve, keeping to out-of-the way hostels and private room rentals listed on craigslist:MexicoCity, hoping against hope for any trace or some kind of other message from him. She even tried reaching out to his employer and a couple other friends of his from the states. They were of little help. Manny had lived a pretty nomadic existence. She'd met Manny's sister once, some military chick, but Manny had told Lucy he wanted nothing to do with his big sister's imperialistic, oppressor ways.

When nothing else materialized, Lucy had begun to drift toward the coast, which is how she'd ended up here.

She took another deep breath, feeling a wave of nausea as the adrenaline began to wear off. No more breaks for self-reflection. Time to find out if all her efforts had paid off.

She set her pack down and began to rifle through the woman's purse, pawing through most of the usual junk, until she hit pay dirt. The woman's thick leather wallet nearly jumped out at her. Taking the clutch in her hand, she opened the metal clasp to reveal cash, credit cards, a driver's license and an American passport.

She stared at the passport photo of the banker's wife for a long moment, before standing to take a look at herself again in the mirror.

Good. She would need to hurry up and dye her hair, of course.

The resemblance wasn't perfect, but it should do.

26

OCULUM'S CORPORATE HEADQUARTERS stood among a row of office buildings running parallel to the Dulles Toll Road. The company name, cast in illuminated letters, ran along the upper story roofline of the building like those of its neighbors.

It was almost midnight. They were barely an hour's ride from the estate in Loudon County. The decision to move on the building without delay had been an easy one after she and Tye told Williamson about what she'd heard in Nathan Kurn's study and played back the recording for him.

Kurn may have been in mourning, but apparently it wasn't slowing him down when it came to covering up his involvement in whatever may have been going on between Oculum and Empyrean.

"What do you think?" Williamson asked.

He was keeping the pickup at an even speed as they drove past the building, checking things out.

As upscale as the scene might have seemed, Raina was unimpressed by the corporate surroundings. Before joining the Army out of high school, she had worked a summer job working as a mail handler in a building just like these. The whole environment had made a strong impression on her—it conjured up images in her mind of some kind of colony for office clones, one of the reasons she chose to join the military and apply for flight school rather than go to college.

"Looks like typical Beltway bandit territory to me."

"Me, too," Tye said. He was already slipping on another utility belt, prepping his weapons and tactical gear.

"One question," she said. "I know these digital records are supposed to be physically secured and protected by encryption and such, but they've got to be part of some network. Why not just hire some hacker, find a way to break through the firewall, and take a look at whatever we need?"

"I've got a guy who might be able do that," Williamson said. "But we don't have time. Whoever is protecting Kurn's secrets may have access to security and encryption techniques that aren't easy to crack and you heard what he said about destroying them."

"Okay. I guess we don't have a choice."

"Which means it's grunt and go time again," Tye said, pulling the bolt back on his gun. He was almost finished gearing up.

It was part of what she appreciated about him. Give the man a power bar and he was ready to take on the world.

"Don't be so gung-ho," Williamson cautioned. "This is Oculum we're dealing with. I'm sure it's not your typical suburban office building."

Tye looked across at Raina. "Well, it ain't Afghanistan. How bad can it be?"

She smiled. "I guess we're about to find out. What are you going to be doing, Major?"

"Overwatch with a satellite video feed I've managed to gain access to. I'll have the outdoors covered and will be on the com. Once you're inside I'll be piped into your audio and video feeds as well."

"Any other intel on the building?"

"There's a full on-site security team backing up the usual front desk uniform guys. Cameras covering just about every angle of the structure, inside and out. If that isn't enough, certain floors have motion detectors activated at night."

"Must be hell on the janitor," Tye said.

"Where's this special data server we're after?" Raina asked.

"My best guess would be housed in a secure area of the basement. Probably not all that far from the company's regular servers."

"How am I supposed to get inside the building?"

"A way they won't be expecting. From above. As soon as I got the call from you out at the estate I had my guy jump online and start digging into architectural plans and anything else he could find. Oculum recently installed an array of solar collectors on the building's rooftop. Power cables going down into the building are well sealed against weather. But there's a utility shed for battery storage with pipes running down into the building. There are also cooling vents that make it relatively easy to fly a MAV into the shed."

"As long as they don't have micro motion detectors."

"Right. From there, you simply follow the pipes all the way down into the basement."

"You make it sound easy."

"I'm sure it won't be, but you can handle it. This is what you've been training for."

"How many floors do I have to pass through?"

"Ten or twelve. If you follow the piping conduit, you should be able to make it all the way down below ground."

"What kind of MAVs will we be using?"

"Hover angel as before. And you'll put up a bigger dragonfly, too, to give you a better view from above. The angel will again be your primary infiltration platform."

"Where are we going to set up?" Tye asked.

"You'll stay together again. I've located a hidden spot between the building's dumpsters and a stand of trees. Might stink a little unless they've already hauled away the garbage for the week, but you should be okay."

"Lovely," Raina said.

"There are bushes, too. They're kept well-trimmed, but they should be big enough to provide decent cover."

"How do we get out of there when the job's finished?"

"Exfiltration will be from the drop off point. A couple of minutes walk from the building."

A couple of minutes. She didn't like the sounds of that. But this whole thing was crazy enough it just might work.

"Can we go over what happens when I make it down into the basement again?"

"Okay, look," Williamson said. "Just like the building, they have to cool this secure room with the server. Which means you'll find ventilation ducts to get you inside the room. Once in the room, you'll need to locate the server and fly through one of the drive slots or vents inside the computer. On a server that size there should be plenty forms of entry."

"That's what has me worried," she said. "Flying inside the computer, I'm liable to set off some alarm or short circuit the whole thing."

"Not if you manage to avoid all the wires and circuit boards. Just like flying in combat, nap of the earth."

"Easy for you to say. Sounds more like trying to flying through a forest full of trees. How am I supposed to acquire the file you're looking for once I'm in?

"That's where it gets a little tricky. The angel you'll be flying comes equipped with its own micro EMP weapon."

"Electromagnetic pulse?"

"Yes. It only has a range of a few millimeters, so no one will even know you're there."

"You want me to fry the company's server?"

"No. The plan is to just temporarily disrupt the drive running the firewall software, at least for a few seconds, make it sneeze if you will, just long enough for us to complete our hack into the system. My IT guy tells me once he's in, he can copy whatever files are there."

"That's insane. How can you be sure it's going to work?"

"I can't be sure. But right now, this is the best shot we've got."

"Won't the pulse knock out the angel, too? It's so tiny."

"The pulse will be extremely focused, microscopic, in fact. It should't impact the hover angel. Unless you happen to aim it in the wrong direction and hit the wrong thing."

"Oh, great. No pressure…What happens then?"

Williamson made a face. "That's it. You high tail it out of there as fast as you can.

Leave the angel behind if you have to. Remember, we're dealing with a high tech company developing its own drone and micro drone technology. Sooner or later, they're liable to suspect what might have caused their firewall to hiccup, although I'm betting they'll focus more on their cybersecurity and software solutions before they start considering a physical breach."

"Won't they detect your computer hack?"

"My IT guy knows how to cover his tracks once we have what we need. The key is to strike before they have a chance to figure out what's going on and get rid of those files."

"Sounds pretty iffy to me."

"It is iffy, Williamson said. "But we're going to have to take some risks, and before this is all over we might end up having to break into a lot more than a secure corporate headquarters." He looked at his watch. "It's now or never, people. I can't keep driving around here all night."

"Where are you going to be with the truck?" Tye asked.

"Half a mile away. I can be back for exfil in under sixty seconds."

"Sixty seconds, huh?" Tye looked skeptical.

"Make it forty-five, if you happen to be under imminent threat of capture or shots are fired."

She and Tye had both pulled on dark hooded sweatshirts and applied camo face paint while Williamson had been talking.

"You missed a spot," Tye said, reaching a pair of fingers up to touch her face and help spread the paint around. He kept his fingers there a moment longer than necessary. She got the message and he nodded.

They reached the entrance to an empty below ground parking garage underneath a different building a short hike down the road from Oculum. Williamson waved a key card in front of the gate pad. The gate rose without incident.

"What is this place?" she asked.

Williamson spun the wheel, turning them toward the back of the garage. "Believe it or not, it used to be an NSA facility."

"Used to be?"

"They moved out a couple of years ago, taking all their spy gear with them, and now it's occupied by several smaller defense contractors. I have friends who work here."

"I guess it pays to have friends then," Tye said.

"But they must have security cameras," she said. "And with that card swipe you just gave them a record of our entering the garage."

"Not tonight," Williamson said. "Already taken care of all that."

Why was she not surprised?

"Good luck, folks," the major said. "This is where I say goodbye."

27

THEY WERE LEFT standing alone in the garage with their weapons and gear.

"Gotta go," Tye said. "I don't like being in here under these lights."

"Roger that."

She followed him from the garage into the shadow of a strip of landscaped cottonwood trees.

She would let him take the lead with the ground approach. It was, after all, his area of expertise. Everything they now needed—laptop with control panel and optical glasses, MAVs housed in hardshell storage case, night vision goggles, and a suppressed MP5 sub machine gun—fit in a camper's style back-pack he had strapped to his shoulders. They also carried Beretta semiautomatics concealed in shoulder holsters beneath their light jackets.

She was already sweating again in the humid air.

They needed to cover about three hundred yards to the spot Williamson had described. From there, the MAVs could climb above the glow cast by the parking lot lights, rising to the roof of the Oculum building.

They trotted beneath the shadow of overhanging trees. A chorus of crickets from an adjacent marsh overwhelmed the sound of the nearby highway traffic. Tye stopped them for a moment, scanning the parking lot ahead for any potential threats.

"Be lucky if we don't get spotted by some local cop and busted as armed robbery suspects," he said.

"Just get us to a spot where we can launch these things."

Treading carefully through a final stretch of tall grass, they reached the place Williamson had been talking about. The dumpster didn't smell as bad as Raina had feared. All remained quiet. The thick bushes gave them plenty of cover.

They set to work unpacking their gear.

"You know," Tye said, "We could just do this the old fashioned way and blast in through the front door."

"Why, so you can add 'domestic terrorist' to your resume?"

"Just trying to expedite matters."

"If it helps, pretend you're a sniper. Those guys have to sit still for hours."

"Right." He lifted the MP5 and attached a magazine. "You do your thing and I'll keep an eye out for trouble."

"I'm on it."

She placed her laptop with the box of MAVs on the back of the now empty backpack Tye had been hauling. She found a comfortable spot to sit and positioned herself before the base of a bush. Then she slipped on her viewing glasses, fired up the computer and placed the control module on her lap.

"Any day now."

"Ready," she said, passing the dragonfly over to him. "Send it."

He did as instructed and, a second later, the dragonfly's infrared camera image appeared on her screen. After watching it take off, she drove the MAV into a steep climb, rising up along the shadowed corner of the Oculum building. Its vertical ascent rate was impressive, even to an experienced helicopter pilot. She watched as the mostly darkened glass office building windows flashed by one after another. Rising above the top floor, the building's rooftop popped into view.

"I'm on the roof."

"Good," Tye whispered. "All clear."

She let the dragonfly continue to climb for another few seconds until it provided a good overview of the roof, and then settled the small drone into hover mode. Its power source was good for at least an hour, giving them ample time to complete their mission. Or so she hoped.

She gently scooped up one of the tiny hover angels and released it into the air.

"Launching angel."

"Tally Ho."

Flying the much smaller MAV to the roof of the ten-story building could pose more of a challenge. The slightest gust of wind or even exhaust from a ventilation system could throw the minuscule drone off course. It could auto-adjust, but only up to a point.

With its nearly microscopic rotors, the angel responded differently to her control when flying outside than did the larger MAVs.

It would feel less like flying her helicopter, Williamson had explained, and more like the art and subtle dexterity of handling a fly-fishing rod—a virtual fly-fishing rod at that.

Raina had never been fly-fishing in her life. But at least the major's description had sounded poetic.

She focused on her controls. The night air here was mostly calm, so at least one thing was working in her favor. Gently setting the controls where she wanted, she watched and waited as the tiny angel climbed up the side of the building.

Like the dragonfly before it, the ascent didn't take long.

But when she crested the top of the building, her video image jerked back and forth and even lurched skyward.

She swore under her breath.

"Trouble?" Tye whispered.

"It's nothing," she said.

The roof of the building must have retained a good deal of heat from the day. The change in temperature between the air above the roof and the surrounding cool night air created a small thermal, a rising updraft that had not been enough to impact the larger drone but could play havoc with the minuscule angel.

Lesson learned—she should have anticipated that. At least the rush of rising air hadn't crashed the drone. She feathered the controls to correct the orientation of her little flyer and the roof came back into focus.

She was too far above the building now. She would have to burn precious battery life and drive the angel on a downward angled descent to steer it to her intended target, but she had no choice.

The dragonfly image in her split screen remained stable. All remained clear on the roof. They hadn't heard yet from Williamson. She hoped he hadn't run into a problem setting up the satellite overwatch.

A couple of concentrated minutes of flying later, she finally had the angel in position.

"I'm at the rooftop shed."

"Roger that," Tye said.

A second later, Williamson's voice rang in her ear.

"Sorry for the delay. Took a little longer than expected to pull up the satellite image, but I've got it now. Everything looks okay from my end. All building approaches quiet."

"Good." She didn't hesitate. "Entering shed."

She drove the angel in through the air vent and was immediately rewarded with a view of the small structure's interior.

There was not much to see. Her camera was still set to night vision and all she could make out was a tangle of pipes and large feeder electrical cables leading to some sort of breaker box. She could see no obvious way of flying down inside the building. Had Williamson's intelligence been faulty?

She buzzed across the shed floor, looking for any opening, but found none. It all seemed solid. She was just about to give up looking and inform the team when she spotted a dark ring around one of the pipes. A shadow maybe? She moved in for a closer look.

There. The ring was no shadow. It was a rubberized collar covering the opening in the floor made by the pipe. On closer inspection, the collar appeared to have slits that formed narrow openings, which meant it didn't form a tight seal around the pipe.

She'd found a way in.

28

TO BE SURE, the crevice in the pipe collar was a narrow, uncertain way inside. But it was an opening. She would have to pick a spot, drop down through the slit, and hope for the best.

She circled the pipe a couple of times, looking for the best angle of attack. Checking her monitor, she noticed she'd already wasted too much time: her angel had less than thirty minutes of battery time left. There was nothing to do but take the plunge.

And plunge, she did—down through the narrow tunnel formed by the widest opening in the pipe collar.

The thermal image immediately opened up into a utility shaft. Williamson had been right.

"I'm inside the building," she informed the others. "Proceeding to the basement."

"Copy." She thought she detected a tone of relief in Williamson's voice.

The hard part now was making sure she had a clear path below and to all sides as she let the angel descend through the shaft. One wrong move could send the angel bouncing off a pipe, damaging the MAV's propulsion system. Or worse, coming into contact with some sort of high voltage wire could potentially fry the little drone, causing it to incinerate or plunge out of control.

She pushed these thoughts from her mind and kept going down. Several more seconds ticked by.

"How's it going?" Williamson asked. He was obviously anxious.

"Still descending," she whispered into her mike. "Remind me to sign up for medical school after this, so I can train to do microscopic surgery."

"You can do brain surgery on me if you hurry it up so we can get out of here," Tye whispered.

She knew how he felt. Standing dogwatch in the dark with an itchy trigger finger was never a picnic.

Here in a suburban office park in Northern Virginia, their enemy—those searching for them—could be everywhere or nowhere at once. Like fighting counterinsurgents in an Iraqi city—on patrol, distinguishing the bad guys from the innocents meant paying attention to the subtlest of things.

She might be battling to avoid disaster in the bowels of a building's ventilation shaft, but at least she could stand back at a distance. If she crashed the tiny drone, the loss was only time and equipment. Tye's world, on the other hand, was always up close and personal. A matter of life and death.

If the worst happened, her world looking into her screen and Tye's standing guard beside her would come crashing together in a hurry.

Nearing the bottom of the shaft, she could begin to see the tunnel opening up into a much larger area stuffed with utility cable junctions, consoles, tanks, and pipes. Reaching the basement level, she found all of these led to a small room with a doorway and more ventilation vents.

The door had a window made of safety glass and through it she could see an empty hallway. She pushed a key on her computer that switched the drones main vision system from low light, night vision to its higher resolution main camera. Speaking of cameras, she spotted a couple of peering security lenses in the utility room and more in the hallway, but she doubted anyone could see, let alone notice, her mosquito-like MAV on their monitors.

At least she hoped that was the case. This was a micro drone research company, after all. Who knew what tricks they might have up their sleeve?

There was only one way to find out. She moved the MAV down to the vent in the door and flew through it into the hall.

And nothing happened. She breathed her own sigh of relief.

"I'm in the basement," she said calmly.

"Copy."

The server room had to be somewhere along the hallway on this level.

She snuck a glance at its location, mapped in a smaller window below her flight control screens; it was marked bright red on the building schematic Williamson had downloaded to her laptop. But, focused on her flying, she wasn't entirely clear of her scale and compass orientation within the overall building structure. She wasn't expecting the door to be marked by a glowing neon sign either.

Wary of surprises, she pushed the angel up to the ceiling where she might blend in against the rough concrete. She scanned the hallway below to get a better feel for what lie ahead.

The floor was made of some kind of tile. There were no lights along the top of the hall, only a few torch fixtures spaced far apart down the walls. Banks of computer servers throw off a lot of heat. The building's owners must have figured the fewer heat generating light sources, the better.

The semi-darkness was working in her favor. No other obstacles appeared to be in her path. Up ahead, on either side of the hall, faint shadows of protruding hinges seemed to indicate some kind of doors to either side.

She was about to fly the MAV forward when a shadow of movement caught her eye. One of the doors up ahead began to open. She held her breath. The drone was in a good position, but she still might be spotted if someone were really on the ball.

Out through the door stepped an armed security guard. He looked to be about Raina's age, mid to late twenties. His gun was holstered and he carried a flashlight in hand, a walkie-talkie strapped to his belt with a shoulder mike, and other gear.

"Problem," she whispered. "Here comes Rambo."

"Guard?" Tye asked.

"You got it."

"He see you?"

"Nope. Let's hope it stays that way."

"Don't move the drone," Williamson said.

"Don't worry. I'm not about to."

She waited as the guard checked the lock on the door. Then he turned and shone his flashlight in through what must have been another window across the hall and checked the lock on that door as well. Guy was obviously making his rounds.

But before she could react, he did something unexpected. He paused and turned to look down the hall in the direction of her MAV hovering just below the ceiling. She could see his face clearly. His mouth broke into a grin.

Had he seen the angel? Maybe, but he made no move in the direction of her drone. He slid his flashlight into his belt instead.

What was he up to? His gaze seemed to be focused on something else.

Then he started to dance.

Well, maybe not dance, exactly. But he did start to twist his body from side to side, up and down, swaying forward and backward as he walked, bobbing and weaving in the direction of her camera. At one point he even high-stepped over something, at another he jumped as if he were clearing a high hurdle, leaning to the side and pushing off the wall.

She continued to watch, fascinated.

"What's happening?" Williamson asked.

"Not sure yet…hold on."

Reaching the end of the hallway below her MAV, the guard reached across his shoulder and pulled his walkie-talkie mike to his mouth.

"Made the beam gauntlet run again, guys. No alarm tripped. That's three for three this shift."

He laughed, obviously pleased with himself. Stepping up to the door, he shone his light into the utility room from which Raina's angel had just exited. Apparently satisfied, he swung the beam over to the wall and opened a small metal door to reveal what looked like a number pad.

A code. Should she risk moving the angel?

She made a snap judgment and adjusted the tiny MAV so its camera could zoom in on the numbers.

Oblivious, the guard punched in a six-digit sequence and pushed the small door shut before turning to walk back in a more relaxed fashion down the hall.

She spoke softly into her mike. "The hallway must be armed with some sort of laser motion detector array. The guard just did a little mumbo-jumbo, dancing through it to avoid setting off the alarm. He called in on his radio to brag about it to the other guards. Must be some kind of competition."

"You think it's sensitive enough to be set off by something as small as the angel?" Williamson sounded concerned.

"In a place like this, the answer's probably yes. But the guard disarmed it." She followed her gut instinct again, pushing the drone forward in order to catch up to the guard and follow along in his wake. Close—but not too close.

"I'm following him. Before he turns the array back on."

"Good work. Did you see how he turned the array off?"

"Yes. There is a keypad and I have the password."

"Outstanding," Williamson said. "Text the code across when you can."

"On its way to you now."

She clicked a box on her optical screen to send the password numbers to Williamson.

The guard continued along the hall. He reached the door from which he'd come and kept going toward the exit at the far end. But Raina stopped the angel. According to the architectural schematic on her screen, this was where she needed to be.

There were no more entrances along the passageway, as far as she could see. She braked the drone to hover in place and waited. The guard made it to the end of the hall and punched in a password again on a keypad. He turned to give one last cursory glance in her direction, before disappearing through the far door.

Raina assessed her situation. At least she knew the space directly in front of the doors was free of the motion array since the guard hadn't disarmed the system when he first entered the hall. The door to her left should lead to the server room.

She was about to turn the angel toward that door when the MAV swung a little to the other side of the hall. Something else in the camera's view caught her eye.

The door opposite the server room had a narrow rectangular window in it, positioned to the side nearest the push plate. The design was otherwise similar to the door to the utility room from which she'd come, except for one thing. This glass was of a darkened hue, making it much more difficult, even if she switched her camera to night vision mode, to see inside.

Still, she knew she'd seen something. The shadow of a large object maybe, like a person moving, from beyond the door. She turned and drove the drone closer to take a better look.

That was strange. She could make out the brightened shape of an image from what looked like a computer monitor, but that was all. Was someone working inside the room? If what she'd seen was a person, they must have been known to the guard. Who else could be working here so late? She needed to investigate further, but she was running out of time.

To remind of her that dilemma, Williamson spoke in her ear. "Any luck yet? Are you in the server room?"

"Not exactly," she said.

"What do you mean not exactly?" Tye interrupted. His voice sounded cool on the surface, as always, but she knew him well enough to detect a slight edge to his tone. Maybe his trigger finger was getting itchy.

"I think someone else is in here," she said.

"In the hallway?"

"No. In the room across the hall. The guard's gone, but I thought I saw someone else. "

Neither of the men answered.

She sensed they were trying to digest this new piece of information. Maybe all she'd seen was a cleaning person or an IT worker pulling graveyard shift.

Either way, she needed to know before trying to break into this top-secret server. She was the one on target at the moment, with the eyes and ears of the tiny drone at her disposal. No one was in a better position to make the call about what to do.

"I'm going in to check it out."

"Affirmative," Williamson said.

She needed to find a way into the room across the hall. When you broke things down to a minute scale, virtually no space was truly impregnable. Look at fleas, for instance, or even microscopic dust mites. They could almost always find a way in.

Backing the MAV away from the door to get a larger view of where she was going, she saw that, unlike the door to the utility room, there was no vent through which to easily fly the angel. There was no key mechanism either. The door must have been opened via an electronic lock. The door looked to be standard issue institutional interior, hollow metal. How about simply going under as she'd done at the frat?

She descended for a better look and sure enough, while it wasn't much, the crack beneath the door was wide enough for her to slip under. As she dropped, the sides of the door resembled a sheer cliff face with a dark overhang at the bottom. That meant that besides the computer monitor she'd seen there was very little light coming from within the room.

She switched to night vision mode again. Carefully, she flew the angel under the door.

"I'm in the room."

"Less than fifteen minutes power remaining." Williamson's tone was clinical. No doubt he was beginning to worry they wouldn't be able to complete the mission they'd come for.

"I should know what we're dealing with in a few seconds."

Who had she seen through the darkened glass? She hovered just inside the door and angled the drone in different directions to take a look around.

The space wasn't large. It looked like some kind of control room. The computer monitor she'd seen through the window glowed directly in front of her. Not much to see there unless you understood lines of computer code. Numbers, letters, and symbols scrolled by as if the system were compiling data.

To her left several computer monitors had been arranged on the wall to form a large display. All the screens were dark save one. But what she saw on that one screen stunned her into silence.

The monitor displayed a video feed of a man strapped into a chair. He stared straight toward the camera and there were wires attached to his head.

But that wasn't the worst part.

She instantly recognized the chair as being identical to the one in which she herself had sat inside Murnell's sphere. She set the angel to hover in place and zoomed in on the screen.

"You seeing what I'm seeing?" she whispered.

"Yes. I see it," Williamson said.

The man in the image looked anything but happy. His eyes were glassy, a line of blood trailed from the side of his mouth, and his head sometimes lolled back and forth. What was going on here? Tye remained silent.

"That's the kind of chair I sat on inside the sphere."

"Not a pretty sight, in this case."

"He looks like he's being tortured or something."

"Maybe. Do you know who he is?"

She took a closer look at the man's face. "Negative. Never seen him before."

"Well, I do. He is, or was, one of the Air Force's top test pilots. I met him a couple of times up at Wright-Patterson."

"You think he's being held here against his will?"

"Hard to say, which is bad enough. But do you see the information box in the corner of the screen?"

"Yes, I see it."

"Can you read what it says?"

"Yeah. The text in the box reads LIVE FEED with today's date and a time counter."

"That's what I was afraid of."

"What do you mean?"

"Whatever's happening on this screen is apparently taking place right now, either in that building or somewhere else."

"Okay." She felt a small trembling begin at the base of her spine.

"I told you I met this guy," Williamson said. "But the man you're looking at crashed an experimental variation of the F-35 in the Nevada desert a couple of years ago. I remember hearing about it."

"What happened to him?"

"There was no ejection from the cockpit, Raina. The pilot you're looking at is supposed to be dead."

29

"I WANT YOU TO see something," Jonathan Ripley said.

"Okay."

Murnell had been summoned to his office again. This time it was at one in the morning.

He was exhausted. After working all day in his lab, he was planning to head back to his National Harbor condo to catch a few hours of sleep. He hoped Ripley's intention wasn't a reprise of the criticisms and second-guessing he'd been hearing all week about what had happened with Sanchez.

But he was relieved to find his superior in better spirits.

"Have a seat on the couch. Let me fix you a drink. The show should be starting shortly."

"Show?"

"You'll see," Ripley said.

The white-haired man poured a couple of tumblers of Scotch and handed one to Murnell.

He had just taken his first sip of the dark liquid, feeling its smoky smoothness on his tongue, when the large screen TV on the wall across from him flickered to life.

"Ah. Here we go." Ripley sipped from his own tumbler but remained standing.

The TV displayed an image of eight or nine people seated around a long dark table backed by a glass wall.

"What am I watching?" Murnell asked.

"It's a corporate board meeting."

"At this time of night?"

"It's an emergency meeting. Supposed to be top secret."

"So naturally you've got a front row seat."

"Naturally." Ripley toasted him with his glass.

"Why is there no sound?"

"Don't worry. I'll turn it up in a minute."

A couple of the people in the room were talking and one of them was pointing to a stack of papers they all had in front of them. It took a moment, but as the man pointing turned toward the camera, Murnell recognized him.

"That's Nathan Kurn."

"Indeed it is. This is the conference room at his office."

"Why am I watching this?"

"What you're watching, Dr. Murnell, is an important meeting about a merger to help secure a big part of your funding. But I'm afraid there's been a complication."

"A complication?"

"Yes. And I thought you'd like to be a fly on the wall."

"What's going on?"

"Understandably with all that's happened Kurn's developed cold feet over Empyrean."

"He what?"

"He's trying to sabotage the merger after what happened to his son."

"That doesn't sound good."

"It isn't." Ripley took another sip of his Scotch.

"You don't sound too concerned."

"Oh, I'm concerned all right. But as I mentioned, there's been a complication."

Murnell thought Kurn's backing out was the complication, but he figured he better wait and see what happened. On the screen, a pair of men in dark suits appeared on the other side of the glass wall.

"Oh good," Ripley said. "The feature's about to begin. Let me turn up the sound."

On the screen, the two men in suits walked through the glass door into the room without stopping or knocking. The sound came up on Nathan Kurn's voice talking, but whatever he'd been saying trailed off at the sight of the men entering.

Everyone else around the table looked up from their papers, their faces registering surprise.

"May I help you gentlemen?" Kurn's tone seemed to have lost its usual swagger.

A pair of uniformed police officers also appeared in the hallway beyond the glass wall.

"Nathan Kurn?" one of the men in the suits asked.

"Yes, I'm Nathan Kurn. What's this all about?"

People were beginning to stand around the table, obviously sensing some kind of a problem.

The questioner's partner was pulling out what looked like a pair of handcuffs.

"Nathan Kurn, you're under arrest for conspiracy to provide material support to a designated terrorist organization....You have the right to remain silent...."

30

RAINA STARED AT her screen. She felt a sudden kinship with the man strapped in the chair.

Why was he just sitting there? What was being done to him?

If what Williamson said was true, the pilot on the screen was a ghost. Were there no remains found at the crash site? Maybe this was all part of some black op. But if so, why was it being conducted here, in the basement of a private company?

A big part of her felt like she'd been brought back from the dead, too. Sometimes, she thought she should have died in the wreck of her burning chopper with Skyles and the others who lost their lives that day.

It didn't really matter if Nathan Kurn or anybody else had some hand in setting the stage. The fact remained she'd been in control of the bird, just as she was in control now. Maybe her being here to see this pilot on the screen was part of the reason she'd been pulled from a certain death. Sitting next to Tye in the darkness of the bushes, she glanced down at her artificial foot.

"Hey. You okay, Rain?" he said.

"Fine."

"You sure there's no one else there in the room with the angel?"

"Not at the moment. Just trying to figure out what to do."

"It's your call," Williamson said.

"This changes the situation." ·

"Yes, it does."

No doubt the major was still trying to process in his own mind what they were seeing. She looked at the window on her screen showing the view from her dragonfly's camera still hovering high above the roof. Then she glanced at the corner of her monitor.

"Everything still looks quiet, but my angel's getting low on juice."

She repositioned the drone to get a better view of the pilot on the screen. "You've recording all this, right, Major?"

"Affirmative."

"I'm going to use whatever battery power I have left to try to find out where this guy is."

"He could be anywhere. They might just be looking at the image on a secure feed."

"But if he's here in this building, I need to find him…"

Before she could finish her sentence, the screen image in Raina's glasses flashed brighter. Almost blinding her. A light had come on inside the room.

"Hold on a sec," she said. "We may have trouble."

Switching back to regular camera mode, she turned the angel to face the wall behind her.

Sure enough, there was another door there. Someone had just opened it and switched on the lights. She reached for the controls to flee, but she was too slow.

"Hello, little angel." A stranger's voice spoke into the MAVs audio feed. A pair of legs and shoes appeared on her screen and her display went dark.

She shook her head to clear her mind and process what she'd seen.

"What's going on?" Tye hissed beside her.

"Aborting mission," she said. "Someone's got our drone."

31

TYE SWORE OVER the com.

"Copy your situation," Williamson said. "You two need to get out of there. Evac in three minutes."

"What about the dragonfly?" she said.

"Forget the MAVs. We're blown."

"I can fly it down."

"Let it go, Raina."

A shout rang out from the far side of the building, someone calling out to a security guard.

"This is not good," Tye said. "Time to move."

But she wouldn't give it up. "Five seconds," she said.

She cleared the edge of the building with the dragonfly and put the MAV into a freefall. It dropped like a stone.

Tye placed his hand on her shoulder. She could feel the strength and tension there. She could also sense the increased activity around the building across the field and she thought she might have heard the sound of a vehicle engine starting.

"Two seconds," she said. Just before the dragonfly reached the ground, she deftly swooped it toward them. "You see it coming?"

Tye's hand left her shoulder. "I got it. Now turn that stuff off and let's get the hell out of here."

She powered down and they shoved everything into the rucksack. Flipping on her night vision glasses, she followed him out from the protection of their bushes. The night was still warm, the air permeated by a damp, wetland smell. Their boots swished through the high grass as they ran.

She followed Tye's dark shape in the green glow of her goggles, his nylon backpack making a chaffing sound against his back in front of her. Above the faint engine noise and their footsteps, she caught the sound of more shouts in the distance.

"Looks like we woke the beast," Tye whispered over his shoulder.

"Uh-huh."

"Weapons hot." He clicked off the safety selector on his MP5. She drew the Beretta out from underneath her jacket and did the same. At least this wasn't Afghanistan or Iraq. But a part of her could hardly tell the difference anymore.

She wondered if the test pilot in the chair had seen combat—most likely he had—and wondered if he'd ever felt the same. She cursed herself under her breath for losing track of her surroundings when she was so immersed in the remote world of flying the angel inside the building.

If they were caught here, she doubted anyone would risk another firefight like the one they'd escaped earlier. They weren't adjacent to an Air Force base and shielded by the wide expanse of the Potomac here; multiple gunshots would no doubt bring police in a hurry.

But after what they'd just seen, who really knew the full extent of what was happening?

At the very least, if hired security personnel or people on Oculum's payroll took them into custody, she and Tye could be tried and sent to Leavenworth. Either that or she'd end up like the test pilot in the chair. Oculum had to be tied to Empyrean, no doubt through Nathan Kurn.

They reached the edge of the field and the cover provided by the tall grass.

"What now?" she whispered.

Their only real choice was to skirt the edge of the illuminated parking lot before them, hoping to remain in the shadows, shielded by the neighboring office buildings. They needed to cross the lot, then another patch of woods to reach Williamson and their extraction point in the parking garage.

"Move or die," Tye said.

Half crouched, they jogged along the dim perimeter of the parking lot lights, hoping to keep a low profile. On the ground, without the freedom of flight, Raina felt vulnerable as she always did. She shook off the feeling and willed herself forward.

They were almost to the other side of the blacktop when, behind them, a security Humvee came roaring around a corner and into the far corner of the lot. They'd been spotted.

"Run." Tye pushed her ahead and moved to protect their flank.

He half spun into a shooting position, still moving swiftly behind her.

She didn't have to be told. She ran as fast as she could up the embankment at the end of the lot and into the cover of the woods on the other side. She turned to see Tye right behind her.

No shots had been fired, but they were about to be in somebody's crosshairs. The Humvee accelerated across the lot straight toward them.

They still had more than a hundred yards to cover through dark, heavy brush to get to the garage where Williamson waited. There was no way they were both going make it. She grabbed Tye by the shoulder.

"What are you doing? We need to move!"

"I'm slowing you down."

"Baloney. I'll carry you if it comes to that."

"You need to leave me behind."

"What?"

The sound of the Humvee's engine drew nearer.

"Go," she said. "We've already talked about this. I've got the best chance of any us to infiltrate Empyrean and find Manny. I'll find some way to reach you."

"You saw what they were doing to that pilot in there. I won't leave you."

"You have to."

She ripped off her goggles and drew face to face with him. There were a thousand things she would have liked to say at that moment, but they were out of time.

The security vehicle was almost on top of them.

"You have to," she repeated.

He stared at her before lifting his goggles from his face. She leaned into him and their lips brushed for barely a second.

Then she felt him pull away. The stock of his gun swept past her in the dark and before she could stop him he was charging back at the Humvee and into the light.

–END–

ABOUT THE AUTHORS

ANDY STRAKA

ANDY STRAKA is the author of the widely acclaimed, best-selling Frank Pavlicek PI series and was named by *Publishers Weekly* as one of a new crop of "rising stars in crime fiction." His other novels include A WITNESS ABOVE (Anthony, Agatha, and Shamus Award finalist), A KILLING SKY (Anthony Award Finalist), A COLD QUARRY (Shamus Award Winner), A NIGHT FALCONER (called a "great read" by *Library Journal*), A FATAL GOUND, A TRIGGER WITHIN, RECORD OF WRONGS (hailed by *Mystery Scene* as "a first-rate thriller"), and THE BLUE HALLELUJAH.

Straka is a native of upstate New York and a longtime resident of Virginia, where he co-founded the popular Crime Wave at the annual Virginia Festival of the Book. A technogeek and fan of all things flying, he is a licensed falconer who has hunted with Red-tailed hawks, Kestrels, and Harris's hawks. He is a graduate of Williams College.

DURRELL NELSON

DURRELL NELSON has worked for over thirty years in the film industry in the capacity of actor, stuntman, screenwriter, director, and producer. He is the director and producer of the film *Texas Rein* and President and co-founder of Beautiful Feet Productions with wife Rebecca.

As a writer, Nelson is a recipient of the prestigious Jerome Lawrence Award for his stage play *Falling Lightly* and first prize winner at the Maryland Film Festival for his screenplay *The Home Game*. Nelson holds an MFA in Creative Writing from Queens University of Charlotte, a Masters of Professional Writing from the University of Southern California and is a *summa cum laude* graduate with a Bachelor's Degree in Business

Finance from Woodbury University. He is an assistant professor in the school of Cinematic Arts at Liberty University.

As a member of the Screen Actors Guild, Nelson has worked on numerous productions including: *Drop Dead Diva, Killing Lincoln, JAG, An American Carol, X-Files, General Hospital, Melrose Place, Blow Out, Passions,* and the mini-series, *Les uns et les autres.*

Connect with Andy Straka Online:

Twitter:
https://twitter.com/AndyStraka

Goodreads:
http://www.goodreads.com/author/show/558166.Andy_Straka

Facebook:
http://www.facebook.com/pages/
Andy-Straka/220894891291320

Linked-In:
http://www.linkedin.com/pub/andy-straka/10/356/754

Website:
andystraka.com